Angel's TOUCH

BY

SIRI CALDWELL

Bella
BOOKS

2013

Bella Books, Inc.
P.O. Box 10543
Tallahassee, FL 32302

Printed in the United States of America on acid-free paper.

First Bella Books Edition 2013

Editor: Katherine V. Forrest
Cover designer: Sandy Knowles

ISBN: 978-1-59493-311-0

About the Author

Siri Caldwell got her start in creative writing in high school writing notes from her parents explaining why she was absent. She has been a health journalist, hydrogeologist, yoga teacher and massage therapist. She lives with her partner outside Washington, DC.

Acknowledgments

Thank you to my massage clients and to my teachers and classmates at PMTI, one of the best group of people I've ever had the pleasure of knowing, not to mention running down the hall with wearing nothing but a sheet. To Ric and Alexandra, for holding their feet in the door to higher dimensions. To Billy, for the construction site expertise. And to the lady from Silicon Valley who had nice things to say about the manuscript while making sure I knew she was very, very straight.

Big thank yous to Karin Kallmaker, for taking a chance on this book, and Katherine V. Forrest, my gracious editor, and everyone at Bella Books for working their behind-the-scenes magic.

And to Jennifer, my angel.

CHAPTER ONE

Megan McLaren didn't know how long she had been sitting at the bar alone chugging cranberry juice, watching the door, waiting for Amelia to show up, but she had just about had enough. One more song and she was going home.

"Want to dance?"

Stellar. She was such a loser that her friend Gwynne was taking pity on her.

"You don't have to do this."

Gwynne thrashed her hips in that charmingly goofy way of hers she called dancing. "What are you doing here, anyway?"

"I ask myself the same question." Amelia knew she wasn't a fan of the Sand Bar. And yet, she had insisted on meeting her here instead of at Megan's house.

Neutral ground—that's what it was. Never a good sign.

She should never have said yes.

Megan jumped off her barstool and followed Gwynne to the two-person dance floor, which was as claustrophobic as the rest of the bar. Anything was better than hooking her flip-flops around that barstool and giving herself a cramp in the shins while she tried not to check her watch.

"Amelia stand you up?"

What do you know, she did have a cramp. "I thought dancing with you was going to distract me from that."

"Is it working?"

"Not really."

Gwynne attempted an airborne spin and stumbled the landing. Laughing, she recovered by throwing her arms overhead in what might be considered a dance pose. "I could teach you this new move I just invented," she wheedled, as if her jump/spin/flail combo were a bribe no sane woman could resist.

"I'll pass."

"You don't know where she is," Gwynne observed. "Do you?"

"I'm guessing she's stuck in traffic." Where else could she be? Piper Beach was at least a three-hour drive from Washington, DC, and Friday-after-work beach traffic was never fun, especially on Memorial Day weekend.

"She hasn't called?"

Megan gritted her teeth. No, Amelia hadn't called. And no, it wasn't like her not to call. She wasn't picking up her phone, either. But no, she didn't think she'd been in an accident. She unclenched her jaw and bobbed her shoulders with an ease she didn't feel. Gwynne didn't need to hear about it.

"Trouble in paradise?"

Yup, Gwynne Abernathy could still read her mind. Unfortunately.

Megan sighed. "I have a feeling she's planning to dump me."

"You need to dump her first, then."

"I'm not sure I've reached that point yet."

"Why not? You have the advantage here. You know what's coming. Why not save yourself some grief?"

"I want to give this relationship a chance."

"Oh, come on. She has the aura of a toad. I don't know why you ever went out with her in the first place."

"Excuse me, we haven't broken up yet. You don't get to trash my girlfriend until *after* we break up. And she does *not* have the aura of a toad."

"My mistake." Gwynne ruined her apology with a wink. "Toads have lovely auras. Very green and healthy."

Typical.

Gwynne managed to insert a spin into her flailing movements without losing the beat, and looked so pleased with herself that Megan had to laugh. Even if dancing with friends was not the plan. Not with friends who were also exes, and who, by the way, had also dumped her.

It had been easier to know what to do with Gwynne. And even then, when it was obvious to both of them that they'd be better off as friends, she hadn't had the heart to break it off. Gwynne, of course, had read her mind and dumped her first.

"I'm trying to remember what it was you liked so much about Amelia."

"We haven't broken up yet, remember?"

"I was looking forward to it so much that I forgot that bizarre detail. She makes you miserable."

"That's not true." Amelia wasn't always the most considerate person in the world, but she meant well. And they had that connection—that zing in the aura when they got close. Not that she could tell Gwynne that. She and Gwynne had strict unspoken rules about what topics they would and would not discuss. Zinging auras did not get the ex-girlfriend seal of approval. "I'm sure there's a cosmic reason why we met."

"Karmic computer malfunction?"

"Karma doesn't malfunction."

"Speaking of malfunctions..." Gwynne nodded in the direction of the entrance.

Amelia Barnett stood just inside the doorway a few yards away, scanning the room. She must have driven straight from the office, because she was still in her work clothes. Her suit was rumpled and her lipstick was long gone, but her short blond hair was still perfectly in place, shellacked into submission.

And someone was with her.

Amelia leaned over to whisper in the other blonde's ear. She didn't touch her at all—not her shoulder, not her arm, not the back of her waist, and definitely not her ass—but the way they were drifting into each other's personal space, she might as well have.

There was no way Amelia would cheat on her in front of her. Was there? She was imagining things. Maybe Amelia gave a friend a ride.

And maybe that friend had thanked her while they were stuck in traffic at the Chesapeake Bay Bridge toll plaza by chewing off her lipstick.

Whoever she was, she followed the direction of Amelia's outstretched arm and headed for the restrooms. Amelia stalked to Megan's side.

"Definitely not green and healthy," Gwynne announced as she made her escape.

"What was that all about?" Amelia watched Gwynne's retreat for a couple seconds before snapping her attention back to Megan. "I need to talk to you."

Megan ignored her unease and reached for her. "Hug first."

Amelia's shoulders softened at her touch. Encouraged, Megan rubbed the muscles between her shoulder blades. Amelia let her head roll back and closed her eyes with a deep sigh of relief.

But when Amelia touched the small of Megan's back, instead of pulling her closer, she straightened, dug her fingers a little too hard into her back, and braced herself.

And Megan knew.

Amelia was going to break up with her. Here, in public. She wasn't even going to apologize for being late tonight and making her worry.

Megan's arms dropped to her sides.

Amelia took her elbow and led her to the bar. She asked the bartender for two of whatever was on tap, skipping her usual rant about their lack of Belgian beer. At least Megan would never again have to remind her that she didn't like beer—Amelia pretended to forget, as if that would magically change anything.

"I don't want to hurt you," her soon-to-be-ex-girlfriend

said, more gently than she had expected. "I know you think we have a past life thing going on—"

Megan cut her off. "I know you don't believe me." Now that it was happening, she just wanted to get it over with.

"Nobody believes that stuff, baby."

Gee, thanks. What happened to *I don't want to hurt you*? Of course, she'd left an important word off the end of that sentence. What she'd meant was, *I don't want to hurt you, but…*

Amelia took a deep breath. "I can't do this anymore. I need to move on."

One good thing about Amelia, she did like to come straight to the point. When she stabbed you with a knife, it was quick. Very humane.

Megan almost didn't feel it.

Amelia took the two beers and joined her new friend at an intimate table in the corner.

Megan watched, stunned.

She wondered if the new girl liked beer.

CHAPTER TWO

When you were new in town, nobody warned you the annual Race to the Beach in Piper Beach, Delaware, was the Race *on* the Beach, because it was so much fun to screw with the tourists.

Kira Wagner's wristwatch beeped, reminding her she was lagging behind her personal best, posted last year at the Seagull 10K. So much for improving on her time. She dodged a wave and put on some speed. Maybe she should start a new list of personal bests for races run under adverse conditions. Sand... mountains...running the Marine Corps Marathon in borrowed combat boots. Maybe she'd include charming a friendly female marine out of her boots as part of the challenge.

She'd have enjoyed *this* challenge if her outer thigh hadn't cramped. At first it was just a twinge, but now that she was nearing the finish line it was becoming harder to ignore. Looked like the visit she'd planned to make to the massage tent was going to be more than just a networking opportunity.

Onlookers applauded as she crossed the finish line. She sagged with disgust at her finish time and followed the seagulls toward the snack table, helped herself to three bananas and a bottle of water, and then stopped by the first aid station for an ice pack to put on her thigh.

She'd been telling herself for months to try a massage, but never gotten around to it. Now was the perfect opportunity. About time, too, because if she was going to open a spa here in Piper Beach, she really ought to know more about the business than just the financials. Somehow she always found time to do the on-the-phone research, but never the hands-on research. The someone-else's-hands-on-her-body research, to be precise. It just didn't sound all that relaxing. She couldn't imagine lying down for an hour without feeling antsy. But it was time to get it over with. The tent was right here. She'd get rid of her cramp, and if she liked the therapist, she'd multitask and ask her if she was interested in applying for a new job.

When Kira reached the head of the line she could see right into the massage tent. Runners lay fully dressed—if you could call running shorts and a jog bra fully dressed—side by side in closely packed rows of massage tables covered in plastic sheeting. Not exactly a spa experience. She bet they were sweaty and sandy, too, like she was—also not a spa experience. But everyone who emerged was starry-eyed. That reaction was exactly what she wanted for her customers. For herself, she'd be happy if someone could get rid of this cramp.

"Any of those massage therapists happen to be Megan McLaren?" she asked the woman organizing the line of waiting runners. Mrs. Jacoby at Smooth Sailing had been quite clear that Megan McLaren was out of her league, but Kira wasn't convinced. The best massage therapist she'd ever met, Mrs. Jacoby had claimed. That didn't mean she wouldn't work for her.

"Right over there." The woman pointed Megan out as a preteen in two lopsided braids brushed past Kira's legs and begged the race volunteer—clearly her mother—for ice cream.

Off to the right, in the row of tables, was a massage therapist who had her back turned to her as she worked. Like all the other massage therapists, she wore shorts paired with an official white

T-shirt with a fluorescent green handprint logo on the back, but unlike the others, she was barefoot in the sand. The wind blowing in off the ocean through the canvas tent's open flaps whipped through her long brown hair and had its way with it. Kira watched, mesmerized. That was going to be one heck of a rat's nest to comb through and untangle at the end of the day.

Kira gulped down the last of her water and tossed the bottle in a convenient recycling bin. "I heard she has a good reputation," she told the volunteer.

"Megan's a sweetheart."

"Is there any way I could get her?" Kira smiled her best I'm-harmless-please-do-me-a-favor smile.

The woman dug out some money for her daughter and sent her running off. "You'd have to wait," she told Kira.

"I don't mind."

She pulled Kira out of the line. "Stand here," she ordered.

Kira waited patiently, trying to look inconspicuous. She scanned the tables to see if she recognized any of the massage therapists from the scouting she'd been doing around town, but her eyes kept returning to Megan McLaren. There was something fascinating about the way she swayed back and forth as she glided her hands up and down her client's legs. Each time she shifted her weight, her whole body moved in a sweeping, primal wave. Kira'd had no idea massage could be so graceful.

It wasn't long before Megan was done with that runner. Kira caught the attention of her guard, who nodded and raised her hand to tell her to wait one more minute. Megan squirted her table with disinfectant and wiped it down, then stashed her towel inside a milk crate tucked under the table. She turned and waved to show she was ready for her next victim.

Kira froze.

That face…

She knew that face. Wow, that was weird. She thought she'd forgotten what the girl in her childhood dreams looked like—dreams that left her flushed and confused. Heat rose to her face as she struggled to push the surprisingly vivid memory aside.

No one had ever measured up to that goddess. Which

was dumb, because, well, she was a *dream*. Something her subconscious made up. How could anyone possibly compete with that?

Sure, Megan had a halo of tangled dark hair framing a round, makeup-free face, just like the girl in her dreams. She had the same quirky elfin eyebrows, the same friendly nose, the same inviting mouth. And no doubt the same amazing body... But there was no way. She must have seen her around town, spotted her in the Piper Beach women's bar or stood in line behind her at the grocery store, and now her face looked familiar and her brain had gotten mixed up. It was some kind of déjà vu. The brain misfiring. No big deal.

"Okay, you can go over there now." The volunteer touched Kira's arm to prod her in the right direction.

Kira wiped her hands on her shorts. They might be moisture-wicking on the inside, but on the outside, the techno fabric certainly wasn't doing anything for her sweaty palms. She considered wiping her hands on her bare skin or on a socially acceptable inch of her soaked jog bra, but that wasn't going to do the trick, either. She made her way over, still trying in vain to wipe the sweat off on her shorts.

She'd be all right. Déjà vu could be disorienting, but it would pass. Before she knew it she was saying hello and lying faceup on plastic sheeting that was just as clammy as it looked.

Megan stood at the foot of the table and enveloped Kira's feet in a sure grip, her hands like miniature hot water bottles. Despite the sweltering air temperature, the heat of her hands was exactly what her body needed. She massaged her arches and her toes, soothed her ankles, and worked the outside of her shins, finding tight muscles Kira never knew she had.

She was too beautiful not to watch. Kira could see the muscles working in her arms, but nothing else betrayed any effort at all. Her chest rose and fell with deep breaths and Kira's own breathing fell into sync with it, pulling her into a state of deep relaxation.

When it occurred to her that she was staring, Kira forced herself to look away and study the pattern of the tent poles overhead until it was time to turn over and lie facedown. What was wrong with her, anyway? It was an embarrassing dream and she was glad she hadn't thought of it in years. No need to act like a jerk.

But it was hard not to let herself get disoriented again, because that touch...there was nothing casual about that touch. Gentle, yes, but wholly deliberate. Megan slid her hands up Kira's exhausted legs with efficient but gentle strokes, flushing the soreness out of first her calves, then her thighs, without any faltering shyness that might have turned her hand on Kira's bare thigh into something intimate. She showed no hesitation as she teased out her sore spots, pushing into them over and over again with a no-nonsense attitude that had Kira closing her eyes and surrendering her body to her. Megan pushed into one particularly sore spot in her hamstrings yet again and Kira almost shivered from the pleasant agony.

She was going to be a wreck by the end of her ten minutes.

"Time's up," Megan said at last, close to Kira's ear. "You can get up when you're ready."

Kira swung her legs off the table and sat up abruptly, relieved to be back in control of her body and anxious to put some distance between her ear and Megan's mouth. She lowered herself onto her feet and immediately noticed how much lighter she felt. Her legs weren't worn-out dead weight anymore. She rose on her toes experimentally, clenching her calves and quadriceps to see if they would cramp. They didn't.

She was impressed. She should definitely try to hire this woman for her spa. Either that or start getting regular massages from her.

Sure. Dream or no dream, that was so not what she wanted from her.

"Hope that helped." Megan rummaged in a tote bag under her table. "I forgot to bring my business cards, but if you're interested in massage I could write my name and number on a piece of paper for you."

She really should tell her she already had her phone number. It was sitting on her desk in her office where, despite

Mrs. Jacoby's warning that Megan would never leave her own successful business to go work for someone else, Kira had placed her at the top of her list of people to contact.

Megan emerged from under the table with a pen. "No paper, but I could write it on your hand."

Writing on her hand—how high school. How...sweet. Instead of ending this charade and telling her she didn't need her number, Kira held out her hand.

She bit her lip at the warmth of Megan's small hand on hers and again at the tickle of her pen across her palm. Pitiful. She was an adult, for God's sake, and had been for quite some time. The touch of a pen shouldn't affect her like this.

And to make it worse, something in her stomach was jumping and cheering and waving a banner, because if the rumors were true and there was no chance of hiring her, then there was no reason not to ask her out on a date. Not that that would really have stopped her. If she had to choose one, hiring Megan was not going to win.

She cleared her throat, feeling a little motion sick from all that gastrointestinal celebration. "I've heard of you."

"Good things, I hope."

"Great things. Well-deserved."

"Thank you."

Kira cleared her throat again. Why did Megan have to look so much like the girl from her dream? Would've made it so much easier. Asking women out didn't usually make her ill. "I know this is probably way out of line, but would you be interested in going out to dinner with me sometime?"

The male massage therapist at the next table turned to look at Kira in surprise, then raised his eyebrows at Megan, no doubt eager to hear her shoot her down.

"I'm sorry." Megan's brusque, businesslike tone made it clear this was how she responded to all wayward clients' requests for dinner, no emotion required.

The flush that appeared in her cheeks betrayed her, though.

Kira felt like a jerk for embarrassing her in front of her colleagues. She glanced at the man at the next table to see what his reaction was, but instead of providing Megan with backup, he had looked away and was pretending to mind his own business. Was that all the effort he was willing to make? Not even a dirty look in Kira's direction? With talent like Megan's—not to mention that sexy, tousled hair—she ought to have someone around who was a bit more on the ball to ward off her admirers.

To be fair, maybe he didn't think Kira was a threat—what with her being a woman and all. Was Megan even gay? Maybe. She hadn't responded with a "What the hell?" but all that meant was that she wasn't shocked by Kira's proposition, and how surprising was that in a place like Piper Beach?

She had to apologize. "Please forget I said anything."

"It's forgotten."

Now that was a nice thing to say. Kira had been about to bend down to retrieve her shoes from underneath the table, but Megan's reply made her look up. What a mistake. She had the most amazing eyes, so full of light they made you wonder if maybe magic fairies were real. She didn't look angry at all. Flustered had given way to apologetic and then to curious.

And so luminous. If Kira were a deer, she'd have been hit by a car by now. Straight women didn't let their feminine power blaze through when they made eye contact. Straight women didn't make her forget where she was, or make her say stupid things like "Really?"

Shit. Did it have to come out high-pitched and breathless like that? Of all the stupid, useless, girly...

Megan didn't drop her gaze. Kira felt behind her for the support of the massage table. It was quite possible that oxygen was no longer reaching her brain.

"Really," Megan said, finally.

No word about changing her mind about dinner. So, okay. She would leave before she made things any worse.

As soon as Megan stopped staring into her eyes and giving her hope.

"Really," Megan whispered, and looked away. Kira thought she saw regret flitter across her face. But when Megan met her gaze again, her eyes had lost that otherworldly look and become cool and distant, the way you glanced at a stranger before gazing past them.

Now it was easy to look away. Kira felt numb. She was being dismissed. People were waiting outside the tent for her to leave so they could have their turn.

"Don't forget your shoes," said the man working at the next table.

She obediently bent to pick up her shoes and socks and caught Megan glaring at him. Kira straightened. Was Megan defending her?

Maybe…

Hope jumped in her chest. "My name's Kira Wagner. I bought the old Starfish Hotel. You can find me there if—"

Megan's eyes remained glacial.

Kira backpedaled. "Ignore me. Thank you for the wonderful massage. It was a pleasure meeting you." She turned and left before she made things any more awkward.

Maybe Megan would track her down.

She seriously doubted it.

CHAPTER THREE

Megan relaxed on her massage table in the massage space that had once been her townhouse's second-floor bedroom as Svetlana Tretyakova Durbridge tapped her fingertips rhythmically up and down one arm, then the other, easing the strain that had built up over a full day of massaging runner after runner at the race the day before.

Svetlana broke the silence. "Volunteer work is great way to meet new people, no?"

Uh-oh. Her friend's Russian accent always became more pronounced when she got excited about something. She should have known Svetlana's husband would fill her in. What did Patrick tell her, anyway? Nothing, that's what. Because nothing happened. When that brave, unforgettable woman asked her out, Megan had said no on autopilot, and that had absolutely been the right thing to do. It was totally unethical to date clients.

"It's all a blur," Megan said, which wasn't technically a lie—because it *was* all a blur. All except for one tiny span of ten minutes that for some annoying reason she could recall by the nanosecond. "One set of legs looks pretty much like any other after a while."

"That's not what I heard."

"You were there. Nothing happened."

"Next time I take table next to you."

"You were close enough."

"I did not think to be two tables away was so very far, and yet, Patrick knows details that I do not."

"That's because your husband is even nosier than you are." He must have blown the incident totally out of proportion.

Svetlana drummed on her body more vigorously with the sides of her hands. "What did I miss?"

"Nothing exciting." Nothing except a fit, tanned brunette backing up against her massage table, gripping the edge of the table behind her for support instead of crossing her arms defensively in front of her chest once she realized that asking her out had been a mistake. She waited for Megan to shoot her down and never looked away.

Megan's heart was the one that had pounded.

"It is not necessary to tell me," Svetlana said, knowing full well that Megan would eventually cave.

And this massage had started out so soothing.

Megan sighed. "If you must know, someone hit on me. It was no big deal."

"Did you reply with good insult?"

"Come on, Svetlana, you know I would never do that."

"I know. Always the professional. But wouldn't it be fun?"

"I'd feel bad about it afterward. Besides, she was very respectful. She backed down right away."

Svetlana kneaded the tight muscles in Megan's forearms. "So, this respectful woman who hit on you, was she cute?"

"I didn't notice," Megan lied.

"Of course you didn't. It is necessary to be professional." Svetlana slid her hands down to Megan's fingers and worked the kinks out. "As you say, it's all blur. All…" She dragged the word out, matching the slow rhythm of her massage as her pitch fell mournfully. "All…forgotten blur."

Megan relented. "She was kind of cute. Very intense."

Svetlana broke into an I-told-you-so smile.

"Don't get too excited," Megan warned.

"Never."

"Have you heard anything about the Starfish Hotel being sold?"

"Starfish? Yeah, some woman is to turn it into spa. Women-only. Kira something. She's asking around, trying to hire idiot to run massage part." Svetlana's hands paused. "This is woman who hit on you?"

"Yeah."

"Unfortunate, as you have sworn off tourists."

"Being new in town doesn't make her a tourist."

"You call the evil Amelia a tourist, and she owns condo here."

"I think I'll be the judge of who my rule applies to."

Svetlana put Megan's hand down and grinned. "That cute, yes?"

"Oh, God," Megan said, remembering how Kira's eyes had drawn her in like a magnet. Well, let's be honest. Much as it pained her to admit it, the first thing she noticed was not her eyes.

Normally she didn't care one way or another what her clients' bodies looked like. Large, thin, splotchy, whatever, she really didn't notice. Besides, clients picked up on that sort of thing subconsciously, and the last thing she wanted to do was make someone uncomfortable. She had been massaging runners all day in that tent, and it was true what she'd said to Svetlana—they did all blur together, just one set of sore legs after another.

Kira's she remembered. In a sea of great legs, Kira's were lean and strong and painfully beautiful. She loved the way you could see the muscles clearly defined, like an anatomy textbook brought to life, and feel their shape under your hands.

Safer to forget she'd noticed.

Safer, but not easy—not with the way her baser instincts kept kicking in every time she thought of her. In all the time she'd been practicing massage, she'd never felt this unprofessional.

"It would be wrong," Megan said. Maybe saying it out loud would help her convince herself.

"Probably," Svetlana agreed.

Megan blew out a deep breath. "God."

"You didn't want to date tourist, anyway."

"Yeah, thanks, that helps."

"Then why you don't trust yourself and go for it?"

Because her instincts weren't trustworthy, that was why. Svetlana had no idea what it had felt like that day she'd passed what she thought was her destiny on the crowded boardwalk and walked right through the woman's aura.

And recognized it.

She had turned back to see who it was. The source of that electricity had stopped to look in the window of a souvenir shop. It was the strangest feeling. She knew this stranger had meant something to her once.

Meant a lot.

The woman—Amelia—must have sensed Megan was staring at her, because she looked over her shoulder and straight at her.

And wasted no time getting her into bed.

"I thought I knew what I was doing when I picked Amelia," Megan said. "I thought it was fate when I met her."

"If you say so." Svetlana stepped back from the table and stretched. "Time to trade. My turn for a massage."

"So much for fate, huh?"

Svetlana shrugged her bafflement.

If fate ever brought her another familiar face, she'd run the other way.

* * *

"What do you think?" Kira asked her dad as she showed him around the dilapidated Starfish Hotel—her new baby.

He'd called earlier that morning to say he was driving out to Wilmington and planned to detour past Piper Beach to see how her latest project was coming along. Kind of like he used to do when she worked for him, except now, when he told her what she was doing wrong, she could ignore him.

Kira led him to the empty roof. It was only four stories up, but they were right at the edge of town, so that was high enough that you could look out over a protected stretch of wild dunes and see the ocean. She couldn't wait to build a rooftop patio up here. "Isn't this a great view?"

He took a few token steps toward the edge of the roof and stopped to mop the sweat from his forehead with a limp linen handkerchief. That's what bandanas were for, in her opinion, but unlike her, he believed in executive attire—including a real handkerchief in his pocket—on the jobsite. Business suits only. He tried, anyway. Catch him first thing in the morning and his pinstripe suit was crisp and his tie tightly knotted, but by afternoon his collar was unbuttoned, his tie was loose, and his assistant was scampering in her three-inch do-me heels to locate where he'd misplaced his jacket.

"No view from the ground floor," he complained. "You're going to lose your shirt on this one."

"You always say that." Ever since she'd quit working for him and struck out on her own, starting businesses and selling them just like he'd taught her to, he'd been full of gloomy predictions of her financial ruin, none of which had come true.

"I was right about that restaurant," he reminded her.

"I didn't lose everything," Kira protested, even though she almost had. She'd helped an aspiring chef open a restaurant in nearby Rehoboth, and ended up taking a big financial hit when the inexperienced chef's cooking turned out to be less than popular. That was the last time she was messing around with a restaurant. Fortunately she'd managed to bail with enough money left to buy this bankrupt hotel and its not-quite-beachfront-yet-still-super-expensive land. Her second chance. She'd fallen in love with the property at first sight.

"You came close," he countered. "How many times do I have to tell you not to use your own money on these projects? Put someone else's money at risk. Find an investor."

"And let that investor tell me what to do? No thanks."

"They won't force you to do anything that's not in your best interests."

"They won't force me to do anything at all, because I'm not taking their money." She knew her father sincerely believed he had her own best interests at heart. He just didn't understand what her best interests *were*.

"You always were stubborn," he said.

"I don't need their money."

"Too stubborn for your own good."

Kira narrowed her eyes at him. "Because women should be meek and do what you tell them to do?"

He raised his hands defensively. "Where do you come up with this stuff?" He shook his head. "I'm just telling you to get a backer."

"I'm my own backer on this one, Dad."

"This one and every one," he grumbled.

Damn right. Kira admired the ocean view that was going to turn her financial future around. This project, unlike her last one, wouldn't let her down.

The restaurant had been a mistake from the beginning, starting with her decision to join forces with the woman she was dating. At the very least, she should have noticed that her girlfriend knew nothing about running a business. Or that she saw Kira as a shortcut to becoming chef of her own restaurant so she could skip the part where she learned how to be a good one.

This project was different. No business partners, not this time. Someone to help her design the spa and later manage it, yes, but no one with a financial stake who would convince her to make decisions she wasn't happy about.

"How much is this costing you?"

"It won't be too expensive." Kira refused to give him numbers, which would only serve as more ammunition. "Some of the rooms are in bad shape—the previous owners closed them off when something broke instead of fixing the problem—but a lot of it's fine the way it is. I won't need to gut the place."

"So you get the retro vibe for free." He looked the roof up and down, his gaze noticeably pausing to dwell on the boxy hulk of the rooftop air-conditioning units, no doubt estimating how many years they had left in them before they had to be replaced. With him, it was all about the condition of your assets, all about the numbers.

"Isn't it great?" Kira said extra enthusiastically, hoping he'd get the hint that he should say something positive.

He eyed her in the same assessing way he'd looked at her rooftop machinery. "You put yourself and your money on the line, you can't afford another loser."

"No, I have a good feeling about this place. This one's going to work out." Let him be grumpy if he wanted to, but with the right renovations and a new business model, this hotel was going to be a success. "You'll see."

He shook his head. "I hope for your sake you're right."

* * *

Megan and Svetlana slowed to a touristy stroll as they approached the Starfish Hotel. It had been in bad shape for as long as Megan could remember, but you could tell it had once looked nice, with interesting architectural details under the weathered, peeling paint. Construction equipment and several Dumpsters sat in the parking lot out front. She wondered if the new owner was renovating or tearing it down. Like everywhere else, people were buying these old properties for the value of the land and ripping everything out, and the city council hadn't gotten around to doing anything but grumble about it. If anyone ever did try to stop a project, they wouldn't get any help from that quarter.

"Okay," Megan told Svetlana. "We've seen it. Let's go." Megan was anxious to leave before anyone noticed them, so she could pretend she hadn't purposely decided to walk down this street to check out this particular construction site.

Svetlana pointed to the side of the building, where Kira Wagner, dressed like a construction worker in blue jeans, a white long-sleeved shirt and a hard hat, was coming around from the back. "Is that her?"

Megan tugged on Svetlana's arm. "She hasn't recognized me yet. Let's pretend we're just walking by."

"No, I think she sees you."

Kira was running toward them now, and not in a half-assed bouncy way that might have indicated a shred of hesitation, but in a real, flat-out run. Like they didn't see her and she wanted to catch them before they left.

She was beautiful when she ran. Fast and fluid and in total command of her body. What was it about some women, that they set off an internal alarm, making her heart race and her gut do…whatever it was doing…because she *knew*—she knew with absolute certainty that they played on her team. Even before Kira had attempted to ask her out, Megan's body had known.

"Megan, wait!"

She slowed. There was no way out of this, was there?

"I think *I'll* pretend I'm just walking by," Svetlana said. "You stay here. And by the way, I don't think ten minutes makes her a client." Svetlana took off while Megan stood rooted to the sidewalk.

"No, wait." Megan looked from Svetlana to Kira and back again. Svetlana couldn't leave *now*.

The traitor turned around but continued to walk away, backward now, wiggling her fingers in a mocking little wave goodbye. *"Do svidaniya."*

She'd pay Svetlana back for this later. What happened to *You didn't want to date tourists, anyway*? What happened to *It would be wrong*? Oh, wait—that was her line. But Svetlana had agreed with her, hadn't she? Some friend.

"Megan." Kira came to a stop. "I'm so glad you came by." She wasn't even breathing hard, and she'd been running in construction boots, powering through like they weighed nothing.

Megan glanced one more time at Svetlana's rapidly retreating form. This would have been much less awkward if Svetlana hadn't pulled a *do svidaniya*.

"Can I show you around?"

"Sure." Megan smiled politely. She really had to learn how to say no.

Of course, it was her own fault for coming by this way in the first place. It was also her own fault that as she followed Kira up to the hotel, instead of paying attention to the construction site, she found herself scanning Kira's posture. It was instinct—a habit she'd picked up in massage school. It was the first thing she did when a client walked into the room.

It was not at all the same as checking someone out.

It was a professional appraisal, that's all it was. It meant noticing with her trained eye that Kira's pelvis was tilted back, which meant her hamstrings would be tight under those formfitting jeans, and could be giving her back pain.

Her fingers itched to find out what was going on in that lanky, well-conditioned frame. Ten short minutes in the busy massage tent hadn't been nearly enough time to search out her muscle imbalances. Athletes were always fun to work on. From a professional standpoint, of course. Megan hung back a step so she could get a better view.

Oh, crap. She squeezed her eyes shut, realizing what she was doing. She really was checking her out. She thrust her hands behind her back and clasped them tightly before they betrayed her. They seemed to have a mind of their own right now, and she knew what they wanted.

Contact.

With those muscles.

Not going to happen.

Kira tugged on the hotel's front door and held it open for her. In the lobby, the carpeting had been pulled up, the wiring was sticking out and stacks of ceramic tile were piled up against one wall. Megan ventured down the hallway to their left and poked her head into one of the rooms. The beds and dressers had been removed, but it still looked like a hotel room. Maybe it was the hotel-like, floor-to-ceiling windows.

She sneezed hard from the dust. "Where's the spa going to be?"

"You heard about that?"

"That you're building a spa? That's the word around town."

"Glad to know my networking worked."

"Better than you expected?"

"It hasn't landed me a spa manager yet, so no." Kira gestured for her to follow her back to the lobby.

A spa manager, right. That's what Svetlana had said, that the new owner of the Starfish Hotel was asking around, looking for someone to run her spa. Megan couldn't imagine why you'd want to open your own spa and not want to run it yourself.

"The spa's going to be in a separate building." Kira led her behind the intact check-in desk, through a door at the back, and into an office. There were stacks of paper piled everywhere—on the desk, on the file cabinets, on the floor. Kira took off her hard hat and shook out her hair like a dog after a dip in the ocean. Her close-cropped hair was so dark brown it was almost black, with a spray of premature gray above the center of her forehead.

"Sorry about the mess. Let me make some room for you to sit down." Kira balanced her hard hat on top of one of the piles on the desk and lifted a stack of papers off the faded pseudo-baroque upholstery of a beat-up hotel lobby chair crammed in the corner. She stood there with the stack of papers in her arms, looking a bit lost, trying to locate an unoccupied surface where she could set it down.

"I don't need to sit," Megan said as Kira started to lower the stack to the floor. "You need all the floor space you can get."

Kira smiled ruefully and hefted the papers back onto the chair. "I do, don't I?" She plucked an oversized sheet of paper from the top of a file cabinet and pressed it against the wall—since there was no room on her desk—for Megan to see. It was a sketch of a single-story building. "This is where the massage rooms are going to be." She pinned the sketch against the wall with one forearm and pointed. "Sauna. Showers. Waiting room. I learned some spas call it a relaxation lounge, but that seems a little over-the-top to me. I think it'll be more relaxing without the cutesy name."

Megan looked more closely at the sketch. It was refreshing to meet someone in the relaxation business who thought the word "relaxation" was over-the-top.

"Indoor swimming pool, fitness room, yoga studio," Kira continued, her finger moving over the layout. "I want live music—piano or harp—in the waiting room, so I need to get someone in here to tell me how much soundproofing I need. I'm also going to need someone to advise me on the size of the massage rooms so they're cozy but not cramped." She paused. "Is there any other furniture that needs to go in the room besides the massage table?"

"You'll want storage space for towels and sheets—like shelves or cabinets. And you'll need a place for clients to hang their clothes, unless they'll be changing in a dressing room and putting on a robe."

"That's exactly what I need to know. Let me write that down." Kira draped the sketch over the mess on her desk and backed away with her arms held slightly in front of her, commanding the piles of paper to stay. Satisfied, she pulled open a desk drawer and found a pocket-sized spiral notebook and a pen and jotted down Megan's suggestions.

"So you don't have a blueprint yet?" Megan said. "You started construction before figuring out what you wanted?"

"Slight miscalculation on my part. But it's a separate building—it's no big deal. I didn't want to hold things up, so I got the crew started on the hotel renovations. They've got plenty of work to do. Fixing up the hotel's going to take a while."

A slight miscalculation? Well, okay, it was nice to know airy-fairy helping professionals weren't the only ones who didn't always have everything planned out. With a project this size, Kira had to have a lot of money on the line. She would have expected her to be more organized.

Kira drummed her pen on her notepad, then stopped abruptly, as if she had made a decision. "Would you be interested in working for me?"

Yeah, right. Megan had to admit it was fun to imagine her opinions might shape what this spa ended up looking like, but give up her private practice? To manage a spa? Absolutely not.

"I did some research," Kira said. "Your competition says you're the best."

"I wouldn't call them my competition," Megan said, dismissing the compliment. Kira had been asking about her? She suddenly felt at a disadvantage. "We're all friends."

"I really want to make this spa a success, and I want to hire the best people to help me. I'd love for you to come work for me. Run the massage side of the business."

So all that talk about taking her out to dinner had been…a business meal? Wow, that was sobering. Kira wanted to hire her. Megan couldn't remember the last time her intuition had been so wrong.

"I'm flattered, but no. I already have a great job."

She almost expected Kira to protest—people always did. Amelia never believed her when she said she was too tired to go out. Clients with fibromyalgia insisted on deep massage when that was the worst thing for them. Even her super-nice, long-term clients begged her to squeeze them in when she was already booked. Everyone wanted something from her, expected something from her. *Demanded* something from her. Demanded she fix them or help them or accommodate them.

But Kira was a class act and didn't press.

Not a single word. Just nodded as if she didn't expect anything less. Like she was going to walk away because Megan had said no. Like she respected her.

And that got to her.

No one was going to give up their practice to work at a brand-new spa, not if they were any good at their job, and a recent graduate wouldn't know enough. It was too bad, because it would be great to have a lesbian spa in Piper Beach. And if Kira didn't get someone soon, her construction schedule was going to be a mess and cost her money she might not have. It had been kind of fun, giving her advice. So she relented.

"I don't mind helping you out a little bit, an hour here and there. Answering these kinds of questions isn't hard."

A spark of hope leapt into Kira's eyes.

"Just questions, though," Megan added, deciding she'd better lay down some ground rules. Kira had said she was looking for someone to actually run the spa, not just help design it. "I have my own business to run, so anything that interferes with that, I won't have time for. That means no interviewing, no hiring, no management duties."

"You've got it," Kira said without hesitation, obviously relieved to get any help at all. "I'll pay—"

"Don't pay me."

Kira's eyes widened. "What?"

Yeah, Megan was kind of asking herself the same thing. Did she really have the time and energy to take on volunteer work? She could already hear Svetlana snickering at her motives. But it didn't feel right to let Kira pay her. Not when she had the feeling that if she didn't help Kira with her spa, she'd find some other excuse to spend time with her, and that excuse would be embarrassingly flimsy.

"I don't know as much as you think. I've never worked at a spa. I'm sure there are all kinds of details I don't know about running one."

Kira didn't look like she was buying it. "You're just going to help me out. Me, your competitor."

"I don't think of you as my competitor."

* * *

Not her competitor? That wasn't the response Kira was expecting. Then again, Megan was probably so good, she didn't have to worry about anyone stealing her clients. "I'm not a threat, huh?"

"I like to think there's more than enough business to go around. Anyway, you'll be catering to tourists. I don't do tourists."

"Why not?" Weren't tourists the only business in this town? How could Megan run a successful business without them?

"They're unreliable."

Kira wondered if she herself was included in that dismissive remark. She wasn't a tourist, but she didn't plan to stay forever. Get this spa up and running, sell it, and move on to the next project, which, chances were, would not be in tiny little Piper

Beach. That was the plan. Some people were good at starting businesses and other people were good at running them. Not that she'd ever tried hanging on to a business for long, but there was no reason to believe she'd be good at both. Guess that made her unreliable.

She really didn't want Megan to think of her that way.

And how fucked up was that? Megan *told* her she didn't want to go out to dinner with her. She was lucky to be talking to her at all. And extremely lucky to have her agree to give her advice about the spa, which would likely involve being in the same room with her on a regular basis.

"I can't tell you how much I appreciate this," Kira said. "And I insist on paying you."

"No. If you pay me you'll start expecting me to spend a certain number of hours working for you, and I don't want to want to get tied up in that."

Geez. Massage schools should teach these minnows better business skills. Megan made her feel like a shark.

* * *

Megan picked her way around Kira's piles of paper and headed for the door, eager to do something more productive than argue about money. "Let's see where you're going to build this spa of yours."

Kira followed right behind her, locked her office door, and directed Megan down the hall and out a side door.

"Where to?" Megan asked.

"The wooded lot next door."

"That's where the spa's going to go? You bought that?" Not that she was surprised. Kira Wagner didn't strike her as the superstitious type. Or maybe, being new in town, she hadn't heard the story about the neighboring woods.

A brief walk through the hotel's side parking lot brought them to a brick wall about waist-high that separated the parking spaces from the overgrown lot. Kira sat on top of the low wall and swung her legs over. She held out her hand to help Megan over. Megan ignored her and scrambled over the wall unassisted, tucking the skirt of her cotton sundress around her thighs with an ingrained move honed by years of practice at avoiding flashing people with what her mother called her unladylike antics. On the other side of the wall, a rough path disappeared into a veil of overgrown vines that strangled everything in sight—pines and oaks and unidentifiable shrubs.

"Come on," Kira said. "I'll show you the spot I picked out."

Megan didn't know how anyone could bounce in those heavy work boots, but Kira managed it. She was like a little girl who skipped and ran when she was excited and played hopscotch on imaginary chalk lines when she was bored, unable to stand still. Megan followed more slowly, making sure she didn't step on any poison ivy. Her sandals weren't going to protect her if she did something stupid. She was so busy watching her step she didn't see the massive fallen tree blocking their path until Kira clambered over it.

Kira waited for her on the other side of the tree trunk. "Need a hand?"

Again? There she was, ready to steady her or maybe even haul her over by the waist if necessary. That was definitely not happening. Not in this lifetime.

"I'm fine. I'm not wearing the right shoes for this, but I can handle this." Megan planted both hands on the tree and waited for Kira to get out of the way.

Now all she had to do was get herself over this thing without snagging her sundress on a branch. Next time she came over here she was wearing jeans. She pressed down harder on the tree, lifted her body weight onto her hands, and vaulted over. Sure, she balanced longer than necessary, but she wasn't going to feel bad about showing off. Kira needed to understand that just because she was wearing a dress didn't mean she had no upper body strength. Not that Kira gave any sign of noticing.

The path didn't continue beyond the fallen tree, but it didn't matter because everything was more open, and you could safely pick your way around the trees without worrying so much about what unpleasant surprise you were about to step on in the underbrush. A beautiful stand of loblolly pines filtered the sunlight.

Continuing on, they came to the edge of a hidden grove where Kira stopped by a yellow surveyor's marker. "Here's the spot. A spa in the woods, with big picture windows. It's going to be awesome."

"The woods aren't as trashed as I thought they would be," Megan observed. "No empty beer bottles. The local kids must be too scared to hang out here and drink."

"What are you talking about?"

"Everyone avoids this place. The real estate agent didn't tell you?"

"Tell me what?"

It didn't seem fair not to have told her. Megan wondered which agent had sold her the lot. "The story is that back when the Starfish Hotel was first built, a woman staying at the hotel was raped and murdered here in the woods. Somehow she managed to stab her attacker with his own knife before she died. Right under the ribs. Killed him with his own weapon."

"Good for her."

"Yeah, except that she ended up dead, too."

"So now everyone thinks these woods are unsafe." Kira didn't look too concerned.

Wasn't she even just a tiny bit superstitious? Megan looked around, wondering where, exactly, the bodies had been found. The hotel wasn't far, and neither was the road. You'd think someone would have heard them. "No one wants to be next."

"No wonder I got such a good deal."

"People have talked about building something on this lot for a long time, but nobody local would buy it."

"Lucky for me, then."

"You don't care about the creepy vibe?"

"You think there's a creepy vibe? If you'd never heard that story, would you honestly think this place was scary?" Kira gestured toward the trees. "I like this place. It's sad about that woman, but I don't think her ghost is hanging around. Not that I believe in ghosts. It feels good here. It feels like..." She rolled her eyes. "Like clean air and ocean breezes and all that wonderful clichéd stuff I'm going to put in my ads. Not like rapists are hiding behind the brush."

She was right, actually. From the outside, it did feel creepy, but here it felt completely different. In all the times she'd walked by on the street, she'd never suspected there was such peaceful, undisturbed wilderness hidden back here.

And Kira was going to clear-cut these beautiful old trees and destroy their magic. So she could build a spa. What a waste. If she wanted to create a healing environment, all she needed to do was preserve what was already here. Get rid of the invasive vines and clear a nature trail.

Kira stared into space with her hands in her back pockets and her elbows out to the sides, lost in her vision for the site. "The minute I saw this, I knew it would be perfect for my spa. It was the same way with the hotel. I walked in the front door and I knew I had to buy it."

Megan knew what she was talking about. Despite its current state of disrepair, the hotel did feel surprisingly welcoming.

"Don't you think it'll be great?" Kira said.

Megan tried to picture herself inside Kira's future building looking out at what was left of the scenery, but all she could think was that she didn't want to be here the day the bulldozers crashed through and knocked down the trees.

Why was this bothering her so much? She had to admit it was a beautiful setting for a spa. And better a small spa than a multistory hotel that would raze the whole site and smother it with a sprawling parking lot. This was one of the last big tracts of undeveloped land in the area. It was inevitable that someone would build here eventually. Yet sticking any new building here, even a small one, felt all wrong. She wandered around, spotting several more of the yellow markers and an ancient solitary boulder that was no doubt destined to be one of the displaced residents.

Sad.

"You've already had a surveyor measure this out?" Megan said.

"Yup."

"But you don't have a blueprint yet."

"It won't be long. The size of the building's not going to change, so why wait?"

A lump formed in her throat at Kira's callousness. Did she not care at all that she was destroying these trees? As she continued to walk, pressure built in her chest, and the sense of doom she'd always associated with this neglected lot increased.

She stopped. Doom was taking it a little far, wasn't it? Maybe the feeling was more like someone's hands pushing her, resisting her. Cautiously, she took a step forward, and the pressure increased again. Weird. Mentally, she scanned her body. Where was the pressure coming from? She couldn't possibly be having a heart attack. She chased a tendril of fear around her lungs, then found the fear hovering over her shoulders like a sweaty linebacker looming behind her. This was ridiculous. Her imagination didn't usually come up with crap like this. So maybe it wasn't her imagination. Could it actually be a spirit? Something left over from the woman who was murdered here? Megan leaned back and relaxed into Mr. Creepy to figure out what he was.

Mr. Creepy and the sense of foreboding abruptly vanished. The pressure was still there, but now she realized it wasn't coming from inside her at all. It was the air, resisting her. Or... it wasn't the air. She was standing in some sort of energy field. And she hadn't even noticed?

Megan turned to face the direction the field was pushing her. That weathered, lichen-covered boulder—that's where it wanted her to go. She moved toward it and immediately the energy lightened. Instead of pushing her, now it drew her, compelled her.

Her hands were on the boulder before she was even conscious of reaching for it. It was taller than she was, an irregular oblong monolith balanced on its small end, yet so solidly planted that there must be several feet of its length buried in the ground. Tingling energy poured into her hands and filled her whole body, charging up her aura with a buzz that made her collapse against the boulder and slide to the ground with her knees bending and her back against the stone and her tailbone smacking into the dirt.

She had a feeling she knew what this was. It was hard to believe it was here, in an abandoned lot where no one knew about it, but here it was.

Kira strode over. "Are you all right?"

"Give me a minute." Megan struggled to her feet and put several yards between her and the stone. As hard as it was to tear herself away, she needed to know if her suspicions were correct. She circled the boulder, opening her senses and sinking her awareness into the ground, tuning in to what lay beneath the surface to see if she could detect other channels of energy. Some people used dowsing rods to do what she was doing. She'd never needed to. She didn't need to hold a pointing stick to help her read the signals her subconscious sent to her gut.

Kira watched her with a bemused look. "You look like you're listening for something."

"Do you feel it?"

"Feel what?"

Megan shook her head impatiently. She didn't need a dowsing rod, but she did need quiet. It would be better to come back later—alone—to get a better read on this, but she was too excited to wait.

There it was. Another current heading for the boulder.

Unbelievable. A ley line in Piper Beach, channeling energy from deep within the earth, zapping it around the globe. She could use this to heal her clients. If Kira hadn't invited her back here she'd never have known. And now...

Kira wasn't going to be happy about this.

"You can't build here," Megan said.

Kira's posture stiffened abruptly. "Excuse me?"

Yeah, that went well. What did she *think* Kira was going to say?

Megan stood up straighter. If she hadn't already agreed to help Kira design her spa, she would definitely have done so now. Because she had to convince her not to build here. She might not be able to change her mind and get her to change her plans today, but if she worked with her and gained her trust, she'd have a chance.

"I know you're going to think I'm crazy, but you have two powerful ley lines running through here."

Kira's eyes narrowed with suspicion. "And ley lines are…?"

"Focused channels of earth energy. They're like the earth's arteries." Megan held her breath, but Kira's face did not cloud over with the usual get-me-away-from-the-crazy-person reaction—which was a relief, because that reaction always hurt, no matter how many times it happened—so she pressed on. "The boulder was positioned on top of the intersection of two ley lines, where the energy is strongest, to magnify the energy."

"You're telling me someone placed that rock there deliberately?"

"Yes."

"Like Stonehenge?"

Megan nodded.

"How can you tell? It doesn't look anything like Stonehenge. It just looks like a random rock."

"It's not."

Kira folded her arms across her chest and glared at the boulder, then at Megan, then back. "I've never heard of Native Americans building stone circles."

"They did believe certain rocks were sacred. And as you can see, this is not a stone circle, it's a single megalith."

"Exactly. It's one rock. The glaciers pushed it around and it ended up here by accident. Nothing sacred about it."

"There's no way it ended up in that particular spot by accident."

Kira coughed. "Because of the energy, right?"

"The ley lines."

"I don't do energy."

"Yeah." Megan crossed her arms, mirroring Kira, and wished she didn't feel so depressed. "I didn't think you did."

Kira gave her a pained look. She did not look particularly happy to have won the argument. Instead, she went over to the boulder, circled it suspiciously, and gave it the kind of solid pat you'd give a dog.

Megan watched her, perplexed.

"Not that I believe any of this, but wouldn't other people already know about this? Why aren't there New Age witches making pilgrimages to my back lot?"

"I don't know." Better not to tell her there would be soon. First Megan would come back on her own, at night, when Kira wasn't around, and get a better sense of what exactly she'd found; then she'd tell the local energy workers. Once they experienced this energy, Kira was going to have a crowd. "Maybe the murder story was started as a way to keep people away from here."

"Why would someone do that?"

"Who knows? In any case, the site must have been forgotten a long time ago. And it's small. The ley lines are strong, but I don't think they extend very far. I've never sensed them anywhere else in the neighborhood. Even if they do extend out, people have built on top of them and destroyed any access. This is an amazing find."

"I can't believe this," Kira grumbled.

"You can't build here. Please. Moving that stone would be…"

"Sacrilege?" Kira supplied the word she was looking for, as if she understood. She seemed to be familiar with the concept of standing stones, not that that meant anything. She was a developer. She was going to destroy this magical site before anyone even had a chance to see what it could do. That was what developers did.

But not if Megan had anything to say about it.

"Moving that stone is not a good idea."

Kira ran her hands through her hair. "You're right, I do think you're nuts. I realize you totally believe what you're saying, but it's nuts. I don't care if there's a vortex of energy or what-have-you here or not. I bought this land so I could build here. And it's going to be an awesome spa."

CHAPTER FOUR

"I'll leave the room now so you can get undressed," Megan said hurriedly, backing out of her massage room before Barbara Fenhurst, her new client, finished stripping.

She shut the door to the converted bedroom on the second floor of her townhouse and checked her watch. Usually she went downstairs for a few minutes to wait, but this client wasn't going to need long to change, so instead Megan waited in the hallway outside the room and clasped her hands behind her back to stretch as she estimated how many minutes—seconds?—she should wait before she knocked.

"I'm ready," Barbara called out from behind the door.

Megan went in and there was Barbara Fenhurst lying on the table, buck naked. She was sure she had asked her to lie under the sheet. It was part of her standard instructions: on the table with your head at this end, faceup, *under the sheet*. Guess she shouldn't have bothered with her line about it being okay to leave your underwear on if you're not comfortable getting completely undressed.

"Let me get another sheet to cover you." Megan headed for the closet. This was not the first time a client had failed to understand the turned-down sheet as an invitation to climb in under it. Most people were nervous the first time they got a massage, and that made it easy to get confused.

"You don't need to cover me," Barbara protested. "My old masseuse never used a sheet."

There weren't many professionals who still did that, now that the industry was regulated and trying to gain mainstream respect, but there would probably always be a few old-school massage therapists who believed healing occurred by transcending societal norms and hang-ups. It was wonderful that they felt so comfortable, but nudity was a lawsuit waiting to happen. You couldn't date a lawyer and not worry about things like that. Oddly enough, it was the one thing Amelia hadn't accused her of being unreasonable about. In fact, Amelia had always been on her case, begging her to be careful. The drape protected against misunderstandings.

Megan pulled a fresh sheet from the top of the stack and unfolded it. "You might get cold."

"I'm fine."

"I'd rather have you draped."

"Really, it doesn't bother me."

Barbara wasn't making this easy. "It's as much for me as it is for you. I'm going to have to insist."

"Oh, all right."

Megan laid the sheet over her and folded down the edge at her shoulders. Barbara immediately moved her arms out from underneath and kicked at the sheet until one foot was exposed. Whether she was too warm or she was trying to make a point, Megan didn't care. The main thing was she was covered. If Amelia ever found out she'd been busted by an undercover cop for alleged prostitution, or sued for sexual harassment... Well, actually, Amelia wouldn't care anymore.

"I've never heard of an uptight masseuse," Barbara said suspiciously. "Are you sure you know what you're doing?"

"Positive."

"I still think the sheet is silly," Barbara muttered.

Megan sat on her stool at the head of the massage table and began milking the tension out of the tight bands of muscle on the sides of Barbara's neck, automatically avoiding the vulnerable soft spots. If only women were this eager to flash her in a social setting. That might be fun. But no, she got the dubious honor of arguing with a naked client whose body she had zero personal interest in.

"So other than the sheet, how are you feeling today?" Megan asked.

"Oh…my back hurts. My neck hurts. My feet. Everything. The doctors don't know what's wrong with me. My acupuncturist said she wants to see me twice a week." Barbara kicked the sheet off her other foot. "I like what you're doing to my neck."

An angel materialized behind them and leaned over Megan's shoulder to see what she was doing. Megan stilled her hands, cradling Barbara's head. As often as she invited the angels to help her in her healing work, she never got used to their otherworldly radiance.

Thank you, she said silently. It was so inadequate for what she felt. Gratitude that they were willing to help her, gratitude that she was one of the rare few who could see them, gratitude that angels existed at all.

The angel extended her arms forward, one on either side of Megan's body, and placed her shining hands on top of Megan's solid ones. They appeared to touch for a moment before the angel's hands passed through her, merging with her, until all that was visible was a faint glow emanating from Megan's form. Her hands grew hot, and her body buzzed with the incredible energy. She channeled that energy into Barbara, moving her fingers in a light circular motion on the back of her neck, feeling the bones and tendons beneath the skin. She could easily get lost in there, drawn in by her fascination for discovering the imbalances she could feel lurking. If she could get at them, the whole structure would self-correct. She sank her fingers around the vertebrae and felt Barbara's arteries pulse, felt her cells breathe, felt the pull of microscopic muscle fibers and connective tissue. Moving her fingers imperceptibly, she ferreted out the wayward tendon at the root of the problem, allowing it to return to its natural relaxed state. Barbara sighed with relief.

When it was time for Barbara to turn over onto her stomach, the angel vanished. Megan stood and held up the edge of the sheet so Barbara wouldn't drag the whole sheet with her and expose herself. She got her settled into the face cradle, folded the sheet down to her sacrum, and tucked her in. She rubbed fresh massage cream between her palms to warm it, then deftly transferred it to her client's skin with broad strokes. She loved feeling the muscles, loved using her hands to ease someone's pain. She positioned her hands on either side of Barbara's spine and pushed down the length of her back.

Something pinched in Megan's sternum—her breastbone— shooting pain through her chest and into her shoulder. Yikes. This was not good. She lifted her hands off Barbara's body and stretched.

Cautiously repositioning herself, she pressed her thumbs into Barbara's upper back, near the shoulder blades. She shifted her weight to push with better leverage, but each time she bent a certain way, something caught in her chest as if a rib were out of place, making it hard to breathe. As much as she tried not to hunch over or move the wrong way, it was almost impossible not to put pressure on whatever it was. This wasn't the first time she'd experienced this type of problem, but it had never been this bad before.

"Right there," Barbara encouraged her. "You found a great spot."

Megan barely registered the compliment. Right now she was more concerned with making sure she could get through the next twenty minutes without hurting herself. And not think about what it would mean if she needed to take a week off. Or more.

It couldn't be too serious if she was able to keep going with Barbara's massage. If she ever got injured so badly that she had to quit massage… She was *not* going to worry about that now.

What she needed to focus on was ignoring the pain and keeping her back as straight as possible to avoid pinching that nerve.

With just a few minutes left in the session, Megan dug her fingers in one more time.

Agony stabbed the front of her right shoulder.

Oh, shit.

She eased her hand away from Barbara's body, wondering which direction was safe to move. Muscles spasmed and pain radiated from the pectoralis minor across her chest and down her arm. She stifled a gasp. "All done," she whispered. Thank God this was her last session of the day. "I'll be back in a few minutes."

Barbara groaned. "Do I *have* to get up? Can't I just lie here all night?"

"Take your time." Megan headed for the door. Occasionally clients did fall back asleep when she left, but today would not be a good day for that. She'd check back in a few minutes, after she washed her hands.

"Wake me up tomorrow, would you?"

Megan was still soaping the massage cream off her elbows when she heard Barbara open the massage room door and wander down the short hallway. So much for falling asleep. She must have shot off the table the moment Megan left the room. Either that or she was walking around in the nude.

"I'll be right there," Megan called out, rinsing off her arms.

Barbara stuck her head in the open door of the bathroom where Megan was washing up. "Hi."

At least her client was dressed. "I'll be right there," Megan repeated. "If you wouldn't mind waiting in the massage room…"

"Okay." Barbara left.

Megan reached for a towel and swiped vigorously at herself, trying to hurry, and squeaked at the sharp pain in her chest. Three of her fingers were numb. She abandoned the towel and dashed across the hall.

"Your house has great energy." Barbara fingered a conch shell she'd plucked from one of Megan's displays of seashells and crystals arranged on pedestals in each corner of the room. She returned the shell and pulled out her checkbook. "Very welcoming. I love it."

Megan picked up her appointment book, gritted her teeth at the stab of pain caused by that small movement, and dropped her book onto the massage table.

"Although I'm not crazy about your walls," Barbara continued obliviously. "I think moss green would look better. My masseuse back in California had moss green walls. Really soothing. I'd be happy to trade you a massage for some house painting."

"Uh, no thanks." Barbara didn't think it was odd to offer to paint her house? Usually it took clients several months before they felt comfortable making suggestions about her personal life. And besides, Megan loved her pale peach walls.

"Suit yourself. Just thought I'd offer." Barbara looked at her sideways like she couldn't believe Megan would pass on her offer. "Great massage, by the way. You have great hands."

"Thanks. Same time next Monday?" Megan flipped open her appointment book and wondered if she would, in fact, be seeing clients at all next week. She kept her doubts to herself. She'd make sure the pain was gone by then.

"I can't wait to tell my acupuncturist all about you," Barbara said. "You two should meet. That reminds me, I'm having some friends over for dinner this weekend and I'd love it if you could come. Saturday? Seven o'clock? I'll give you directions."

"Sorry, I make it a rule not to socialize with my clients."

"Oh, come on. Why not?"

"It helps me keep this a safe space for my clients," Megan explained. "If we tried to be friends, then you might worry about whether I like you or not. I want you to relax into the massage and not worry about keeping me entertained."

Barbara looked confused. "You don't like me?"

"Of course I like you."

"I invite my co-workers to my house all the time."

"Being friends with a co-worker is not the same thing as being friends with your massage therapist."

"Sure it is. Heck, people even *date* their co-workers. Happens all the time. Nothing bad happens."

Usually nothing bad happens. Megan doubted anything she said would convince her, but she had to try. "Your co-workers don't see you naked." At least, she hoped they didn't. Considering how they'd started their first massage, she could be wrong. She continued before Barbara could contradict her. "What if it was your boss? The therapist/client relationship is very intimate and also very unequal. I want this to be a healing experience for you. That means we have to have rules. The rules protect you. They make this a safe place for you emotionally. And they protect me, too."

Understanding did not dawn in Barbara's eyes.

"My boss has seen me naked in the hot tub."

Perfect.

* * *

"Let me give you a massage," Svetlana urged Megan over the phone. "Friday afternoons are cursed, anyway—I never get any appointments. I'll have hours free to fix your sternum."

"I appreciate it, but..." Her pectorals were always tight. Bending over a massage table was like doing pushups all day, and all the stretching in the world never seemed to be enough to counter that. And if anyone was going to work on her it was Svetlana. They traded frequently, and she felt safe with her. But anytime anyone, even Svetlana, got close to her chest muscles, her body tensed against the touch and she ended up tighter than before. Obviously, she had issues.

"Why you don't let me help you?" Svetlana demanded. "I can help. I'm putting you down in my book for three o'clock."

Megan gave in.

* * *

Svetlana's office suite was the perfect space for her and her husband—two treatment rooms, a restroom and a waiting room with utilitarian chairs and a bubbly Zen fountain. Inside the massage room, Megan relaxed on her back while Svetlana leaned over her and tucked her into a navy blue sheet with a race car print.

"Can you believe these sheets?" Svetlana complained. "On sale, Patrick tells me. I now learn it's not safe to let husband loose at outlet mall."

"There's really nothing wrong with—"

"What about solid color, I tell him. What about white? These sheets are for children."

"At least they're soft," Megan said, glad she was in charge of picking out her own supplies.

Svetlana sighed and switched on Megan's favorite music—a quiet blend of birdsong with wind chimes and flute—and turned the volume down extra low. "So how was your day?"

Megan rotated her wrists, stretching out her forearms. "Someone told another one of my clients I can see angels, and now she wants to know if they have a message for her. I told her I've never heard an angel speak, but she doesn't believe me."

"What kind of message?"

"You know, a message. Inspirational guidance. Celestial advice."

"No one ever asks me for divine guidance."

"Be grateful. People ask me all the time."

"Why you don't make something up?"

"You mean, lie?"

Svetlana waved her hands around encouragingly. "Get book of angel messages and pick message that sounds good. If they notice it came from book, tell them you ask angel to guide you to correct page."

"I'm a massage therapist, not a tarot reader."

"It make your clients happy."

Megan shifted uncomfortably on the massage table. "It would be taking advantage of their trust."

"Why? It's all a gimmick anyway, no? You can call it angel therapy or what you like, but it's still massage. It's still your hands on their muscles, no?"

Yes, it was her hands; yes, it was her intuition. But despite what Svetlana might think, the angels weren't a gimmick. They were real. With the angels providing extra juice, the healing was more profound than what she could do on her own.

Svetlana positioned one hand on top of the other with the heel of the underneath hand placed firmly on Megan's breastbone. She sank her weight ever so slowly, deep…deep…deep into her chest until the pain made further conversation impossible. Megan stared at the familiar medical posters illustrating the human musculoskeletal system without seeing them. Svetlana pressed harder.

Wasn't that deep enough?

Becoming a professional massage therapist had ruined massage for her. She knew too much. She couldn't stop herself from analyzing Svetlana's technique, and how could you fully relax when you wanted to micromanage the whole experience? Some days she could shut it out and enjoy being on the massage table, but today was not one of those days.

To be fair, Svetlana was doing everything right—at any hint of defensive clenching in the muscles, she paused and let up a bit on the pressure. When she sensed Megan was ready to let her back in, she continued pressing.

Exactly what Megan would do herself. The only difference was that Megan preferred to use a lighter, gentler touch with her own clients, while Svetlana prided herself on not doing relaxation massage. With her body weight leveraged onto her arms, she was a lot stronger than she looked, and that was saying something, because Svetlana was built. Clients never fell asleep on her table. Blacked out from pain, maybe, but not sleep.

Megan stayed with the pain as it radiated out along the path of her ribs and seeped into her lungs. It hurt to breathe. The edges of her field of vision turned to gray. She wondered if she was going to pass out, and if Svetlana would notice she was no longer conscious.

In the grayness, a vision of a feral girl gradually came into focus.

The girl was emaciated and wore nothing more than a loincloth. She didn't look anything like her, but she knew she was looking at herself. Herself in some other lifetime.

She swung an ax at a tree and hit it with a satisfying thunk. She had built this ax herself—sharpened and polished the stone, then lashed it with rawhide to a club—and it was performing well. Her brothers teased her for being slower and weaker than a man, but the fact was, there were plenty of others willing to clear boring vines. She preferred to swing at trees.

The trees and brush would be left to dry in the sun, the elders would predict when the rains would come, and on the augured day, the dry kindling would be set on fire, turning that patch of forest into fertile ash for planting.

The day came, the skies flashed, and the fires were set. But something went wrong.

The rains never came, and now the whole forest was on fire. Deer stampeded downhill toward the river. She followed them, fleeing the wall of heat that chased her through the parched forest, but she wasn't fast enough, she couldn't breathe…

Something cracked under Svetlana's hand.

Megan blinked back to the present. It wasn't the crack of bone. It was the fascia—the net-like tissue that held all the body's parts together—softening and stretching under the pressure of Svetlana's palm. Things were moving in there that hadn't moved in years. Like the cartilage where her ribs attached to her sternum. Nauseating when you were on the receiving end.

She tried to take a deep breath, but her chest wouldn't let her. Svetlana let up a little, adjusting the pressure, staying completely present even as tears leaked from the corners of Megan's eyes. That was the great thing about working with someone who was good at this job—she didn't have to worry about scaring her off if she got emotional. Her body relaxed. She might bitch to herself about Svetlana's deep work, but this was what her chest needed. Svetlana waited for her to inhale one more time, then rode her exhale down, sinking to her previous level of pressure. Megan's heart raced. She stayed with the feeling and waited to see if it would dissipate. It didn't. It got worse, almost to the verge of panic. Her vision clouded again. There was no sign of the burning forest. Instead, the gray darkened and solidified into the shape of massive stone columns.

The ground shook violently, knocking her to the stone floor beside a blazing hearth. The earth heaved again. Voices shouted to each other to run, but they were not shouting to her. She had to stay. She had been chosen. The goddess would protect her against Poseidon's temper. The goddess would protect her... She stumbled to her knees and prayed the temple would not collapse, that the sacred flame would not be extinguished, for that would bring down a curse upon the city. If it wasn't already cursed...

Her vision swam. She found herself in a cobblestone town square in another century, squeezing her eyes shut to block out the sight of the pyre and the excited crowd.

A twig snapped.

Smoke filled her lungs and paralyzed them. She was gasping and she couldn't...

"That's too much," Megan said abruptly.

Svetlana stopped pressing, but kept one hand resting lightly on Megan's breastbone. Standard procedure; but irrationally, Megan wanted to slap her hand away. Instead she sat up and doubled over, clutching the sheet to her breasts.

Svetlana let go and leaned over her with concern. "Are you all right?"

Megan waved her away. "I guess I wasn't as ready as I thought I was."

"It is necessary to work on this scar tissue. You told me you cracked sternum when you were a kid, yes?"

"When I was three."

Megan pressed her fists, still clutching the sheet, to the center of her chest. She'd had a client once who'd been in a car accident tell her that a cracked sternum could be seriously painful, but Megan didn't remember any pain. She'd fallen off a jungle gym, and what she did remember, with total clarity, was how time had frozen still. The impact couldn't have lasted more than a second, but for what seemed like an eternity there was no sound, no people, no movement—just her on the ground in that profound silence, flat on her back with the breath knocked out of her, too stunned to cry, staring into the eyes of an angel.

Just went to show that even the best parenting was no match for the forces of karma that shaped kids' lives. Most people thought karma was cosmic payback. Cause and effect. It wasn't. It was cause and effect and effect and effect and effect. A groove in the dirt that got worn down so many times it became a canyon. Leftover habits and memories—any baggage you hadn't let go of—that became ingrained, forming a blueprint for the shape of your life. Her fall wasn't a punishment, but it was no accident: It was her karma's way of re-creating the trauma she carried over from previous lives. Knock her off the jungle gym with a slip of the foot and bingo!—she was all set for a lifetime of blocked energy in her chest. God forbid she should forget what it felt like to suffocate. Oh no, fate made sure her lungs and chest would hurt in this life, even if she couldn't remember why.

"Will you be able to work?" Svetlana asked.

"I think so."

Maybe a hot bath would feel good after all the ice she'd been applying to her chest. It was really a horrible place to have to stick an ice pack, but not as horrible as not being able to do her job.

* * *

Later that night, Megan sat cross-legged and barefoot on a pillow on the floor of her bedroom, gritting her teeth against the jolt of pain that shot through her chest when she shifted position. With every hour, the pain was getting worse. She ignored it and focused on meditating. One way or another she was going to make this pain go away.

Except as soon as her heart rate began to slow, red-orange flames intruded upon her thoughts, engulfing her.

She shook her head in frustration, trying to get rid of the image. What use were these disturbing flashes of intuition? If only they came with a voice that said, "This is how you're fated to die, so be careful," or, "This is how you died last time, and there isn't a damn thing you can do about it." Even if she knew whether the images were from the past or from the future, what was she supposed to do with the information? Track down the person who killed her and forgive them? Become a firefighter? Learn to flambé? What exactly was the point?

"What!" she shouted at the universe.

If there was some spiritual lesson she was supposed to learn from this, it would be nice to have the teacher's answer key.

Her doctor had prescribed painkillers, suggested lots of rest, and said if the pain in her chest and the numbness in her arm continued, they could look into other options. The chiropractor wanted to see her again in two days to continue work on freeing the nerves she'd pinched. Svetlana's massage had helped, but an hour later the pain was back. No one knew exactly what was wrong. Megan could tell what they were thinking, though—that whether it was a pulled muscle or a torn ligament or a wrenched disk, injuries took time to heal.

Weeks.

Maybe months.

Months of not having a job. Months for her clients to abandon her and discover someone else.

Months. Maybe years.

She wouldn't be the first massage therapist to get injured and never make a full recovery, and be forced to change jobs, do something more financially secure—something boring and unfulfilling, like most of humanity. Kira Wagner wanted to offer her a job like that.

She clenched her fists and rammed them into her thighs. She didn't want to be manager of Kira's spa. She wasn't ready to lose her clients and start over. She wasn't ready to end her career.

And she wasn't going to.

Because she was going to fix this.

Taking a deep breath, she turned her vision inward, past the flames, and found her inner spark. She felt it glow, and expanded it, flooding herself with its white, sparkling light. She ran the specific energy current that would release her karma and untie the knots that bound her to her past—the past that had created this injury. Flames appeared again, hot against her eyelids. She steadied her breath and continued. No need to react. Karmic patterns were a habit, after all, and habits could be broken. Whatever this karmic memory meant—and perhaps it meant nothing—she could free herself. She could let it go.

She might feel like she was burning, but in reality she was sitting alone in her room in no danger at all, and trying to push away the fear would only make it embed itself more deeply. She had to face it. She had to lower her barriers and let herself feel the screaming pain as she burned.

She would burn until she was dead, and then it would be over.

CHAPTER FIVE

"I need to reschedule your appointment," Megan said over the phone for the eighteenth time, relieved that she was almost done working her way down her list of next week's clients.

"Why?" Barbara Fenhurst—number eighteen—demanded.

"I injured myself." The words were a little easier to choke out after so many calls, but they still made her mad.

Meditation had not helped. Even the painkillers didn't help enough to let her kid herself that she'd be able to work through it. Much as she hated to do it, she'd decided to cancel her appointments for a week and give her body a chance to heal.

"That's annoying," Barbara said. "I'm going to miss you so much."

"I should be better in a week." She sure hoped so, because some of her clients were in serious pain and they needed her.

"If I have to miss my next appointment then I want to make an extra appointment to make up for it. Do you have any openings Wednesday after work?"

"I have you down for your regular time slot on Monday, but other than that, I'm booked."

"How about Wednesday morning?"

"I'm sorry, I've been rescheduling everyone and I'm already overbooked for the week."

"Don't you want the extra business?"

Megan tightened her grip on her phone and hoped she wouldn't say something she'd regret. She knew Barbara's massage was important to her, but to be honest, there were other clients she wanted to make time for who were in more serious pain. Besides, Barbara shouldn't be making her feel guilty when there was no guarantee she'd be seeing *anyone* next week. It was times like these when it would be nice to have an assistant to make her calls for her, someone who could talk to her clients without feeling torn between wanting to help and knowing there was a limit to how many massages she was physically able to give.

"I'm flexible," Barbara said. "You can squeeze me in anywhere."

"I wish I could. How about scheduling your extra session for next month?"

"Next *month*?" A note of hysteria entered Barbara's voice. "All right, but I want to make sure you have me down for every Monday through the end of July."

"Okay."

"How many weeks is that? Six? Seven? Can I get one free?"

"I'm sorry, but no."

"Don't I deserve one free session for the inconvenience of canceling my appointment?"

"I'm really sorry." She did wish she could do something to make it up to her clients, but discounts meant more work for less money, and more work—even though she was going to be super-careful about her body mechanics when she got back to work—meant more chance of injury. And injuries she definitely couldn't afford.

"Not even for your best customer?"

Barbara Fenhurst just didn't know when to quit.

* * *

That night Megan had no evening appointments—since she'd canceled them all—so she headed over to Kira's hotel around seven. She had planned to return to the ley lines in the pitch-dark to avoid any potential run-ins with attractive, annoyed landowners, but decided to take a chance on going early. The construction crew would be long gone, as would Kira, and because it would still be daylight, she'd be able to see where she was going in those woods near the hotel, which would be nice, because the last thing she needed was a sprained ankle.

She found the path easily. The fallen tree wasn't as easy to clamber over because her injury made it too painful for her arms to support her body weight, but in her ratty jeans and sneakers and T-shirt she could make her legs do most of the work without worrying about snagging nicer clothes.

She went straight to the monolith, but this time was careful not to touch it. She'd investigate it later, after she mapped out where the ley lines were. No sense in knocking herself out with an energy surge first thing.

She closed her eyes and, with an ease that came from years of practice, shifted instantly from her everyday awareness of normal physical reality to a state of consciousness where her body was not a solid, physical presence, but a net of crisscrossing lines of electricity. Where her physical body ended, the electrical currents continued, hooking into the larger web of energy that was the earth itself. Energy flowed out of her and into her, sparking along different channels.

Slowly, she walked around the standing stone, feeling her way, tracking the energy. She felt her aura click into place each time she stepped onto one of the leys. Just as she'd thought, there were two intersecting ley lines that met underground inside the stone, creating two entry points and two exit points. She opened her eyes and noted their position. She chose one of the streams of energy and followed it across the wooded lot, walking in slow motion, her back very straight, her eyes unfocused as she tuned in to the energy. It wasn't a straight line, but a shallow wave, undulating left and right. When trees got in the way, she walked around them and picked up the trace on the other side. At the far end of the lot she turned around to face the stone. She could almost see the path of energy shimmering.

What if Kira moved the building over? Kept the monolith where it was and built at the other end of the lot? But no, the lot was too small, and the way the leys crisscrossed it, there wasn't any one spot that was big enough to accommodate a building without interfering with the lines.

The noise of twigs snapping and footsteps approaching made her turn.

* * *

Kira recognized Megan in the distance and tripped over a tree root.

What was Megan doing here?

She laughed silently at herself. She knew what Megan was doing here. Causing problems.

Kira had just gotten back from dinner when she'd caught a glimpse through the trees of someone sneaking around on her property. Sure, Megan said the locals avoided the place, but how many people did that really cover? Most people here were tourists. She had followed, expecting to find a group of teenagers who were going to have to loiter somewhere else. She didn't know if discovering Megan here instead was better or worse.

Megan stood motionless and ethereal in the summer evening sunlight, her gaze unfocused and distant. Kira approached and stopped a few feet away, unsure what to say, thrown off by Megan's complete lack of any sign of having noticed her.

Megan was the one who broke the silence. "Didn't mean to trespass," she said.

"You're not trespassing," Kira said, recovering her ability to speak. "You work for me, remember?"

Megan blinked and opened her mouth. "I—"

"At least I hope you do," Kira added, because maybe she didn't want to help her with the spa now that she knew those energy lines were there.

Megan shook her head. "You won't need me if you don't build your spa."

Kira came closer, drawn by the certainty that they *should* work together, no matter what Megan thought. "I'm building it," she said gently. As much as she didn't want to force reality on Megan and wipe that dreamy look from her eyes, she wasn't going to lie to her.

Megan gestured to the woods surrounding them. "You don't realize what a treasure you have here."

"I *do* realize what a treasure I have here. I have a place to build." And a beautiful, earnest woodland creature spouting nonsense at her. "I'm trying to do something good, create a beautiful place for women to vacation. I'm not the villain here."

"You don't understand." Megan's eyes were more focused now, harder.

Kira blew out her breath in frustration. "Why can't I build on these lines? Assuming they exist. They're energy, right? Won't the energy still be here if I stick a building on top of it?"

"When you build on top of a ley line, the energy's still there, of course, but it becomes harder for us as human beings to access it. Man-made structures dilute our perception of the energy. Steel, any kind of metal, water running through the plumbing, electrical wiring—it all disrupts the energy and scatters it."

"How do you know that?"

"I can tell that the channel—at least our perception of it— was weakened when it was paved over and electrical power lines were put in. Now that I know the leys are here, I can sense them out on the street, but they're very hard to detect. I can't feel them at all anywhere else in the neighborhood."

Not that she understood how seemingly normal, rational people could believe in this stuff, but Kira had met enough strange women over the years to have heard some of this mumbo-jumbo before, and what Megan was saying didn't make sense. "Weren't ancient temples purposely built on power spots like this one?"

"Many of them were. But they were designed using sacred geometry to enhance the power instead of interfere with it, and they were places of worship."

"A spa's kind of spiritual."

"Nice try."

"Why not? It's healing."

"It's not the same thing. It'll be a business, not a church."

"A spiritual business." That was stretching it. She didn't actually have any plans to give her spa a spiritual aspect, but anyone who sensed so-called "energy" could surely find the spiritual side to any business.

Megan pursed her lips, obviously seeing right through her bullshit. "The ancients knew how to use stone to harness this energy. We don't. Please don't build anything here. It's a powerful site and it would be a shame not to preserve it."

"Look, I'm sorry you're not happy with what I'm doing, but we're not talking about an endangered bird—we're talking about something that most people would agree does not even exist."

Megan's face went blank, her emotional armor sliding into place.

Kira's heart clenched. What was it about this woman that she couldn't stand to hurt her feelings? She hated how Megan was looking at her, but it was impossible to do what she was asking of her—to cancel construction of the spa and throw away her investment in the land. If Kira were her father she wouldn't even waste time arguing about it.

"I need to go home." Megan turned and headed for the fallen tree that marked the way out.

"I'm heading out, too." Kira joined her, matching her stride for stride. She turned her head to look at her, but Megan stared straight ahead, shutting her out. As they stepped around a tree, Megan pushed a low-hanging branch away from her face and winced as it ricocheted behind her.

"That branch didn't hurt you, did it?" Kira touched Megan's arm and pushed her wild hair out of her face, searching for scratches.

Megan stared at her with luminous eyes. Her hairline was

incredibly soft and warm and… Whoa. Okay. Stop. Take a step back.

"No scratches," Kira mumbled, explaining what her hand had been doing lingering on Megan's sweet, delicate face.

"The branch didn't hurt me." Megan turned away and continued along the rough path.

"You looked like you were in pain."

"I'm fine." They reached the fallen tree and Megan paused. "You first."

Kira clambered over and waited for her. Megan followed more slowly, using her legs to haul herself up. It was clumsy, and yet last time she'd seen that Megan was quite capable of climbing over that tree—and of looking damn good doing it. So why was she having so much trouble now?

"Would you like a hand?"

"I'm fine." Megan jumped down. She stumbled when she landed, almost pitching into her. Kira held out her hands to steady her, but Megan angled her body away from her, and Kira, rebuffed, pulled away.

"Are you hurt?"

"I didn't fall," Megan protested.

Kira persisted. "Not from your jump. Are you hurt from something else? You're moving like something's wrong."

"I'm fine."

"Would you stop saying you're fine? You don't look fine. You look like you're in pain. Let me take you back to the hotel. I have painkillers and a first-aid kit if that'll help."

"I'm *fine*," Megan insisted.

Kira threw her hands in the air and let out a growl of exasperation from the back of her throat. "Fine." Some people just couldn't accept help.

They walked the last few yards back to the parking lot in silence.

"Back in the office I have a box full of sample products that people send me," Kira said. "They want me to sell their stuff at the spa. Mostly skin care, but there's other cool stuff in there, too. I know I saw some pain-relieving gel. Maybe you could take some of it home with you and test it out, see what you like."

Megan laughed, then pressed her hand to her chest and grimaced as if laughing had dislodged a rib. "You never give up, do you?"

"I know—you're fine."

"I am." Megan rubbed her breastbone.

So it was her chest that hurt. From the way Megan had gotten herself over that fallen tree she'd suspected it was something in her upper body, maybe her shoulder. "Can you please tell me what happened to you?"

"I think I sprained something."

Kira gave her a puzzled look. How did a person sprain their breastbone?

"I thought at first I might have broken my clavicle—my collarbone," Megan explained. "But the X-rays didn't show any fractures. So that's positive, I guess."

"Did you put ice on it?"

Megan traced the edge of her breastbone with her fingertips and dug in again and again, making herself flinch each time. "Yes, and it was a horrible place to put an ice pack."

"It looks like it hurts."

"It kills," Megan admitted.

"Maybe if you stopped pressing on it so hard…" Kira fought the urge to take Megan's hand in her own and kiss her fingertips until they relaxed so she'd stop hurting herself.

Megan continued the aggressive self-massage. "I had to cancel a week of clients, and I'm worried a week might not be enough."

No wonder she was upset. How badly hurt was she?

"I said before that I'd be happy to pay you for the advice you're giving me. Hire you as a paid consultant. If you're not able to do any physical work for a while, you might want the money. So please, let me pay you."

"I appreciate it. I really do. But I don't want you to pay me. I have some money saved. I'll be okay."

"I *want* to pay you."

"Look, if you really want to, you can pay me back by

referring your friends to me when I recover. I might have lost some clients."

Kira had to smile at Megan's twisted offer. Maybe there *was* a spark of competitiveness inside that generous heart.

"What I'm more concerned about is the people who are in pain who depend on me," Megan said.

"There are other massage therapists."

Megan stared at her, probably wondering if she'd just been insulted, then nodded. "Good point."

"Come on inside with me and I'll get you that gel."

They headed back to the hotel and into Kira's office. She pulled out her big cardboard box of sample products, squatted next to it on the floor, and dug around for the sample tube of pain-relieving gel she'd tossed in there when it arrived in the mail a couple weeks ago.

Megan waited in the doorway. "What's in there? Scented soaps?"

"You can smell that?"

"You can't?"

"Sure, but my head is practically inside the box. They're candles, by the way, not soap." She looked up and saw Megan take a step back. "They're wrapped in plastic…"

"Doesn't matter."

"You don't like the smell."

Megan wrinkled her nose.

Kira pulled the candles out to identify the source of the problem and read the labels aloud. "Pine, lavender, sandalwood, vanilla…"

"It's a little much," Megan said.

"So much for my idea of you taking this whole box home with you, then."

"Don't you want to try out your freebies yourself?"

"It's not really my thing." She rummaged some more in the box. "Oh, look, here's the gel." She pulled it out and also snagged another item that caught her eye. "You might like this beanbag pillow thing. I think you heat it up in the microwave like a heating pad. For later on this week, when you're done inflicting that ice pack on yourself."

"Thanks." Megan stepped into the office and leaned over to take the two items from Kira's outstretched hand, unsuccessfully stifling a small squeak of pain.

The sound made Kira's gut hurt. She wanted to wrap Megan up in a blanket and take care of her until the pain went away. "The pillow doesn't smell too much like perfume from being in with all the scented stuff, does it?"

"No, it's okay." Megan started backing toward the door.

"Watch your step." If they were going to continue to meet in her office, she was going to have to organize some of the junk she had piled on the floor and find somewhere else to put it.

"I should get going," Megan said.

"If you need to take the week off to rest, we can postpone our next powwow. We don't need to meet until you feel up to it."

"I'll be fine."

She was fine, huh? Now there was a surprise.

Megan leaned against the doorframe. "I'll actually have plenty of extra time to meet with you this week, since I won't be seeing clients. We can talk about alternatives to your building a spa on that land."

Kira rocked forward onto her toes and pressed through her thighs to stand up. She sighed. "You're going to tell people about the energy, aren't you?"

"Yeah."

"I'm going to be overrun by woo-woo types."

"Maybe they'll want to stay at your hotel," Megan suggested. "You could turn this into a tourist attraction."

"I bought that abandoned lot so I could build a spa on it."

"It could be a real draw. There's no other lesbian hotel in the country that has what you have right here, if you don't cover it up. There are tons of crazy women like me who would love to come here and experience this energy."

"I never said you were crazy."

"You said you were worried I would tell all my woo-woo friends about this place."

"Woo-woo's not crazy."

"Right." Megan rolled her eyes.

Kira couldn't help but smile. "It's not crazy. It's…different."

"You don't have to be polite."

"I'm not being polite. I'm going to bulldoze your rock and that's not going to be polite at all. I just think we have a different way of dealing with the world. Your way is charming."

"Not charming enough, obviously," Megan muttered.

"Interesting?" Kira ventured.

"Uh-huh."

"I wish you would believe me."

"I'd like to, but it's been my experience that people who use the word 'woo-woo' generally think I'm deluded when I talk about energy fields. But it's okay if you do. I'm used to it."

"It's not okay." If she didn't feel so comfortable around her, Kira would have been more careful not to annoy her. Although she was kind of cute when she was annoyed.

"Then you won't build your spa on this spot."

"That would be financial suicide. It's not an option."

Megan turned away, stumbling over one of Kira's piles of junk. "Yeah," she muttered. "You definitely find my point of view interesting."

* * *

A sliver of moon shone through the pine trees behind Kira's hotel, peeking out through passing clouds. Megan clicked off her flashlight and let her eyes adjust to the dark.

Without the ley lines, this was nothing more than a neglected, overgrown, wooded lot. That was how Kira saw it—as a nothing-special plot of land waiting for her to build something. A place that Megan was a fool to care about. In the dark it was easy to believe the rumors about that poor woman who was murdered, or that bad guys hung out here waiting for girls to wander into the shrubbery where no one would see them being attacked. Mr. Creepy was there again, breathing down her neck.

Megan sank to the ground next to the standing stone. The cushion of pine needles that blanketed the sandy soil released the faint scent of pine, so different from the overpowering smell of Kira's sample candles. She crossed her legs and leaned back against the stone.

Energy from the stone flooded her the instant she touched it, and the uneasy feeling of danger vanished. How could she possibly be afraid of anything when she had the strength of the lifeblood of the earth flowing through her? The power was unbelievable. And this time, Kira was not going to interrupt. This time she was alone, and she had all the time in the world to see what this energy could do.

Consciously she merged her inner light with the energy of the standing stone, then channeled it all into the cause of her chest and shoulder pain, whatever that cause might be. The thing kept moving, evading her, slipping away each time her beam of energy touched it.

Eventually her legs grew stiff. She massaged the feeling back into them, adjusted her position, and became still again. The leys weren't helping as much as she'd hoped. She could feel their power, but either that power wasn't enough to release the karma causing her pain, or she didn't have the skill to channel it, or she wasn't able to reach the requisite level of deep surrender.

She opened her eyes, pondering what to do next. And blinked. Hundreds of twinkling pinpricks of golden light glowed in the darkness like drifting bubbles lit from within. Angels. Hundreds of them. She'd never seen so many in one place before. One by one, the bubbles popped and morphed into glowing female forms, some as small as butterflies, some twice the size of a person.

They were beautiful.

Magical.

She stared until their brightness hurt her eyes. Her sternum throbbed. Was it possible they had come to take away her pain?

She pushed that thought from her mind before the angels could pick up on it and be offended. Of course they weren't here for her. They were here for their own angelic purposes, and she just happened to be lucky enough to witness it. She craned her neck upward, taking in the beautiful enormity of it, and noticed something she couldn't believe she'd missed. Behind her, a silvery thread of energy extended from the top of the standing stone up into the sky, disappearing into the night. It glowed faintly in the dark, and angels were shooting down it like they were going down a water slide, joining the others. Soon she realized the arriving angels were not drifting around randomly, but were lining up along the two leys, hovering a few feet above the ground.

Eventually the funneling of angels from God knew where slowed to a trickle and one of them spoke, although it was impossible to tell which one it was—the words seemed to come from several directions at once.

"Don't let anything happen to this crossroads." The sound was like a glass harmonica—or were they called glass harps?— where a table of wineglasses filled with different amounts of water made music when the rims were rubbed—except someone forgot to tune this one. And broke a glass. And plugged it into a guitar amplifier. Megan fought the urge to clamp her hands over her ears to block the painful vibration.

She'd never heard an angel speak before. Had the energy of the leys unlocked some hidden potential in her? Fine-tuned her psychic hearing? Or was it standing on the leys themselves that allowed her to hear them? Her friend Gwynne—the only person she knew who could hear angels—had never mentioned how disconcerting their voices were. If the whole choir of angels thing was for real, then she hoped to God that was not what they were gathering here for, because that much sound just might make her lose her mind.

The angels continued to hover over the leys, silent now, and gradually the shock wore off and the words sank in. *Don't let anything happen to this crossroads.*

Sure thing. Nothing like a little added pressure.

The angel who was closest held her arms out to her in a gesture that was both pleading and welcoming, but mostly sad. What would happen if Kira built here? Was this a portal where angels came to earth? Would moving the standing stone destroy the portal?

"I'll do my best," Megan promised.

A wave of caring and compassion rushed from the angel's hands and hit her with such force it was almost violent. It wasn't the same as the energy she'd filled herself with earlier, the energy she'd drawn from the ley lines and the standing stone. This energy was warmer and more chaotic, and it built and built and built, brighter and hotter than anything she'd ever channeled. She sat up straighter, trying to keep the flow of energy from overwhelming her. Her body heated like it was going to melt away and all that would be left would be a core of white-hot light, too bright to look at.

The combined angel/ley energy changed, gathered itself into a sphere that contained her whole body, and started pressing inward. It found the glob of fear that was the survival-level root of her chest problems, the karmic patterning that had cracked her sternum to begin with, and pressed on it from all directions at once, trapping it, compressing it until it was a fist, a BB, the smallest speck of darkness. Megan stopped breathing for the longest time.

Then the speck of fear imploded.

It didn't spew darkness; it spewed light—blinding, frightening, world-destroying light. An uncontrollable chill tingled up her spine as her buzzing energy system realigned itself.

The light receded; her spine sagged. She started breathing again, and peace seeped through her jangled nerves. Something had happened to her. Something big. But what, she wasn't sure.

CHAPTER SIX

"My pain is completely gone," Megan told Svetlana as they walked through town to Kira's hotel.

Megan shifted her tote bag, which held gardening gloves and a pair of pruning shears, to her other hand. She'd invited a few people to meet them by the hotel to check out the ley lines, and afterward they were going to clear some of the overgrowth from around the standing stone to make the place more inviting.

Svetlana tried on the gloves she'd loaned her and modeled them without much enthusiasm. "Pain is gone because you sat by this mysterious stone?"

"There were angels there. Lots of them. They lined up on the ley lines, and then…I'm not quite sure what happened. They hooked up to the energy of the ley lines and zapped me with it and broke through a blockage."

"And now you're healed?" Svetlana sounded confused. "I never know what it is necessary to think when you talk about angel. You seem so rational about everything else."

Megan swung her arms, twirling her tote bag, showing off how good her shoulder felt now that she could move it without worrying about pinching a nerve in her chest. After all the frustration of not being able to heal herself, not being able to find anyone else who could help, and not understanding why, she was almost giddy at being pain-free. "I haven't felt this good in ages."

"Then I'm glad for you," Svetlana said firmly. "The energy is amazing, yes? You think I'll feel it?"

That was a good question. Megan hoped that anyone who knew how to work with energy would be able to take advantage of the ley lines to magnify their skills. Whether someone like Svetlana, who was not an energy healer, would be able to sense the ley lines, was a separate issue, and she was afraid the answer would be no. "We'll find out soon enough."

"I wonder because maybe this energy is what is necessary to help me astral travel."

Megan stopped swinging her arms abruptly. "You're interested in astral travel?" Practical, medical-minded Svetlana? "Since when?"

Svetlana tugged disdainfully at her borrowed gardening gloves, which were probably too small since they didn't seem to want to pull off. "My grandmother, she had the ability. She used to visit my grandfather with this astral travel after he was exiled to Siberia. When I was young girl, she tried to teach me, but I didn't have the knack."

"I had no idea you were into that sort of thing."

"Only curious."

"Don't be. Astral travel's dangerous."

"What could be dangerous about it?"

Megan stared. Sure, what could be dangerous about your mind abandoning your body? "You're leaving your body unguarded."

Svetlana shrugged nonchalantly. "My grandmother never had problem."

"How is this better than calling someone on the phone?"

Svetlana looked incredulous, as if Megan, of all people, should understand. "Phone call is nice, but it's not real visit. I have not seen my parents in years. I miss them."

Megan gave a dismissive shake of her head. So much for Svetlana being the practical one. "I wouldn't recommend it."

She didn't think she had much to worry about, though. Chances were good that if Svetlana had already tried astral travel under the guidance of her grandmother, and hadn't been able to do it, she wouldn't be able to do it now. No ability—no danger.

* * *

"Here it is." Megan waved toward the standing stone and stepped out of the way so everyone could get a closer look.

They clustered around the monolith, trying to sense what she had sensed, each in her own way. Vanessa dangled a quartz pendulum, Dara walked back and forth in slow motion holding dowsing rods, and Svetlana, who couldn't sense energy, put her hands on the stone, examining its shape. Gwynne merely mouthed the word "wow" and retreated to stand next to Megan.

"Dara's going to hurt someone with those dowsing rods if she doesn't open her eyes," Gwynne commented under her breath. "What did she make them out of? Coat hangers?"

"Be nice. Just because you can see without tools…"

"Well. She *is* on the right track," Gwynne conceded. "But what good she thinks her rods are doing if she doesn't look at them, I don't know. Kind of defeats the purpose. How is she going to know which direction they're pointing?"

What was up with Gwynne today, making her so irritable? Actually, Megan had a pretty good guess. People like Dara Sullivan often wished they could see angels and auras the way Megan and Gwynne could, but those abilities set them apart. Watching Dara fumble with her dowsing rods, and knowing Dara was one of the better energy healers—well, sometimes it got lonely.

"So, what do you think?" Megan asked.

Gwynne was dipping a toe in and out of one of the energy streams with a fascinated look on her face. "About the ley lines?"

"Yes, about the ley lines. Unless you have more to say about Dara. Like you noticed her eyes were closed because you can't stop thinking about what color they are?"

"You must be out of your mind. Sitting on these leys last night must have fried something crucial."

"It's possible," Megan said easily. "The power here is incredible."

"It is," Gwynne agreed. "And you know what else? Something weird is happening with that standing stone." She sauntered over to the monolith, careful to stay out of range of Dara's swinging dowsing rods.

Megan followed. "What is it?"

"There's a funnel of energy anchored to the ground under this stone, and it's not a ley line. It has an angelic residue."

"I know. I saw angels traveling down it."

"I wonder what it is." Gwynne tilted her head thoughtfully.

"The angels called it a crossroads."

"Whatever that means. But I can see why they like to hang out here. It's a powerful spot. I'll have to come back."

"You don't have an uneasy feeling you should leave?"

"A spell of ward?" Gwynne looked startled. "No. Do you?"

"I thought I did, briefly, the last time I was here." She figured her encounter in the woods with Mr. Creepy could have been the manifestation of a warning spell—a psychic Do Not Enter sign. But she trusted Gwynne's intuition, and if Gwynne didn't sense a spell, maybe it was something else. "You really don't sense it?"

"Maybe it's masked by the uneasy feeling I have that I should get out of here before you set me up on a date with Dara Sullivan."

"Shh." She hoped Dara, who was approaching with her eyes still squeezed shut in concentration, hadn't heard.

Gwynne scrambled out of Dara's way. "You sure it wasn't the rumors about this place giving you the heebie-jeebies?"

"The murder?"

"Yeah."

"I don't know."

Dara came to a halt in front of them, opened her eyes, and lowered her dowsing rods. "Thanks for showing us the stone."

"No problem," Megan said. "Are you going to stay to help us pull poison ivy?"

"I wish I could, but I jammed my thumb yesterday playing volleyball." Dara held up her injured hand. It looked swollen. "I know I shouldn't play, but…what can I say? I'm an idiot. I have two clients tomorrow and I need to save my strength."

"You're not going to cancel them?" Megan suggested. Yeah, like she was one to talk. How many times had *she* canceled on a client when she really should have? Not nearly enough. "You don't want to overdo it and get permanently injured."

"I'll push through. I don't want to lose what few clients I have."

Megan winced. "I understand."

"I might have to cancel my gig at Avalanche, though. I work there four nights a week giving free back rubs. Free for the patrons, I mean. The club pays me. Not much, but it's good advertising. But it's hard on the thumbs." Dana clasped her hands together in beg mode. "Would you be willing to cover for me sometime this week?"

"Sure," Megan said. "How long is your shift?"

"It's only an hour. It can get pretty hectic, though."

"Is Friday one of your nights? I could help out then." She didn't love Avalanche's throbbing, too-loud dance music, but an hour wouldn't kill her.

"I could take a couple nights, also," Svetlana volunteered, overhearing their conversation.

"Thanks," Dara said. "That would be fabulous."

* * *

Kira surveyed the site of her future spa and stuck her hands in her pockets. She wasn't surprised that Megan was back. And what do you know, she'd brought a bunch of her woo-woo friends, just as she'd predicted. She was starting to wish she'd never brought her here. Would have made life so much simpler.

Even worse, they were weeding. Weeding! You didn't weed a construction site. Why bother, when heavy machinery was on its way, and would strip the soil of any and all greenery? Weeding was something you did to a garden, or maybe a park. Some place you wanted to take care of. Someplace you were trying to protect.

Exactly what she'd like to avoid.

Megan had her back to her and was tugging with both hands at a vine of poison ivy that had grown up a tree trunk. She wore a cropped T-shirt and shorts, her only protection a heavy-duty pair of gardening gloves. It wasn't enough. What if she pulled that vine off and it fell on her face? Or brushed against her bare arms? Poison ivy was nothing to fool with. Kira watched anxiously as Megan successfully pulled the vine free. When she started to tackle another one, Kira kicked at some brush to make it rustle, annoyed that Megan hadn't noticed her. Megan still didn't notice.

"Please tell me my construction crew's not going to get here tomorrow morning and find you chained to a tree."

Megan turned around. She wiped the sweat off her brow with the back of her arm, holding her gloved hands well away from her body. "Now there's an idea."

No. There was *not* an idea. Not that she was ready to start work on the site, but once she was, tree huggers could hold up construction for weeks. Kira groaned. "You're messing with me, right?"

"We're totally serious."

"Please don't do this."

"You're not really starting construction tomorrow, are you? Patrick went down to the county office for me and said you don't even have the permits yet."

Shit, this was sounding worse and worse.

"I'm not a big-time developer," Kira said. "You bankrupt me, someone a lot worse is going to get this land at a bargain price and do God knows what to it."

"We're not going to bankrupt you." Her friends started

to object, but Megan shushed and flapped at them until they quieted down.

Kira relaxed a fraction. At least one of these nuts was willing to see reason. Not that Megan was a nut, exactly. Maybe a small one. A pistachio. That was it—a loveable little pistachio. The arm flapping was certainly adorable. Now if only she would forget the tree hugging idea. And stop clearing poison ivy.

"We'll work this out." The look in Megan's eyes, like she wanted to connect with her on a gut level and find out what made her tick, was almost enough to make her want to discuss a compromise—if it meant they had to spend more time together hammering out the details.

Almost.

"How's your injury?" Kira asked quietly. "A couple days ago you couldn't use your arms at all. And now…" She gestured toward the pile of vines at Megan's feet. "You look like you're doing great."

Megan smiled, and Kira suddenly worried that telling her she looked great might not have been the smartest thing in the world, because the way the pistachio's smile slowly got wider and wider made her think she had just ceded her the upper hand. She didn't know how yet, but somehow she had just made a mistake.

"I'm guessing it wasn't the pain-relieving gel," Kira said.

"No," Megan said. "It wasn't." She spread her arms wide. "And you're right. See, my chest doesn't hurt anymore."

Kira cleared her throat. She could do without an invitation to look at Megan's perfectly lovely chest. "I can see that."

"It was the ley lines. And some…well, mostly it was the ley lines. I sat here last night and their energy healed me. Like that." She snapped her fingers mutely with her glove. "I woke up this morning and the pain was completely gone."

Kira had to admit she didn't look like she was in pain. The way she'd been tugging on that vine, no one would ever guess that two days earlier she'd been unable to move her arms at all without flinching. But she found it hard to believe her property had anything to do with Megan's supposedly miraculous recovery.

"I'm glad you're not hurting anymore." That part, at least, was the truth.

"The healing energy here is amazingly powerful. It's worth protecting."

And again with the nut factor. The pistachio didn't give up, did she?

"I'm sorry to disappoint you, but I'm not changing my mind."

* * *

Megan yanked at more poison ivy and tried not to feel like a failure. She would have more chances to change Kira's mind. Just because Kira had walked out on her without listening this time, didn't mean she wouldn't succeed the next time. She *would* succeed. She had to. The angels were counting on her. But it hurt that Kira had actually turned her back on her and left.

Gwynne tossed her gardening gloves on the ground. "So."

Megan stopped what she was doing and waited for whatever was coming next, even though she wasn't really in the mood to talk right now. It was bad enough to fail without doing it in front of an audience.

Gwynne glanced over her shoulder as if she wanted to make sure no one would overhear. "You're in love with her, aren't you?" she said in a low voice. "With Kira Wagner?"

"What? No."

Gwynne gave her a look.

Oh, for God's sake. She'd been expecting Gwynne to have something to say about Kira, but not…not this.

"I'm really not."

"No, I think you really are."

"You're wrong." Megan gave Gwynne her best I-don't-know-what-the-heck-you're-talking-about look. Whatever she felt for Kira, it was not love.

Gwynne snorted. "I don't think so."

CHAPTER SEVEN

When Kira saw Megan arrive in the hotel driveway, she ran outside with her clipboard to meet her, pulling up short when she realized Megan was in the middle of a phone call.

"Like I said, I don't have any openings until the day after tomorrow. A one thirty and a four o'clock. Maybe you could tell me what seems to be—"

Kira took a step back, but Megan held up one finger and motioned her closer. She covered the phone's mouthpiece. "This'll be over in a minute."

Kira stayed put and pretended to review the list attached to her clipboard. Megan's hair was a mess, as usual. If it were hers, she'd pull it back in a ponytail. But she was kind of glad Megan didn't, because there was something really sexy about seeing it so mussed. She'd always had a weakness for unmanageable hair. Or, to be more accurate, unmanaged hair—the kind that got all messed up because you were the active, outdoorsy type and didn't think it was natural to shellac your hair in place, no matter how limp or frizzy it got from the humidity. Growing up, she had always been mildly freaked out by her mother's perfectly groomed friends—women who honestly thought they looked ugly without makeup, even when there were no men around to impress.

Of course, it helped that the girl in her long-ago dreams had wild hair, too. Megan looked so much like her, especially when her hair misbehaved. It reminded her of those dreams, of how tangled the strands got over the course of a long night, and how the girl had been so much more sure of herself—and more sure about what she wanted to do with Kira—than Kira herself had been back then. The dreams had been both enlightening and—because her dream girl wasn't real—endlessly frustrating.

She wasn't dreaming now, though—not the old dreams. Megan was heart-poundingly real—tell-your-friends-to-call-back-next-year-because-you'll-be-busy-not-sleeping real—and Kira had a pretty good idea what she wanted to do with her.

If she'd ever let her.

Megan held the phone away from her ear and shot the mouthpiece a look of disgust. She pushed her wonderful hair away from her face and switched the phone to her other ear. "I don't do nine p.m. appointments."

This caller was *arguing* about when her next available appointment was? Take it or leave it, honey—don't be obnoxious. Kira couldn't wait to hear her soft-spoken angel inform her caller that she was *not* going to squeeze anyone in.

"Look, Joe, I think you have the wrong idea about me." Megan's voice hardened, but she wasn't angry—not yet. Her tone reminded Kira of her high school chemistry teacher asking the class to settle down.

Wait a minute...the wrong idea? Kira's jaw locked.

"I do therapeutic massage. For wellness and injury rehab. I'm sure you understand why I won't see you." Megan turned off her phone and put it in her back pocket.

Kira stared at her, wondering how she could look so unfazed. *She* had been mad thinking the guy just wanted to change Megan's schedule, when in fact he had been—

"Did that guy just try to hire you for sex?"

Megan rubbed her forehead. She looked like she was fighting a headache. "He was scoping out the situation," she acknowledged.

Unbelievable. She'd been hoping she was wrong. It was too gross to think about. "Why didn't you hang up on him?"

Megan looked up at her from between her fingers, then returned to rubbing a spot directly above her eyebrows. Her eyes were half-closed in pain. "I did."

"I meant why didn't you hang up on him sooner."

"I didn't want to be rude."

"*You* didn't want to be rude?" Kira would have had a few choice words for any man who phoned *her* for sex. She didn't see how Megan could stay so calm about it. "*He* was rude to *you*." She hoped this didn't mean Megan really was straight and she was used to getting propositioned by men in weird, inappropriate ways. That would be so unfortunate.

"It's not completely his fault. If prostitutes give normal-looking massages before they massage guys' dicks, then how are these guys supposed to know who's who?"

Kira tried not to gag at *that* visual.

"They call me because they're honestly making an effort to find out whether sex is one of the services I offer. I'd rather they try to find that out on the phone than in person."

"In person?" Who did these guys think they were? Kira fought the urge to grab Megan's phone to see if the guy had been stupid enough to call from a traceable number.

"I've never had a problem," Megan assured her. "I don't take same-day appointments—that alone tends to cool them off. And I'm pretty good at screening them on the phone. I know the code words they use."

Yeah, it wasn't hard to figure out why. She knew the code words because some jerk-off had used them on her, and she had innocently breezed right over the innuendo until one day one of those guys didn't buy the innocent act and made it frighteningly clear what he wanted. And now she knew the code words.

Christ.

Kira pushed her hands deeper into the pockets of her jeans

so she wouldn't reach for Megan's phone and call the jerk back. Megan obviously didn't think this guy was a problem, and that was her decision to make. She was the owner of her own business, not some entry-level hotel registration clerk on her first day at work. She had a feeling Megan wouldn't appreciate her interference.

"Don't they ever get mad when you won't give them an appointment?" Kira asked, unable to let it go. "What if one of them tried to hurt you?"

"I try to be nice when I turn them down. It seems to work."

"You shouldn't have to be nice to them."

"They're real people, too."

How could Megan be so forgiving? There were good eggs and bad eggs, and the bad eggs needed to be kicked to the curb because they just didn't get how to act like normal, respectful human beings, especially when they had sex on the brain. "I work all day with men—I know what they're like. I'm being realistic. I mean who in their right mind does that, anyway? Paying for sex? With someone they don't know? That is totally a male concept."

"Nothing's ever happened. I'm telling you, I know how to handle these guys."

"I cannot believe you have to put up with that crap."

Megan smiled weakly. "To be honest, this was not what I imagined I'd be doing when I dreamed of becoming a massage therapist."

Yeah. It wasn't what Kira had imagined her doing, either. "How often do you get calls like that?"

"Not often."

Which could mean anything. Kira led Megan up the driveway, through the lobby, and into her office, her feet hitting the ground with an impact she could feel all the way up her legs. How Megan handled her phone calls was none of her business. Not that that was going to stop her from feeling furious. But it might stop her from arguing about it.

She picked up a stack of spa brochures from her desk as they walked in and peeled one off the top to hand to Megan. They were samples from the competition, both local and from around the country. The one she'd just given her was from Peaceful Moments down on the boardwalk. "I want to go through these with you."

Megan flipped over the glossy card stock. "This is Mary's brochure? I like the graphic."

Megan was too nice for her own good. Too nice with problematic guys, and too nice with her colleagues in the industry. No sense of self-preservation.

"Why am I not surprised to hear you compliment our competition?"

Megan snagged three more brochures from the stack, more interested in checking them out than in acknowledging Kira's comment.

Right. Back to business.

"I want to make a list of everything we should offer and what equipment we'll need," Kira said.

"You do realize I've never worked at a spa, right?"

"Heck, you've got to know more about it than I do. I've never even had a massage. Well, except for the one you gave me at the race tent."

Megan looked up from the brochures and squinted at her in dismay. "Then why in the world are you opening a spa?"

"I got bored building medical offices and I got burned opening a restaurant. I wanted to do something fun this time."

"Even though you don't know anything about spas?"

"It's not that different. I know about construction and permits and all the state and county regulations you have to deal with. The specific type of business doesn't actually matter that much. I researched the financial aspects. I know the laws governing the spa industry in the state of Delaware, and I know what my costs are going to be."

Megan shook her head and reached over to take another brochure from Kira's stack. "An aesthetician would know more about this than I do. Beauty treatments and I don't mix."

"That's why you're perfect for this job."

"That's why I'm *not* perfect for this job."

Kira was used to people doubting her business plans, and was used to dismissing those doubts as she would a complaining muscle during a run. It was a fact of life that if you pushed yourself hard, some people were going to say you were unprepared. She'd never felt shaken by a mere look.

"I *want* a massage therapist," Kira explained. "Not an aesthetician. I'm not in the manicure business. I want this to be somewhere women come for good food, clean air, exercise classes and to-die-for massages."

"And spa treatments."

"Yes."

"Hmm." Megan flipped open the next brochure and scanned it quickly. "I really think you should experience a spa treatment before you try to sell one."

"I agree with you. I do. I just haven't gotten around to it." Kira wished she didn't sound so defensive. She just didn't think she was the spa type. If she needed to relax, she'd rather go for a good run than lie down and have someone smear scented crap on her face.

Megan's massage in the tent had felt good, though. She wouldn't have minded if *that* had lasted longer than ten minutes. So maybe she *was* the spa type—at least for leg and foot rubs, if not for facials—and just didn't know it yet. Or maybe it all depended on who was doing the massaging. Megan was clearly amazingly good at her job.

"How about I make an appointment with you for a massage?" Kira suggested.

It was the perfect solution. Her lack of hands-on experience seemed to be a sore point, so this would make Megan happy, and she could guarantee herself that a massage, as long as it was with Megan, wouldn't be a waste of time. It would also give her a chance to make a small financial contribution toward repaying Megan for her advice.

Megan refused to meet her gaze. "My friend Svetlana is great with athletes. I think you'd really like her better." She pulled a business card out of her wallet and wrote Svetlana's name and number on the back.

Great. Had she been so sweaty and rank after the 10K that Megan was too revolted to touch her again? Megan was so sensitive to smells… Or was it asking her out that had ruined any chance of ever getting a massage from her? This was bad. If Megan had men calling her up for prostitution, asking her out may have triggered some toxic memories. Maybe Megan was scared of her. Kira took a step back, suddenly grateful that Megan was even willing to be alone in a small room with her talking about brochures.

Megan tossed Svetlana's number on top of the stack of brochures Kira was still holding. Kira plopped the whole thing down on her desk and slipped the business card into her back pocket. "Thanks. I'll call her."

"It's not that I wouldn't love to work with you—" Megan started.

"You don't have to explain."

"I didn't mean to hurt your feelings…"

"You didn't."

Kira tried not to look hurt so Megan would stop looking so guilty. She had no right to feel hurt. Appalled with herself for making Megan nervous, yes. Hurt, no. She would call up Megan's friend Svetlana and hope that one day Megan would forgive her for being an ass.

"So let's talk about saunas," Kira said, hoping the change in subject would make Megan more comfortable. "Do people really want a sauna when they've been out on the beach all day?" She flipped through another pile of papers on her desk and found the printout showing how much saunas cost to build and operate. "Of course, we will have off-season guests."

Megan looked at her with her mouth half-open as if she couldn't quite figure out what to say—either about saunas or about rejecting her.

Kira showed her the printout. "I need to do a survey, find out what local women want from a spa."

"What if they say they want manicures?" A hint of a smile twitched around the corners of Megan's mouth.

Good. She didn't look guilt-ridden anymore. Kira smiled

back at her, mesmerized by the way Megan's amusement played out on her face. A powerful, invisible force pushed at her between her shoulder blades, urging her closer.

"They won't."

Megan rewarded her with a bark of laughter that she quickly bit back, the tip of her tongue slipping between her lips, wet and pink and immediately gone, back under control.

God.

"Any suggestions for where I should do my survey?"

"How about Avalanche? I'm supposed to work there Friday night, subbing for a friend. Giving mini-massages," Megan explained. "You could ask the women who show up."

"Okay, sure. That sounds like a good idea."

So Megan wasn't afraid to go to a nightclub with her. A *gay* nightclub. This was...interesting. Kira sank into her wheeled office chair, suddenly dizzy. Of course, she wasn't going *with* her. This was a work-related outing.

What else did she expect?

CHAPTER EIGHT

Piper Beach had the Sand Bar, a hole-in-the-wall women's bar not far from the boardwalk, and it had Avalanche, built in a converted warehouse, where men outnumbered women five-to-one. That was five too many for Kira's taste, but it had good music. She could hear the beat from halfway down the street.

At the propped-open door, Megan introduced herself to the bouncer as Dara-the-massage-therapist's replacement for the evening, and he waved them both inside through a flurry of soap bubbles that spewed from a nearby bubble machine and into the club, where hundreds of sweaty, dancing bodies glowed under black light and a multicolored light show.

"Where to?" Kira asked.

"I'm not sure. We could stop by the bar first if you want something to drink."

Megan led the way around the perimeter of the cavernous dance floor toward the bar, visibly flinching when they passed an amplifier.

Kira found an unoccupied spot at the bar. "Do you want anything?"

"Not right now, thanks."

Kira ordered a beer. While they waited, a swishy shirtless college boy squeezed in next to her and thrust a few moist dollar bills at the bartender. Kira drew Megan close to keep her out of range of his flying sweat, but Megan swatted at her and she let go.

Now there was an ego boost.

But wait—there was an added bonus. A friend of hers was standing a few feet away and had witnessed the whole thing. Kira grimaced.

She'd met Shayna Denning a year ago when she was living nearby in Rehoboth, struggling to keep her failing restaurant afloat, and Shayna had immediately adopted her into her wide circle of friends.

Shayna walked over and saluted her with her beer. "You always did have a way with the ladies, Kira." It was clear from the way she grinned back and forth at the two of them that she thought they made an adorable couple. "Who's your friend?"

"Megan McLaren, Shayna Denning," Kira introduced them with a vague gesture. Shayna was being way too obvious as she checked Megan out and no doubt committed the details to memory. Kira gritted her teeth, even though she suspected Shayna's only interest in Megan was in providing a full report to their other friends. They were counting on her.

"Someone who can put up with the great Kira," Shayna shouted over the music, moving closer and holding out her hand.

Megan accepted the handshake. Shayna held it longer than necessary. She always did shit like that, trying to push her.

"Go away, Shayna."

Shayna nodded knowingly, refusing to acknowledge Kira's hostility. She turned back to Megan. "You've got your hands full, girl. So what do you do for a living? Lion tamer?"

"Massage therapist."

"No kidding." Shayna immediately dropped her joking. "Can you do anything about my back?" She reached her arms behind her head and twisted around to show her. "It hurts right here when I look over my shoulder to back the car out of the driveway."

Kira had never seen Shayna look so serious—it was like witnessing a doctor's appointment. She had been bracing herself, expecting Shayna to say something offensive, and instead...this.

"When you look right or left?" Megan asked, immediately all concern.

"Left. Like this." Shayna demonstrated.

Megan mimicked the movement and touched her spine like she was feeling something in her own body to help her identify the problem. She pulled Shayna farther from the bar to an area that was less crowded so she could knead her shoulders, then the back of her neck.

Shayna's eyes were half-closed and she looked like she might groan with pleasure at any moment. Amazing how quick people were to con a massage out of Megan.

"You lucky dog, Kira," Shayna teased.

Kira suppressed the urge to hurt her friend.

It didn't take long for other people to notice what Megan was doing. A woman in a Piper Beach souvenir T-shirt sidled up to her with a hopeful expression, kind of like a dog whining for a treat.

Kira was not a dog person. She glared at her.

"I'm next," the woman announced.

"*I'm* next," protested another woman. She locked the first woman into a deep kiss and used the distraction to angle herself into the front of the line.

"You cut in line," complained the victim of the kiss, sliding her hands from her attacker's face.

"You let me in."

"I did not."

"You're drunk, honey."

"I just remembered why I broke up with you."

"Looks like my shift just started," Megan said, continuing to massage Shayna's neck as more supplicants materialized.

"Aren't you supposed to officially set up shop somewhere?" Kira asked. For now, people were waiting in a semi-civilized line, but it wouldn't take much for the situation to turn into a free-for-all.

"Dara said it's not that organized." Megan performed some massage maneuver with her elbow, acting completely unconcerned about the potential chaos behind her.

"They're throwing themselves at you."

"They'll settle down."

Kira wasn't convinced, but could see she wasn't needed. And her territorial instincts were getting out of control. She needed to calm down. This was not a date. And she had a job to do, so she might as well get started. She turned to the closest woman in line. "While you're waiting, would you be interested in filling out a brief survey?"

"Sure." The woman took Kira's pen and her one-page questionnaire and commandeered the back of another woman to use as a temporary writing surface.

Kira lined up several more takers and quickly ran out of pens. While she waited for her surveys to be filled out, she chatted with the other women in line, getting their opinions on what they wanted from a spa and what they liked and didn't like about the hotel they were staying at. She did her best to give them her undivided attention, but part of her brain kept abandoning the job, preferring to keep Megan in her peripheral vision and watch her work.

If this were a date, and not Megan's job, Kira would have taken her by the hand and dragged her onto the dance floor to lose the fan club. But this was not a date. This was Megan feeling sorry for her and letting her tag along while she worked. This was Kira willing to do anything that involved spending time with her, and then foolishly getting her hopes up. So now she was here handing out surveys while her date—correction, pseudo-date—okay, friend, really—business acquaintance?— was ten feet away with her hands on another woman. Served her right.

* * *

Megan looked up from yet another set of shoulders and noticed Kira on the far side of the room, leaning against a wall, watching her. When had she taken off, anyway? The last time Megan had glanced over at her, she'd been effortlessly schmoozing her way down the line, coaxing everyone into giving her their heartfelt opinion on spas and God knew what else—their conversations had been getting pretty animated. Megan had stopped watching when she realized that the sight of Kira's firm backside in well-worn, tight-fitting, blue denim cutoffs made her hands slow to a stop on her clients' shoulders. Those cutoffs were shorter than anything Megan would dare to wear, and the frayed edge suggested they might inadvertently get even shorter. Kira and her toned legs could get away with it, though. Just thinking about it, Megan's hands started to slow. She should take up running. It obviously did great things for your ass.

And she was supposed to be working—not daydreaming. Not staring, not wanting…

She pulled her wristwatch from the pocket of her comfy massage pants—she never wore her watch on her wrist when she worked, because it got in the way—and checked whether it was time for her to stop yet. Except she couldn't remember what time she'd started. The merciless pounding of the music must have scrambled her brain and made her lose track of time. Or maybe it was the daydreaming. And the staring. And the wanting. No problem. It wouldn't hurt to do a few more people just to be safe. Then she'd figure out a way to get out of here without starting a riot.

She put her hands on the next set of shoulders and suppressed a sigh. Could it be any louder in here? Thank God the state of Delaware didn't allow smoking indoors in public places anymore or she'd be in serious trouble, because the smell of stale beer and sweat was about all she could handle in the odor department, especially when combined with a noise problem. She could handle it, though. She'd come a long way from the frightened five-year-old whose mother had dragged her to party after party, prying her kid's fingers off her leg, refusing to admit defeat.

"What do you say, Megan?" her mother would prompt, urging her forward. The sparkly rhinestones on her mother's skirt dug into Megan's palms, but she hung on hard, too scared to remember what she was supposed to say to the lady who leaned forward, cooing, bringing the malevolent force of her perfume closer, trapping her in an unwanted hug.

"Say hello. Say 'Hello, Mrs. Winaker.'"

"Hello, Miss Win," Megan mumbled, keeping her head down.

The lady released her and beamed. "Aren't you adorable? And what a very pretty dress you're wearing."

"What do you say, Megan?"

Thank you. Megan knew what she was supposed to say, but no words came out. Except then they did—the wrong words— because curiosity got the best of her. "Why is your baby hiding in there?"

Mrs. Winaker blanched.

"What are you talking about, Megan?" said her mother. "Mrs. Winaker doesn't have a baby."

"He's hiding," Megan explained, pointing at the lady's belly. Couldn't they tell he was in there? She had felt him when the lady hugged her. Definitely a baby. But getting an adult to understand what she meant was never easy.

"I apologize, Ellen. My daughter has an overactive imagination."

Megan burst into tears at her mother's disapproval.

"But she's right, Nancy, I am pregnant," said Mrs. Winaker. "I…I haven't told anyone yet. I didn't think I was showing. How could she possibly know such a thing?"

Good question. How could she touch Mrs. Winaker's flat stomach and know she was pregnant? How could she sense her ten o'clock appointment had cancer? How could she feel sex and drunkenness bombarding her from all over the crowded club? Megan shut her eyes against the incessant flash of colored lights and dug her thumbs into her client's levàtor scapulae. Not much had changed since she was little enough to hide behind her mother's legs.

Her gaze darted across the room and instinctively found Kira. There was no way Kira could tell, from that far away, how she was feeling, but she immediately straightened up at the eye contact and, beer bottle in hand, strode purposefully toward her through the throng of convulsing bodies. Somehow she knew it was time to rescue her.

Kira arrived by her side and leaned close so she wouldn't have to shout. "Didn't you say you only had to work an hour?"

"Give or take." Megan patted her client on the shoulder and sent her on her way.

"It's been an hour and twenty minutes."

Megan fingered her wristwatch and pulled it out of her pocket again. "I wasn't sure. I thought I'd do one more before I quit."

Kira gave her an assessing look. "You're tired. You could call it a night right now."

She *was* tired. Some of these women were in a lot of pain, and the pain had crept into her own body as she touched them. The patchouli somebody reeked of had given her a headache. Too much more of the noise and the smells and the emotional backwash and she might collapse from overload. She was surprised Kira knew her well enough to tell.

Kira draped a protective arm around her shoulders, apparently forgetting that when she'd tried this at the bar an hour ago, Megan had pushed her away. Megan sagged into the support of Kira's body.

"You did your hour," Kira said. "Want me to help you clear them out?"

"Thanks, but I can do it myself."

"I'd be happy to do it for you."

"I'm fine." Megan stepped out of the comfort of Kira's arm.

Kira shifted her stance and slid her hands into her back pockets, her hands moving slowly from hip to rear. That hand on the hip thing looked sexy on her, especially in those cutoffs. So did the hands in the back pockets thing. Megan bit her lip. She must be tired if she was thinking this way.

Kira raised her voice to address the women who were still waiting in line. "Thanks a lot, ladies. We appreciate your business and hope you'll be back tomorrow night, because we'll have another fabulous massage therapist here giving free back rubs at—"

Kira looked questioningly at Megan out of the corner of her eye and surreptitiously held up nine fingers. Megan nodded. She shouldn't let Kira do this, but she didn't have the energy to stop her, and besides, Kira was doing a great job.

"Nine o'clock to ten. I know you're going to love her. Her name is—"

"Svetlana Tretyakova Durbridge," Megan prompted.

"Svetlana Tretya-what?" Kira broke off and muttered at Megan. "Did she have to tack on her husband's name to that mouthful?"

"Svetlana Tretyakova Durbridge," Megan announced loudly to the group.

Not to be sidetracked, Kira returned to her spiel. "Svetlana's really great."

"You're not leaving, are you?" someone pleaded.

"Sorry, ladies," Kira said. "That's it for tonight. I know you'll want to check out the bar for our specials, and we'll see you tomorrow."

"Bummer," someone else shouted.

Kira pulled Megan away from her fans and over to a private corner under the balcony. She offered her the beer she still had in her hand. Megan shook her head.

"Want to leave?" Kira said.

Megan's throat tightened and she blinked several times, too quickly. She hadn't expected Kira to understand how easily she got overwhelmed in places like this. She had taught herself from an early age to tolerate as much chaos as she could and to expect to be criticized when she couldn't. "I need to talk to the manager before I go. And you don't have to leave with me." She nodded toward Kira's beer. "You haven't even had a chance to finish that."

"Don't worry about it. Are you sure you're okay?"

"I'll be fine as soon as I run to the restroom." That was the one place she could partially escape from the sensory overload, short of going outside, and she needed that right now.

* * *

Kira glanced down at her feet and noticed how she was standing: feet planted firmly apart, arms crossed in front of her chest. Was she seriously guarding the door to the restroom? Yes, that was exactly what she was doing, and she had a feeling Megan wouldn't appreciate her protective crap. She'd been told over and over again by a string of ex-girlfriends that if they wanted a macho attitude, they'd find a man. That just because they looked femme, didn't mean they couldn't take care of themselves. Goddamn *Charlie's Angels*. She *wasn't* a man. Somehow they always knew how to push her buttons. Well, they'd be happy to see their complaints had sunk in.

Kira stepped away from the door and forced her arms to uncross and drop to her sides.

A couple of women she recognized from the line for Megan's massages walked up to the restroom door. They paused when they spotted Kira.

"Keeping her all to yourself?" one of them asked.

Kira clenched her teeth, incensed. If she had to watch Megan get hit on, she didn't think she could take it.

"Yes," she bit out. It was the best way to get rid of them.

I wish was more accurate, but she was not about to go down that road. The thought of Megan coming home with her... It stole the breath right out of her lungs.

Didn't stop her from giving those women the evil eye, though. She didn't want them coming back and corralling Megan into another back rub, because Megan wouldn't turn them away, even though she was exhausted. She was too nice for her own good.

The women wandered away. Smart crowd.

Before she could threaten anyone else, Kira strolled to the bar and got Megan a glass of seltzer with ice and lime— something she remembered seeing in one of the spa brochures she'd been collecting. Honestly, if it were her, she'd drink a beer to relax. But Megan hadn't wanted her beer. So maybe this seltzer would do the trick. If she was lucky, lime juice was a spa rejuvenating secret. Kira eyed the highball glass in her hand. Yeah, right. When had the word "rejuvenating" entered her vocabulary, anyway?

* * *

Megan leaned over the shared sink in the club's graffiti-covered restroom and splashed cold water on her face. She pressed her wet hands over her eyes and took several deep, calming breaths that did nothing to ease the pressure in her forehead. She felt guilty about how long she was making Kira wait, but she kept her eyes closed and breathed, trying to talk her body into overcoming its exhaustion.

When her face was dry and she emerged from her sanctuary, Kira was leaning against the wall outside the restroom talking to Shayna, who relieved her of the door before it could swing shut.

"She's got great hands, Kira. Must be nice getting free massages every night." Shayna winked at Megan as she headed into the restroom, letting the door swing shut behind her.

Kira's jaw visibly clenched. "If I hear that innuendo crap one more time…"

Was Kira defending her honor?

Kira glared at the restroom door. "Shayna can be such a jerk."

"She's your friend, right? I'm sure she didn't mean to insult me. She thinks you have a girlfriend…" *Okay, don't choke on that thought…* "And she's happy for you."

"One who's talented in bed," Kira fumed.

A rush of warmth hit her abdomen. No one had ever reacted like this before. She was so used to being told she was too sensitive that she didn't know quite what to do. She smiled wanly. "I'll take that as a compliment."

"You're not offended?"

"I know she didn't hear it from you, since we've never slept together."

* * *

If only Megan knew how much she wanted to do just that. Which was probably why Shayna's teasing had pissed her off so much. Pushing that thought from her mind, Kira offered Megan the glass of seltzer with a slice of lime wedged on the rim.

Megan hesitated before taking the glass, eying it warily. "Is this a gin and tonic?"

"Seltzer with lime."

Megan broke into a grateful smile. "Observant, aren't you?"

"Don't you mean presumptuous?"

"It takes an observant woman to connect the dots." She raised the glass to her lips and took a sip. There was something intimate about watching the way she hugged herself with her free arm, cradling Kira's gift and rounding her shoulders expressively, trying to eke out every ounce of comfort she could. Kira's heart twisted.

"Perfect." Megan took another sip. "How did you know this was just what I wanted?"

"Lucky guess." Kira couldn't explain it to herself, even. All she knew was there was something about Megan that filled her with a tenderness she hadn't felt in a long time.

"The ice is good." Megan drained the glass and eyed the ice as if she were deciding whether to salvage it. She glanced around. "Looks like no one's waiting to pounce on me for a massage. I was expecting people to track me down."

"Why would they?"

"You *were* convincing," Megan conceded. "You made it sound like you were with the management."

Kira thought she detected a hint of criticism in Megan's voice. "The real management won't mind." She didn't really give a shit about what she'd done—either about her management impersonation or about her little encounter with Megan's groupies outside the restroom—an encounter that would remain unmentioned.

"Let's hope not." Megan put her glass down on the closest empty table. "Because I need to go talk to the manager now and get paid."

"Want me to go with you?"

"I'll just be a minute. Do you want to wait here?"

"No problem."

When Megan returned, Kira folded the completed surveys she'd been looking over and tucked them into the back of her waistband. There were several requests for body mud and several more for yoga, and one for a beer waterfall, which didn't surprise her, considering the venue.

"You ready to go?" Megan asked.

Actually, no, she was not ready to go. Not until she found out whether Megan's invitation to join her here tonight was one hundred percent work-related, or whether there was some small part of her that would say yes to dancing. She was almost certain Megan would say no, since the first time they met she had shot her down when she suggested dinner—and dinner was a lot safer—but it was worth a try.

"Do you dance? Since we're already here…"

Megan's eyes widened. "Okay."

Kira's jaw dropped. She should have had faith. Extroverts were entertaining, but they were too easy to figure out. The quiet ones had a way of surprising you.

She took Megan's hand and led her to the edge of the dance floor. It was probably a bad idea to touch her, but she couldn't help herself. Megan got to her on a level where logic didn't always rule. And speaking of logic, she had no idea why Megan had agreed to dance with her, although it was just like her to be sweet and generous and… Wait. Kira let go of Megan's hand. She didn't want her to do this out of politeness. "If you don't want to…"

Megan recaptured her hand.

Kira melted. It was still entirely possible that Megan was just being polite, but she let herself pretend it was more than that. All her senses focused on Megan's powerful grip on her hand. Amazing how such a small, delicate hand could be so strong.

She pushed her way blindly through the crowd, Megan at her heels. Grudgingly, the mass of bodies ceded them a few square inches on the dance floor. Megan moved her hips to the throbbing beat. Their bodies swayed and swiveled in unison, close enough to feel the heat of each other's bodies, but not touching except for that one hand, palm to palm, fingers intertwined.

Megan was a good dancer. Slinky and graceful and smiling like she was having a good time. Smiling at *her*. God, if she could feel this happy from Megan smiling at her when they weren't even on a real date, she was afraid to think about what would happen if they *were* on a real date. Because passing out would just be embarrassing.

A couple of blondes tried to squeeze past them without coming unglued from each other. Megan faltered and fell off the beat and the color drained from her face. The taller of the two blondes paused and stared at Megan in surprise.

"Amelia," Megan said.

Kira frowned at the intruders and stopped dancing. She took a step closer to Megan.

"You're dating another massage therapist?" Megan blurted out. "No offense, Cynthia," she added, acknowledging her target's companion for a microsecond before redirecting her anger. "What happened to the woman you were with at the Sand Bar the night you broke up with me?"

"Oh, you mean Carol. That was nothing serious."

Okay, definitely the ex.

"I can't believe this," Megan continued. "You said I was too weird. You said all massage therapists were irrational."

"Cynthia's different." Amelia smiled at her new girlfriend, who rubbed one hand up and down her back like a supportive massage therapist girlfriend straight out of Shayna's ridiculous fantasies. "She's not out on the fringe the way you are."

Megan squeezed Kira's hand, hard.

"And she's not too stubborn to take my advice. She's willing to improve."

Kira took a menacing step forward. "Megan doesn't need improvement."

Megan stopped her with an insistent tug and Kira shut her mouth.

"Would taking your advice have changed anything?" Megan asked bitterly.

"Contrary to what you seem to think, I tried to make things work."

"By dumping me? I see."

"I tried," Amelia snapped. "We can't all be a damn saint."

Kira moved so she was standing behind Megan and wrapped one arm around her waist, hoping Megan wouldn't stop her. She pulled her pretend date's ass to her hips, front to back, away from Amelia. Not grabbing her, not desperate the way Amelia was clinging to her sidekick—who had the grace to look nervous, but not the grace to look embarrassed—just a firm grip with one arm. A nice possessive gesture that said *back off* without violating Megan's personal space.

Or at least that was the idea. It wasn't actually working out that well, because she probably *was* violating Megan's personal space, seeing as how her entire body was pressed up against her, and because holding Megan this close felt unbearably good. And that was going to make it difficult to think straight.

Oh well. To hell with thinking straight. Kira locked eyes with Amelia to make sure she was watching, then moved her pelvis to the techno beat, grinding into Megan's backside. And what do you know, Megan mirrored her every move perfectly, as if they'd been dancing together for years. She might have even felt her giggle. Maybe when this was over, Megan wasn't going to smack her after all.

What had possessed Amelia to break up with this sexy, amazing woman? She almost felt bad for her. To make such a serious error in judgment…

"Don't keep Megan out past her bedtime." Amelia gave them a condescending smirk and moved off into the crowd.

"Forget about her," Kira told Megan, her lips grazing her ear.

Megan stroked Kira's forearm where it lay wrapped around her waist and continued to shimmy her hips to the music. Kira kept hold of her, tightening her grip with an involuntary shudder. She watched over Megan's shoulder as Amelia got lost in the crowd. *That's right, Amelia, go away. Go dance with your deluded girlfriend and leave Megan alone.*

She clung to the warmth of Megan's back against her chest, breathing her in. She knew she had to let go, but she didn't think she could. If they weren't in public she would be extremely tempted to turn around and ease her to the floor and press her body against her and work very, very hard to find out exactly how to make her scream.

This was not good news.

As long as Megan wanted to keep dancing she'd be okay, but what did she think was going to happen when it came time to stop? A little preventative thinking a few minutes back might have been called for.

Megan rotated in her grip, their legs and hips and chests still close, but no longer touching. She raised her hand to the side of Kira's face and traced the line of her jaw. "Your jaw's tight."

Whether it had been tight before or not, Kira had no idea, but Megan's caress did nothing to relax her. If anything, it made her clench her jaw tighter. Megan's touch was innocent and gentle and feminine. Not to mention irresistibly arousing. And Kira didn't have the right to hold her this way. She should let go.

Instead, she leaned into Megan's hand. Megan curled her fingertips around her jaw with a featherlight pressure that she probably didn't even realize drew her closer. Kira moved her head in a barely visible hitch of invitation, the only warning she could give. And kissed her.

She hadn't intended to do more than brush her lips against hers in a gentle, tentative, not-quite-sure-of-her-reception kiss.

But Megan's lips were warm and hungry and not at all guarded, so instead, she lost her mind. She thrust her tongue into her mouth and it felt like the best decision she'd ever made in her entire life.

Megan's hands found their way under her shirt and up her back, pulling her closer. Kira tucked her hands into Megan's pockets and fit their hips together. Their legs bent and swayed to the music pulsing in her veins, and Megan's hips matched her beat for beat. They moved like one body and kissed with a searching, possessive need.

Megan tasted just like her dreams, clean like the ice cold water she could never gulp enough of after a long, hot run. But Megan couldn't be the one from her dreams—it didn't make sense that she could have dreamed of her so long ago. Reality didn't work that way. But it felt like her. So familiar. So *right*.

What the hell. Maybe reality did work that way. She was willing to give the mysteries of the universe the benefit of the doubt.

Because as it turned out, reality was much, much better than her dreams.

Megan twined her leg around Kira's, pulling them off balance, and Kira stumbled and caught her footing, managing not to fall. Megan didn't seem to notice. She kept kissing her, kept rubbing her inner thigh against her. Kira tightened her grip and let the feel of Megan's body sear a memory into the deepest fibers of her being at every single point of contact. Nothing existed but her heat and her taste and the way she kissed her like the kiss would never end.

Until a half-naked man bumped into them and Megan sprang back. Kira reached for her, but Megan put a hand up to stop her.

"I can't do this," Megan said abruptly.

No. Kira's body ached for her across the space that separated them.

"You're a client."

What? "I'm not a client."

"The 10K…"

Kira's mind spun, trying to adjust to Megan's sudden change of heart as club lights played across her body in weirdly inappropriate patterns. Her words didn't even make sense. "That doesn't make me a client. That tent—that was an assembly line in there. Half those people you wouldn't even recognize again."

"I know, but...I shouldn't." Megan looked deflated and apologetic. "I could lose my license if I'm not careful."

The troubled look in her eyes—and the unspoken trust that Kira would understand—knocked the fight right out of her. She could never try to force Megan to do something that made her uncomfortable, not if she wanted to be able to live with herself. Although she had to say that as far as excuses went, the losing her license thing was bogus. No way did she qualify as a client. But none of that mattered if Megan didn't want her. It was hard to process, but that was what Megan was telling her—she didn't want her.

She'd been showing off for her ex. What a waste.

So, okay. She could respect that. She wasn't a man. She'd worked with enough Neanderthals to know that men always wanted the woman who was out of reach, the woman they had to chase, and once they got her, the excitement was over. They missed out on a lot, thinking that way. Because she had a feeling that once Megan let her into her life, the excitement would only get better.

Unfortunately, it didn't look like she was going to get to find out.

CHAPTER NINE

Megan opened her front door and looked past the courtyard toward the street for Esther Bonney, her ten o'clock appointment, who was about to be late.

She spotted a familiar gray Taurus. Wasn't that Barbara Fenhurst's car?

Before she could wonder if she'd written down the wrong name in her appointment book, Esther drove up, parked and hobbled out of her car, the arthritis in her knees slowing her down more than usual.

Megan left her door open and went over to help Esther with the walk from her car.

"Thanks for your reminder call yesterday." Esther gripped the support of Megan's extended arm. "Can't count on my memory anymore, and I'd hate to miss an appointment with you. Now the dentist, that I don't mind missing."

"How's the arm?"

"Hurts a bit."

"You don't have to be stoic around me, you know."

Even though Esther wore long sleeves to hide the compression wrap, Megan could tell her right arm was twice the size of the other one. Several years ago a mastectomy had saved her life, but it had left her with severe lymphedema. At least nowadays they didn't remove all the lymph nodes as a matter of course. But surgeons still had this attitude of *I saved your life, what more do you want from me?* They cut the cancer out and if you complained about pain or infection or loss of function, well, that was the price you had to pay for not dying. It was a price women were willing to pay. But that didn't make it right.

When they got upstairs and Esther was settled on the massage table, Megan elevated her arm and massaged it with the lightest, gentlest touch possible. Pressure would only aggravate the swelling. She brushed the arm over and over again, encouraging the excess fluid to flow toward the chest and leave the arm. The scent of the arnica massage cream filled the room.

By the end of the session the edema had visibly improved, and that meant the pain should be better, too. Megan sat on her stool behind her client and rested her hands on either side of her head. Like a mother tenderly stroking her sick child's hair, she soothed her with slow circles on her scalp and forehead. Megan's eyes lost focus, making Esther's skin smooth out and her face become rounder, more youthful. It wasn't hard to imagine her as a little girl racing around the beach with her arms open wide, screeching with delight.

Megan held the healing image in her mind and radiated love into Esther's energy field. She realigned what she could, noted where there was resistance, and, with the pressure of her hands, invited her to let go. She positioned her hands at the base of Esther's skull and waited for her to drift into the stillpoint—a gap between breaths, between heartbeats, between thought. A moment of pure stillness, where time followed different rules and deep healing occurred. She loved holding the stillpoint, feeling loving but detached, because when she was in that space, it was impossible to get sucked into her client's problems. Or maybe it was the other way around: When she got sucked into her client's problems—or her own problems—it was impossible to be a channel for pure love.

Which was why she was having trouble staying in the stillpoint. She was pulling herself out of it each time she thought about what happened at Avalanche with Kira. And she couldn't stop thinking about it.

That kiss was a mistake. Kira had been so nice to her the whole evening. She looked so hot, too, in her tight shorts. The music was great, and what with all that pretending they'd been doing to make Amelia jealous, she'd gotten carried away. Way too carried away.

It had felt so natural to meet Kira's lips, to let her tongue in, to revel in the way her hands tightened on her ass to pull her closer, so desperate for her. Megan had felt pretty desperate herself. It had taken quite a while before she remembered where she was and why she didn't want to do this.

Inviting Kira to go to Avalanche with her had sounded like fun at the time...and yeah, it *had* been fun. Too fun. Somewhere along the way she'd left her ethics at the door and forgotten Kira was a client.

Clients were off-limits. For good reason.

She couldn't see a woman's personality clearly when that woman was a client, because it was all infused with that heart space she worked from to create healing. She loved her clients, every single one of them. She loved them because it was her job to set aside her personal prejudices and see them as innocent and lovable. Once she had looked at someone through that lens, that image was hard to shake. She wasn't sure she could ever see them any other way.

And her clients couldn't be objective about her, either. They raved about her because they saw her at her best, and because she helped them. They didn't see her when she was tired and cranky and had other things to do. It was an illusion, and that illusion caused problems outside of the massage room.

Which was why she should have pulled back the instant she realized Kira was about to kiss her. There'd been time.

Time which she'd spent mesmerized, dizzy with yearning as

she caressed Kira's taut jaw, watched her lower her gaze, and felt her hesitate, knowing she was coming closer, knowing she was going to kiss her, wondering what it would be like.

Instead of thinking.

Thank God her brain had kicked in eventually.

Maybe they could just forget the kiss ever happened. Kira might agree to that. She was desperate for her help with the spa, and wouldn't want to complicate their working relationship. They'd treat it like an accident—an accidental bumping of the lips. That accidentally turned into an irresistible soul kiss.

Yup. That would work.

Kisses that brushed against her soul were easy to forget. Not that she'd ever come across one before…

Well, she was sure it was possible.

* * *

It didn't take long for George—Kira's foreman—to confirm her suspicions. She liked to check on the construction site and assess the hotel's progress every day, even on weekends when no one was around, so when she'd stopped by after her early Saturday morning run and noticed a stack of several large coils of copper pipe had disappeared, she'd immediately called George to assess what else might have been stolen.

George checked all the areas under construction as Kira followed close behind. "Looks like that's all they took," he said.

"Were they watching the delivery?" Kira had been in this business long enough to know she had to budget for some worksite theft, but it galled her every time—especially since these pipes had been delivered less than twenty-four hours ago. She'd almost been late meeting up with Megan at Avalanche the night before because she'd been waiting for the delivery and the truck got stuck in Friday afternoon beach traffic. Like that was a big surprise. She'd *told* them not to do it on a Friday. Her crew had gone home for the day and she had waited for the truck. Eating pizza out of a cardboard box, wondering when the truck was ever going to get there, knowing she was going to inconvenience Megan if it didn't arrive soon… It had been a frustrating way to start the evening. And all for nothing.

She stomped down the hall. The plumbing was never going to get finished at this rate. They were already behind schedule. Did she need to hire a guard to stay overnight? Copper pipes weren't a sexy, big-ticket item—not like the $60,000 backhoe that disappeared from one of her dad's worksites—but they were untraceable and easy to resell. At least nothing else had been taken. Long before she'd started construction, she'd run the numbers and calculated that a security guard would cost much more than whatever her potentially stolen building supplies were worth. She didn't want to be proven wrong.

George followed as she headed for the lobby. "I can get what we need. I know a guy—"

"And buy back what they stole? No thanks. I'm not providing them with a market. Tell me what we need and I'll order it. And when the new pipes come in, tell the guys I want that plumbing installed as soon as possible."

"Might not make any difference. I heard the guys working on that house down on Oak Drive got their copper pipes ripped right out of the walls. Took the toilets, too."

Kira rubbed the hinge of her jaw, trying to get it to relax. She should get some tips from Megan on how to do that. Although as far as she knew, Megan was shit at it. The last time her favorite massage therapist had touched her jaw they had ended up kissing, and that kiss had jolted her like a shot of pure caffeine, intense enough to give her the shakes. It had certainly not left her feeling relaxed.

Not that she was complaining.

She rubbed her hands over her face and hoped her foreman hadn't noticed that her lips were parted, still tingling from the aftereffects of their contact with Megan the day before.

"Think positive, George."

"Yeah, sure," he grumbled. "It's your money."

"Positive," she reminded him. She wasn't in the habit of giving up, and she wasn't going to start now. She'd sleep at the hotel herself if she had to.

When they were sure nothing else was missing and George took off, Kira went to her office and tried to get some work done. Her current string of bad financial luck had started over a year ago, with Lizzy. Maybe if she hadn't found Lizzy so sexy, she would never have taken her up on her offer to open a restaurant together. If it hadn't been for the way she let her look down her very nice cleavage, she might not have talked herself into sinking money into an industry that was notoriously unstable instead of sticking with what she was good at. If only she'd had Megan's strength of character and made some personal rule about not dating potential business partners, that whole fiasco could have been averted.

To be fair, she *had* been ready for a change. Lizzy and her dreams of being a chef and having her own restaurant happened to come along right when Kira was getting bored of building doctor's offices. There was no guarantee that anything she tried at that point would have succeeded. Still, it was hard to believe lust hadn't had something to do with her mistake. Lust that died before the restaurant ever opened.

Megan wouldn't have gotten involved with Lizzy. And if Megan's standards of integrity weren't so admirable, she could be enjoying her company right now. She could be sleeping in late with her dream woman in her arms, blissfully unaware of what had happened at the hotel, instead of stewing because she had to order plumbing supplies she had already ordered once before.

She supposed eventually they'd have to get out of bed so Megan could see her massage clients. And yeah, Kira had to work, too. But not if she really didn't want to. She could afford to take a day, or a week, to do nothing but roll around naked with her very sexy girlfriend. It had been a long time since she'd had a reason to take advantage of being her own boss.

Unfortunately, it was going to continue to be a long time, because Megan was unlikely to invite her to crawl into her bed anytime soon. Optimistically speaking.

Megan thought kissing her was a mistake.

That was so not how Kira felt about it.

Well, okay, the kiss was a mistake if it had scared Megan off. But if you could ignore the repercussions... Definitely not a mistake.

She could still feel Megan's fingers on her jaw, her other hand gripping her shoulder, her mouth setting off demolition charges that threatened to make Kira lose her balance even before she hooked her with her leg.

Why had Megan suffered an attack of conscience and pulled away? The abruptness of it had reminded her of something. Something that danced at the edge of her brain that she couldn't quite remember. Kira shook her head in annoyance. That massage after the 10K was only ten minutes. How could that count as a professional relationship? If she had known getting a massage from her would have such frustrating consequences, she would have run out of that tent before Megan ever saw her.

* * *

Megan was eating spaghetti at home Saturday night when the phone rang and she almost didn't pick up. She changed her mind when she saw who was calling. Kira.

She didn't know what in the world she was going to say to her. Her body went hot and cold just thinking about the way she felt pressed up behind her with her arms around her waist, dancing, or the way she'd looked at her in that slow-motion instant before they kissed—her hesitation, and then her sharp intake of breath.

And then her kiss. It hurt to think about that kiss.

Too bad she hadn't spent any time thinking about what to say to her the next time they talked. Which was turning out to be sooner than she'd thought.

"Kira?"

"Your friend—the Russian one?" Kira sounded anxious. "She needs help. Can you come over?"

What was Svetlana doing with Kira? "What...is she drunk or something? Where are you? What happened?" Megan located her sandals and her keys while she talked.

"I'm in the woods by the hotel. You know, at your magic rock." She could almost see Kira's jaw clench in annoyance at finding one of Megan's friends on her property.

"Okay, I'm on my way." She locked her front door behind her. "What's wrong with her?"

"Who the hell knows?"

Megan got there ten minutes later. Svetlana lay crumpled against the boulder that marked the intersection of the two ley lines, her body curled in a fetal position, her face pale. Her eyes were open, but glassy, and didn't react to the presence of the people around her.

"She was screaming," Kira explained.

Megan rushed to kneel at Svetlana's side. The instant she touched her shoulder, an oily darkness made her recoil. Svetlana remained motionless, frozen in the grip of…something. She wasn't sure Svetlana even knew she was there. Megan wanted to hug her and warm her and make her feel safe, but she couldn't bear to touch that darkness again.

"You tried it, didn't you?" Megan said softly.

"Tried what?" Kira asked.

Megan retreated to where Kira stood watching. She sighed. "She must have tried to go out of body. I warned her not to."

"I don't even know what that means. Is she going to be okay?"

"Yes. Did you call her husband?"

"I asked her for the phone number, but she didn't seem to be able to talk. That's why I called you."

Megan pulled out her cell phone, punched in the number, and handed the phone to Kira. "Ask him to come over, but try not to scare him."

Kira nodded.

Megan circled Svetlana cautiously, assessing the problem. When she heard Kira say goodbye to Patrick, she held out her hand for her phone, ignoring the flutter in her stomach that kicked up the minute she entered Kira's airspace. So inappropriate. Kira passed her the phone without touching, and

Megan curled her fingers around it and hit speed dial. She was going to need reinforcements.

Patrick Durbridge arrived in record time. He immediately dropped to the ground and pulled Svetlana's unresponsive body onto his lap and wrapped his arms around her, his head bowed to hers. Gwynne showed up a few minutes later, giving Kira a brief glance that Megan found hard to read. Without getting too close, Gwynne leaned in Svetlana's direction to get a good look. She tensed, but so briefly that Megan would have missed it if she hadn't been watching for some kind of reaction, then shrugged it off and whistled like she was admiring a prize-winning fish.

Patrick interrupted his murmured words of comfort to glare up at her in irritation. "Do you mind?"

Gwynne shrugged and sauntered over to Megan's side.

"What do you think?" Megan nodded in Svetlana's direction. "You see it, right?"

"Yup. Do you?"

"I feel it." The sense of malevolence clinging to Svetlana was hard to miss—much worse than the fleeting apprehension she'd felt the day she'd first discovered the ley lines. She was kind of glad she couldn't physically see—the way Gwynne could—the leech that had grabbed Svetlana. Sensing it was bad enough.

"It's a big one," Gwynne agreed, not sounding too concerned.

Svetlana twisted violently away from Patrick's embrace and threw up. It was the first time she'd moved since Megan had arrived. Patrick held on, his expression grim, smoothing her hair and keeping it out of her face.

"I don't know what's wrong with me," Svetlana cried, then threw up again.

At least she was talking now. Patrick sure was able to bring her around fast. That was one advantage of not being perceptive enough to detect the spirit plane—he could hold her without being repulsed by her new noncorporeal companion. He could sense that she wasn't herself, but he most likely had no idea what was going on. Beyond the obvious physical symptoms, of course. Fortunately, holding her was enough to snap her out of her astral dissociation and back into her physical body.

Patrick wiped her mouth with the edge of his shirt as Svetlana clung to him, her face pressed to his chest.

"What happened?" Patrick asked her.

"I felt like someone grabbed me."

"Someone attacked you?" Patrick reared back, his face a bright, blotchy red.

Svetlana shook her head angrily, as if by forcing the movement she could make him understand. "No one was there. I imagined it."

"You were screaming," Kira reminded her.

"I...I guess I...how do you say? Flipped."

Patrick pulled her into his arms again. "Kira said you passed out. Are you sure no one hurt you?"

Svetlana threw up again, turning her head away from him just in time. "I don't understand. Why I pass out? Why I vomit?"

"You picked up a hitchhiker," Gwynne explained.

"A what?" Svetlana clutched Patrick's arm.

"Something bad," Megan said.

"But not serious," Gwynne insisted.

"Are you sure there isn't a more down-to-earth explanation for this?" Patrick demanded, directing his ire at Gwynne.

"Psychosis?" Gwynne suggested sarcastically.

"Is demon, no?" Svetlana whispered.

"Of course not," Megan said, although *demon* was actually a pretty good name for it. It wasn't surprising, really, that that was the word that would come to Svetlana's mind. But there was no need to make her more scared than she already was. "You don't believe in angels, so don't start believing in demons, okay?"

Svetlana looked dubious. "How I get rid of it?"

"We're going to do that right now," Megan said. "That's why I called Gwynne. She's better at this than I am."

And the sooner they got it out, the better. Svetlana was actually lucky she had attracted such a big one, because the small ones were harder to spot, and better at insinuating themselves into a person's life. People felt like they weren't themselves, that they were more negative and angry, but they never figured out the real reason why. Anger was easy to dismiss. Throwing up was harder to ignore.

"Can you move away from the boulder?" Megan suggested.

Patrick helped Svetlana stand, and they stumbled a few yards away from it.

"Good?" Patrick asked.

"Yes. But you're going to have to let go of her, Patrick. We don't want to pull the hitchhiker out of her and have it jump into you."

Patrick's nostrils flared. He let go but held his arms out, not trusting that Svetlana wouldn't fall. "I think she should sit."

"I can stand," Svetlana protested. "Dizziness will pass."

She swayed, and Patrick caught her arm.

"Maybe I sit." She bent her knees and sank to the ground.

Megan stationed herself behind Svetlana with her legs planted wide apart and her arms spread out to the sides. Gwynne stood opposite her, positioning Svetlana between them.

Patrick left Svetlana's side and parked himself next to Kira—who stood a few yards away between two trees—to watch. "I don't understand any of this," he told Kira, crossing his arms in front of his chest.

"Join the club," Kira said.

"Svetlana's never been interested in energy work. And now this."

"Patrick?" Megan said. "Are you going to help us?"

"I thought you said… Wouldn't I just be in the way?"

"I didn't mean leave the area. You have a connection with Svetlana that no one else here has."

"That would help?" Patrick stood up straighter and uncrossed his arms.

"Possibly. You got her to the point where she could talk and stand up."

"We don't need him," Gwynne said dismissively.

"It wouldn't hurt," Megan argued. Gwynne might be confident they could handle this thing on their own, but Megan wasn't one to discount the power of an emotional bond.

Gwynne looked Patrick up and down. "His emotions are all over the place right now, and he doesn't know what he's doing. God knows what would happen."

Megan shot him a look of apology.

Patrick held up his hands, palms out. "I don't think this is the right time for me to be learning how to do this. You two are the experts. This isn't the time to experiment."

* * *

At first it seemed to Kira as if Megan and Gwynne were doing nothing—perhaps meditating—as they stood facing each other on either side of Svetlana, although she definitely got the sense that they were both focused on how to help her. Then Gwynne began prowling and waving her arms around, herding an invisible something around Svetlana's body.

"Come here," Gwynne muttered, clenching her fingers around her invisible target and yanking on it with vicious, forceful tugs that made it easy to believe she was grabbing something more than just empty air and pulling it out of Svetlana's body. "Slippery bastard."

"Aren't they all." Megan circled Svetlana with her arms out in front of her like a blind woman feeling her way, tracing the shape of the air.

Gwynne adjusted her grip and kept tugging. Abruptly she let go and stared at her open palms in shocked disbelief. "Meg, quick! It's escaping!"

Gwynne had let it slip out of her hands? Kira's gut tightened. As if armoring herself against this hitchhiker thing would be any use.

If it was real.

Which it wasn't.

Not that she had a better explanation for what could have made Svetlana sick. When she'd heard a scream coming from the woods next to the hotel she'd rushed over to make sure no one was being attacked. By the time she'd gotten there, Svetlana was on the ground hugging herself and moaning, looking like she'd either seen a ghost or broken her arm. Kira hadn't expected anyone to actually go for the ghost explanation.

Megan dove to one side as if she were blocking a soccer ball from getting into her goal. "Relax. I see it."

"You do?" Gwynne dodged in the same direction.

"I meant that figuratively. It's got body odor like you wouldn't believe. Stinks worse than a sweaty man."

"Men stink? I feel like I might have heard you mention that…oh…once or twice. Or has it been a million times? I forget," Gwynne said. They exchanged a teasing glance. It wasn't intimate, exactly, but it held a shared familiarity that made Kira's insides twist with jealousy.

"Gag me." Megan made a sound from deep in her throat that was half choking, half laughter.

"Think she's a lesbian?" Gwynne shot the words over her shoulder at Kira with a crooked grin. "I bet Svetlana doesn't think our friend here smells bad. She likes manly pheromones."

"Please tell me you ladies are focusing," Patrick begged.

Kira couldn't blame him for being worried. She didn't know whether he believed there was an invisible force at work or not, but either way, she'd be freaking out if her wife looked that pale.

"We're focusing," Megan reassured him. "But this won't work if we let ourselves get scared. Hitchhikers love fear. They hook into it."

"Besides, there's nothing to be afraid of," Gwynne said.

"We've got it under control," Megan added.

"If you say so." Patrick still looked worried.

"This is how it got me?" Svetlana asked. "But I had no fear until after."

"They're attracted to the light, too," Megan said, "because light casts a shadow. The hitchhiker was probably drawn to the intense light of the ley lines and then found something in you to lock on to."

"Something in me? *Nyet!*"

"Everyone's got unloving places in their heart," Megan said gently. "It could have gotten anyone."

"Ready for us to finish this sucker?" Gwynne interrupted.

Svetlana nodded.

"We need to weave a stronger net around it," Megan told Gwynne.

"I know. I pulled on it too soon."

Gwynne backed up with her arms waving around and Megan joined in like a mirror image, perfectly matching her every move, as if there really were something there they could both see, something they were circling and binding.

"Sorry I yelled," Gwynne said quietly to Megan, winding her arm around some part of the thing's body, hopefully its neck.

"No problem." Megan's nose wrinkled in disgust as she moved cat-like, stalking and pouncing, intent on her invisible quarry.

Could she really smell it? Kira didn't smell a thing.

They worked well together, anticipating each other's movements. They'd done this together before, she was sure. Many times. It was not a comforting thought. Gwynne Abernathy was so much more Megan's type than Kira would ever be. They shared an imaginary world that Kira wasn't cut out to believe in. Yet she couldn't look away.

"This is so much faster than doing this by myself," Gwynne observed.

Megan started to hyperventilate. "It would be even faster if you would—"

"I know, I've got it." Gwynne smacked her palms together an inch away from Svetlana's face, startling her enough to make her jump, but probably intended for the hitchhiker, maybe to dislodge it. She pulled on their invisible quarry with the imaginary rope they had tied it up with, cautiously changing the angle this way and that, as if she really were trying to pull an oddly shaped object out of Svetlana's body without snagging it on a vital organ. "Got it." Gwynne raised it in her hands triumphantly, like an offering made to the sky. As her hands floated down, Kira could almost see their victim dissolve and drift away on the wind.

Megan stumbled forward and collapsed with her head on Gwynne's shoulder.

Was she okay? Kira started forward, then halted. Gwynne knew her better than she did. Megan might not welcome her butting in, especially since she didn't understand what was going on.

Gwynne patted Megan on the back. "You okay?" she asked, echoing Kira's thoughts, her tone more gentle than Kira had heard her use with anyone else, even the puking Svetlana.

"Tired. It's been a while." Megan freed herself from Gwynne's arms and turned to Svetlana. "How do you feel?"

Svetlana looked dazed, but it was nothing like the scary blankness she'd sported earlier. "Better. Thanks."

Patrick knelt at Svetlana's side and wrapped her in his arms, shutting out everyone else.

"I'll get everyone something to drink." Kira excused herself and headed for the hotel, where she kept all sorts of drinks and snacks for the construction crew. The sun was starting to go down and they could probably use a few flashlights, too.

She only got a few yards out of earshot of the others before Megan caught up with her and fell into step beside her on the rough, narrow path.

"I'm glad Svetlana's better. I was worried about her," Kira said, her skin prickling from Megan's nearness.

"You got more wackiness than you were counting on, didn't you?" Megan said. "I don't know what possessed you to call me instead of an ambulance, but I'm grateful that you did."

"Yeah, I'm not sure either. But you might want to watch it with your use of the word *possessed*. I've seen you in action now."

Megan came to a stop so Kira stopped too, and turned to see what was wrong.

"Did I freak you out?" Megan searched her eyes for her reaction.

"Of course not."

"I thought you might not want to talk to me after what happened last night."

Kira puzzled over what to say to that. She'd worried that now that the crisis with Svetlana was over, Megan might remember that kiss. It was why she'd been in such a hurry to escape to the hotel for drinks and flashlights. Hadn't worked too well, actually, since here Megan was, bringing it up. What was she supposed to say? Would the truth make things worse?

The truth was, that kiss had not lasted nearly long enough. And when a kiss was that perfect, you couldn't just turn your back on it and say okay, one kiss was all I wanted.

She could still taste Megan's lips, still feel her softness and her eagerness and the heat of her body, but it wasn't enough. There was so much more she wanted to know. Like what made her laugh, and what did she think about when she lay awake late at night, and was she as opinionated about other things as she was about where she should build her spa? And yeah, normal getting-to-know-you kinds of questions would be nice, too, like...oh, who cared?

She stared into Megan's fathomless eyes and knew she was lost. Her heart fell off a cliff and into a canyon she couldn't climb back out of.

Kira rubbed the back of her neck. "Yeah, about that..."

What the hell. If she did make things worse, she'd find a way to fix it. So she told her the truth. "I still want to talk to you. Of course I still want to talk to you. More than talk to you." Her heart hammered. "I know this might not make you happy, but I haven't given up on you."

"Um...that might not be such a good idea."

"Yeah, I was afraid of that." But it didn't change how she felt.

* * *

The next morning, Kira was out running on a quiet, sparsely traveled road past miles of cornfields when against her better judgment, she reached into the zippered back pocket of her running shorts for her phone and hit speed dial for the number she already—God help her—knew by heart. If she was lucky, Megan would be busy and not answer, and not check her call log, and Kira could hang up and finish her run and pretend this moment of insanity had never happened.

"Hello?"

Kira cautiously moved her thumb away from its position hovering above the button that would end the call. "How's Svetlana doing?"

"Much better. I was just going to call you."

"You were?" Maybe things weren't going to be as awkward as she thought. Megan actually sounded like she wasn't mad at her.

"Svetlana wants to thank you for helping her out instead of having her arrested for trespassing, and I thought maybe we could all get together for dinner. Tonight. Our treat. Well, hers, really. We decided you'd be more likely to say yes if I was the one who called you."

Wow. Really?

"So, um…" Megan said into the awkward silence. "We're still friends, right?"

"Absolutely."

"Friends have dinner together, right?"

Well, actually, friends who were trying not to kiss each other again were usually better off not seeing each other at all for a few weeks. But hey, she could probably use a little more agony in her life right now.

"Sounds fantastic," Kira managed.

CHAPTER TEN

Kira snacked from the complimentary basket of still-warm, freshly fried shrimp chips, dipping them into Piper Thai Restaurant's famous peanut sauce while she waited for Patrick, Svetlana and Megan to decide what to order. She pushed the basket of chips in Megan's direction and Megan passed it around the table. Kira opened her menu again, closed it, and sat back and studied the ornate décor, wondering idly if she'd ever have the chance to design a room that called for red and gold drapes.

Megan's hair was pulled back in a sleek ponytail. She'd wondered in the past why Megan never put her hair up, but now it was killing her to imagine what it would take to convince her to allow her to pull off that rubber band—or what it would take to convince her to let her weave her fingers through her hair until it was as disheveled as it must look first thing in the morning before she was fully awake.

But she knew where she stood. Megan had told her that kiss had been a mistake. That she didn't date clients. And Kira didn't want to pressure her to violate her ethics.

That didn't mean she wasn't hoping there was a way around them.

"How's business?" Kira asked Patrick, trying to make conversation and stop thinking about Megan's hair.

"Same old story," Patrick replied. "Women prefer a female therapist; men prefer a female therapist."

"That leaves what? Horses?" Kira said.

"Believe it or not, horses do get massages."

Kira blinked in surprise. "But can they pay?"

Svetlana looked up from her menu. "It's big bucks."

Patrick poked her with his elbow. "Don't get any ideas, honey. I'm not doing horses."

"Patrick hopes for male athletes," Svetlana said. "Sports massage."

"That's my marketing focus," Patrick explained. "When they see results, male athletes can overcome their paranoia that they might get turned on by a man's touch."

"Especially when they don't believe woman is strong enough to massage their big, tough muscles," Svetlana added.

"That's because they haven't met my strong, tough wife." Patrick squeezed Svetlana's biceps and she preened, making a muscle against his hand.

Megan didn't have biceps like that. She was strong, but it was a stealth strength that took you by surprise, and Kira loved that.

"What about advertising in the gay paper? I see ads for male massage therapists in there all the time," Kira said.

Patrick patted his wife's arm and let her go. "It's not a bad idea, but you may have noticed the guys have to say 'non-sexual massage' in their ads. That's insulting. What other health care provider has to put that in their ads?"

"Patrick's a little sensitive on the subject," Svetlana said. "He's organizing campaign to convince phone company not to list escort services under 'massage' in phone book."

"Do people still use phone books?" Kira said.

"They're not even escort services," Megan complained. "They don't escort people."

"Bastards," Patrick said. "Scaring the shit out of idealistic young women who graduate from massage school eager to love and heal the world. I don't want Svetlana to ever have to listen to some moron ask her to finish him off. It makes me sick."

"I agree." Kira had felt more angry than afraid when she overheard Megan on the phone with that guy, but now the reality of what she faced was starting to sink in. Sweet, fragile, trusting Megan. Who somehow was tougher than she looked, tough enough to not feel threatened by those creeps, tough enough to try to educate them instead of hanging up on them. "Is there any way I can help? Talk to the Chamber of Commerce? I know a lot of businesspeople in the state."

"Fantastic," Patrick said as their waitress arrived to take their order. "We'll talk."

"Has Megan given you a massage yet?" Svetlana asked Kira as Patrick told the waitress what he wanted.

"No, she hasn't." Kira looked pointedly at Megan. So it wasn't only Shayna and company who assumed that being friends with a massage therapist came with perks, and didn't believe her when she insisted it wasn't like that. First of all, what they really meant was *dating* a massage therapist came with perks—and she and Megan were unfortunately not dating. And second of all, it wasn't a massage she wanted from Megan, not anymore. She couldn't care less about getting a massage. All she cared about was getting a chance to taste her lips again. If she could officially quit as a client, she would.

"Why you don't do this?" Svetlana scolded, looking back and forth between Kira and Megan.

"You know I have, Svetlana, you were there," Megan protested.

Svetlana was at the Race to the Beach? Kira recognized Patrick—he was the one who gave her that my-daughter's-too-good-for-you look when she asked Megan out—but she didn't remember seeing Svetlana.

And suddenly Kira realized what Svetlana had really meant: That in her opinion, Megan had *not* given her a massage—not one that counted, anyway—and maybe this was her way of telling her she saw no reason why Megan couldn't date her.

Not that it mattered what anyone else thought. All that mattered was what Megan thought. End of story.

"She's very good," Svetlana singsonged.

Kira snapped her napkin out of its tortured origami. "I won't let her."

Svetlana's eyes twinkled. She obviously knew exactly what *that* meant.

"I haven't offered," Megan muttered.

"You do massage?" asked the petite Asian waitress jotting down Patrick's order.

Megan nodded.

"It pinches when I do this." The waitress tucked her order pad in her apron and raised her arm to demonstrate, pointing to her shoulder with frighteningly long fingernails painted hot pink with pale pink plumerias. "Right here. Do you think massage would help?"

Megan pushed back her chair, stood up, and reached for the woman's shoulder. "May I?"

She nodded, and Megan pushed her thumbs into the joint, exploring. It was amazing how quick perfect strangers were to throw themselves at Megan's mercy. First Shayna at the club; now this. What was it about her that made total strangers open up to her and ask her for help?

"Ow." The waitress craned her neck to see what was happening.

"That hurts, huh?" Megan continued her exploration, inching her fingers across her upper back.

"Medial deltoid?" Svetlana suggested.

"Could be thoracic outlet," Patrick said. "Test her neck."

"Her neck is fine," Svetlana argued. "Hold your neck normally, miss."

"Don't look at what Megan's doing. Look straight ahead," Patrick said.

The waitress complied.

"See?" Svetlana said. "Neck is aligned correctly."

"You can't tell just by looking." Patrick snagged Svetlana's fork and used it to gesture at the waitress. "Miss, are you having any pain in your forearms? Hands?"

Megan raised her hands in the air and stepped back. "Would you let me do this, please?"

Patrick and Svetlana exchanged guilty looks. Svetlana reclaimed her fork and playfully ran the tines down his bare arm, murmuring something in Russian that—judging from the expression on Patrick's face—meant she was seriously considering continuing down other parts of his body.

Kira tuned them out and watched Megan, who had placed her hands on the waitress's shoulder again. Megan's eyes were lowered in concentration, her fingers moving almost imperceptibly, pressing.

"The doctor told me I have bursitis," said the waitress.

"Thoracic outlet," Patrick muttered, for some unfathomable reason not completely distracted by his wife. "They think everything is bursitis."

"What's thoracic outlet?" the waitress asked.

"Oops." Patrick covered his mouth.

Svetlana laughed at his look of chagrin. Over what, Kira had no idea. She looked to Megan for a clue as to what he'd said wrong.

"Practicing medicine without a license again, Patrick?" Megan teased.

"Oh, fine," Patrick grumbled. "Let me rephrase that. I feel some tightness in your shoulder…"

Megan smirked. "Do you now? From all the way over there?"

The waitress glanced around as if she were having second thoughts about getting involved with these crazy people. "The doctor told me to stop carrying plates above my head," she said, clearly trying to bring the conversation back onto familiar ground.

"Did that help?" Megan asked, returning to full customer service mode.

"How can I stop if I never started?"

"It's certainly possible that you have bursitis," Megan said, "and if you do there's not much you can do except rest, but—"

"Ow, ow, ow."

"Sorry." Megan rubbed soothingly at the spot.

The waitress looked over her shoulder again, forgetting her instructions to not turn her head. "What was that?"

"That's what's making your shoulder hurt," Megan said.

"But that doesn't hurt my shoulder—it hurts my back."

"Hold on." Megan braced herself with one hand on the front of the woman's shoulder and pressed into the spot again, hard.

"Don't hurt yourself, Megan," warned Svetlana.

Megan ignored her. "If I press hard enough with my thumb, you'll feel the pain shoot into your shoulder."

The waitress gasped.

"Feel it?"

She nodded.

"Don't waste your time rubbing your shoulder. Rub here instead. You have trigger points in your rotator cuff. Right here." Megan touched the spot on the shoulder blade where she'd been pressing. "Massage will definitely help."

"But it is necessary to tell your massage therapist where the problem is," Svetlana added. "Because practitioner who only does relaxation massage will not understand how to help."

Megan dug a business card out of her purse. "Supraspinatus," she said, writing it down on the back of her card.

"Thanks." The waitress rotated her shoulder experimentally. "It feels much better."

"I'm glad."

She examined Megan's card and slipped it into her apron pocket before casting an anxious glance in the direction of the kitchen. "I'll take the rest of your orders now. And if there's anything you need, let me know. I mean it."

They ordered quickly and their waitress dashed off. Kira suspected there was going to be a big smiley face drawn on their bill. She angled her head toward Megan. "This happens to you all the time, doesn't it? People tell you their medical problems."

Svetlana answered for her. "All the time."

Kira frowned, annoyed at the intrusion. No, that was unfair of her. It was only natural that Svetlana would know about Megan's life. They were friends. They'd known each other for a long time before Kira came on the scene. But still, it made her jealous. *She* wanted to be the resident expert on all things Megan. She wanted to know her past, and her parents' names, and her favorite pizza topping, and the color of her sheets, and whether she secretly preferred jazz to that spacey massage music. She wanted to know everything.

Megan picked up her water glass. "Sometimes I think I have a sign above my head that says 'Good Listener.'"

She was right about that—there was something in her face that was incredibly open and friendly. No wonder people came to her with their problems. You could see in her wide-set eyes and in her gentle way of interacting that she genuinely cared.

Patrick cleared his throat and Kira glanced at him, disoriented. Had she missed part of the conversation? Svetlana swatted him.

Kira glanced back at Megan, who raised an eyebrow at her. Was she staring? She hadn't meant to. Megan shook her head but made no move to look away.

What the hell happened at the club the other night, anyway? She'd thought that kiss was the last one she was ever going to get from Megan. Now she wasn't so sure, because Megan might be trying to look mad, but her eyes gave her away. Her eyes were like sunlight. It was amazing how good that felt, to just look into her eyes and be dazzled by the magic shining from her soul. Kira's grin stretched out of control. She was sure she looked lovestruck, but she didn't care. Patrick would either have to look away or get over it.

But, oh, my, God, those eyes were going to get her into trouble. How was she supposed to keep things professional if mere eye contact was enough to make her forget why she'd ever agreed to keep her distance?

CHAPTER ELEVEN

When they left the restaurant, the gray skies that had threatened rain all day were unleashing a downpour. Megan paused under the awning outside to give Svetlana a hug goodbye, awkwardly trying not to bump her with the folded umbrella looped over her wrist.

Svetlana wasn't the touchy-feely type—despite what she did for a living—so Megan was surprised when she turned to give Kira a hug, too. "Thanks again for helping me yesterday," Svetlana told Kira. "You called the right person."

"Glad I could help. I had no idea Megan knew how to banish evil spirits."

The strain on Kira's face belied her light, joking tone. She wished Kira was more comfortable with what she'd witnessed, but at least she wasn't trying to pretend the whole thing had never happened, the way Megan's mother had always done, somehow managing to convince herself her child's embarrassing behavior was all the product of an overactive imagination.

"It was a surprise to me, too," Patrick said, his eyes on

Svetlana. "Let's hope this never comes up again." He pulled his keys out of his pocket, took Svetlana's hand, and together they dashed through the rain to their car.

Kira shrugged into her rain jacket and zipped it all the way up. Her shorts disappeared under the bottom of the jacket, emphasizing the bareness of her tanned, muscular legs. "It looked like you and Gwynne were old pros at handling Svetlana's problem. You must work together a lot."

"No, not really." Megan glanced away from Kira's legs. Did they have to talk about Gwynne right now? "It's been a long time since we've done any work together."

"I wouldn't have guessed. You had that finishing-each-other's-sentences thing going on."

So those two were keeping an eye on each other, were they? Interesting. It made her forget that Kira thought she was crazy. No, wait...what was it she called her? *Different*.

Megan opened her umbrella and held it over Kira's head. "I'll walk you to your car." Kira's raincoat had a hood, so there was no real need for her to offer. She wanted to, though. She could walk her to her car, and maybe on the way they'd get chilled from the rain and decide to stop somewhere for coffee.

Except sitting across from Kira at a cozy little table after dinner might feel like a date. Sipping coffee and gazing at her over the rim of her cup might feel like a date. Being alone with her might feel like a date. And she needed to make sure this didn't turn into a date.

"Where did you park?" Megan asked.

"I didn't bring my car."

"Let me drive you home, then."

Kira adjusted her hood and stepped out onto the sidewalk, away from the shelter of Megan's umbrella. "I can walk."

Megan jerked her umbrella back, hurt. Again. Five minutes ago inside the restaurant Kira was staring into her eyes like she wanted to pull her into her arms, and now she refused to accept a ride when it was pouring down rain?

"I'll drive you," Megan insisted. *I'll behave myself*, she added silently. She'd keep both hands on the steering wheel and not even look at Kira's gorgeous bare thighs, no matter how close she was in the passenger seat. They'd talk business and she'd try not to enjoy it too much when Kira pretended to be a ruthless businesswoman who'd never be nice to a competitor.

"Thanks, but no."

There was something in Kira's eyes she couldn't identify. She wished she could touch her—hold her hand, even—so she could use her weird abilities, which worked best through physical contact, to sense what Kira was feeling and understand what was going on.

And that was no way to think about a client and a friend. Because hand-holding would lead to running her hands up her arms and cupping her face and stepping into her personal space and kissing the explanation out of her.

Which would be out of line.

Which was exactly why Kira didn't want to accept a ride from her, wasn't it? Kira was holding the line. The line that *Megan* had drawn. She felt like a jerk.

"At least take my umbrella." Megan held it out but Kira refused to take it.

"You'll get wet," Kira said.

"And you won't?"

"I'm a runner. I'm used to being out in the rain. Sometimes I even do it on purpose."

The air smelled tangy with ozone, which meant the storm was about to get worse. Kira didn't have to be a selfless idiot. Megan was the one who had drawn the line and she was going to re-draw it. "It's storming and it's dark out. Come on, my car's not far."

Kira looked away, into the darkness, her hands shoved in her pockets.

Megan pursed her lips as the hollow feeling in her stomach turned into a knot. So she'd get rained on. She hoped Kira wasn't refusing a ride for her sake, but really, if Kira didn't mind getting wet, why should she argue? She didn't have to force her to accept her help. She wasn't a client on her table asking her to solve her problems.

Megan gave up. "I'll go," she said.

Kira didn't turn around. "I'll go with you."

* * *

With her windshield wipers smacking furiously, Megan pulled into the parking lot of the complex of squat three-story garden-style apartments where Kira lived. Each unit was clustered around an open stairwell and had its own miniature balcony.

"Svetlana lived in one of these apartments her first summer here," she told Kira.

"How did she like it?"

"She liked that it was affordable." Svetlana had been one of the hundreds of Eastern European teens who were lured to the Delaware shore each summer to fill unglamorous jobs like waitressing, lifeguarding at hotel pools, selling chocolate-covered frozen bananas, and taking tickets at putt-putt courses because there weren't enough locals to fill the demand. She was already in the hole from airfare just to get here, so she did what everyone did—squeezed in with as many of her new acquaintances as possible in short-term rentals that they furnished with plastic lawn chairs. "She shared the apartment with five other women."

"They fit six people in here? These apartments are all one-bedrooms."

"She slept on the floor. She said she was used to living in a small apartment in Moscow and the close quarters didn't bother her."

"Did she at least have a mattress?"

Megan's heart warmed at Kira's concern. She wanted her friends to like each other. "You sound like Patrick. When he found out, he couldn't wait to get her out of there."

Kira looked at her like she was clueless. "Patrick just wanted to sleep with her without an audience."

Okay, so maybe Kira wasn't a complete angel of concern.

"Do you like it here?"

"I don't spend much time here," Kira said. "As soon as we're done working on the plumbing and the electrical at the hotel, I'm moving into a room over there."

Megan braked in front of Kira's building. "I guess you don't worry too much about separating work and home."

"I move around a lot. Usually it doesn't seem worth the trouble." Kira unbuckled her seat belt. "But if my job involved questionable men coming to my home and getting naked, I'd make the effort. You should think about getting a real office."

"I think about it," Megan protested. "But I don't have any problems working at home. Besides, everything is so expensive around here. I can't afford to rent office space on top of what I already pay for my townhouse, not unless I raise my fees—and I don't want to do that to my clients." She slid the gearshift into Park and draped her left hand over the top of the steering wheel. "So I'll see you later?"

Kira paused with her hand on the door handle. "Want to come in for coffee?"

Megan's fingers clenched spasmodically around the steering wheel. *Not a date*, she reminded herself. Driving her home was not supposed to turn into a date. She pressed her foot harder, unnecessarily, on the brake. Coffee and dessert near the boardwalk—whether in a dimly lit restaurant or in the bright glare of an ice cream shop—would have been dangerous enough. Coffee in Kira's apartment, just a few feet away from her bedroom, was…was not something she wanted to dwell on right now. She wished she could tell whether the tension buzzing in the enclosed space was mutual or whether it was all one-sided, but Kira's face was unreadable in the darkness inside the car.

"Okay." Megan shifted back into gear, wondering how worried she should be. "Do you have decaf?"

Right. As if staying awake was what she was worried about.

They found a parking space in the visitors' lot and Megan shared her umbrella for the dash to the entrance. A futile gesture, now that the rain was coming down in violent gusts and her umbrella was in serious danger of flipping inside out, but Kira didn't rebuff her, and that made her happier than it should have. Kira also didn't hold her arm or touch her hand to steady the umbrella, but that was probably for the best. There was enough electricity in the air from the lightning storm without her huddling any closer.

When they got inside and up the stairs to her second-floor apartment, Kira stripped off her raincoat and relieved Megan of her umbrella. She gestured vaguely toward the living room couch and headed for the tiny kitchen. "I have some herbal tea in here somewhere if you want that instead of coffee."

"What kind?"

"I don't know, herbal? It comes in a red box."

While Kira disappeared into the kitchen, Megan looked around. The main living area held a couch, an ancient television, a dining table with two plain wooden chairs, and not much else. No personal knickknacks, no art, no clutter, no dust. Did she always live like this, or was most of her stuff in storage? She hadn't been exaggerating when she said she didn't spend much time here. She couldn't sense Kira's imprint at all in the emotional debris left behind by the apartment's many previous occupants. She closed her eyes and, with a whoosh of an exhale, swept her arms in a breaststroke-like motion through the emotionally clogged air, clearing it out until the apartment felt as psychically clean and unburdened as Kira had tried to make it look.

"You okay out there?" Kira called out from the kitchen.

"Yup."

Megan nodded with approval at the smoke detector and sprinkler. Scanning the ceiling for smoke detectors was a bad habit, but no one could accuse her of being neurotic if they didn't see her do it. She moved one of the chairs and climbed onto it so she could take a closer look.

She was still standing on the chair, holding the smoke detector's lid open and examining its inner workings, when Kira walked in with two mugs of tea. Megan blushed with embarrassment. Not that this was a date, but no relationship guru would recommend invading your host's privacy as a way to make a good first impression. Butt at eye-level, no less.

Kira stopped outside the kitchen doorway and stared up at her, unsmiling—at her face. Steam rose from the mugs she held in either hand. "What are you doing?"

"Checking your smoke detector." Megan snapped the lid shut, careful not to dislodge any wires. "You have the dual-action kind that detects smoldering fires as well as open flame. That's great."

"I know what kind of smoke detectors I have. You do know what I do for a living, right?"

"Sorry. Guess that was kind of nosy of me." Megan should have left it at that. Instead, she listened to herself in horror as her mouth continued. "When was the last time you changed those backup batteries, anyway?"

"I replaced them when I moved in. They're new." Kira put the mugs down and stared at her strangely.

"Good. Great. That's great." God, her mother had been right, warning her that people would think it odd if they ever noticed how many smoke detectors the McLarens had in the house. Her mother had threatened to take them all down the day a fourteen-year-old Megan blew weeks of her allowance on an eight-unit value-pack of smoke detectors, taught herself to use a drill while her parents were at work, and went wild. You'd think they'd appreciate being safe.

But she'd always known she was the only one in the family who took the threat of fire seriously. When she was five years old, she packed her stuffed animals in a backpack and kept it by her bed because her mother said if there was a fire she was supposed to run outside right away and not get her animals and not look for Mommy or Daddy, just run outside, so she wanted to be prepared. She wanted to save her kitty, too, but Tiger wouldn't stay in the bag. "Leave the door open for Tiger if you have to run out," her mother said. "The cat will find her own way out."

Kira reached up to help Megan down from the chair. Megan didn't need help but she took Kira's hand anyway, probably because she was still flustered over being caught nosing around. When she stepped down and Kira didn't immediately let go, she looked up at Kira's face, then down at their hands, remembering how good this had felt when they were dancing. She hated limp handshakes that shrank from her touch, or elderly socialites who frowned at her as if a firm handshake was unladylike. Kira's grip was wonderfully strong, as strong as her own, and the joining of one forceful grip with another was solid and electrifying. Like they were meant to hold on to each other like this.

Before things could get awkward, Megan consciously relaxed her hand and tried to pull away, but Kira wouldn't let her. O…kay. Kira rubbed her thumb against her hand. She hadn't done that at Avalanche. Megan bit her lip. Damn it, she needed to free her hand. Either that or give in to the heat that was bubbling up in her chest and making her break out in a sweat. And kiss her to make it stop.

To make it stop—yeah, there was a logical plan. Kira continued with her slow stroking, loosening her grip so she could slide across Megan's palm and between her fingers. Megan swayed on her feet.

It was Kira who finally put a stop to it and broke contact. Megan sank onto the couch, afraid she might pass out.

Kira retrieved one of the mugs from the table and passed it to her. "Hope you like Cinnamon Sensation."

"That's the tea you couldn't remember the name of?" Megan commented weakly. "What's the sensation part?"

Kira's smile made her sorry she'd asked. "Licorice, I think."

There was no coffee table in front of the couch, so she placed the hot mug on the floor by her feet to wait for it to cool. Now her hands had nothing to do.

"Personally, I have my doubts about the name." A sexy drawl crept into Kira's voice. "I think that's why I can never remember it."

Megan's fingers tightened, aching to mesh with Kira's. How could she miss that feeling so acutely after mere seconds? She dug her fingers into her thighs, then realized Kira was watching. She sat on her hands.

"I got this spa supply catalog in the mail today," Kira said, her voice back to normal and her teasing smile suddenly gone.

She pulled the catalog from a basket by the front door and came back and sat next to Megan on the couch. "Would you mind going over it with me?"

"Sure." Megan grabbed Kira's pen and notepad from her, relieved that Kira had taken mercy on her and returned to business mode.

"Kelp body mud," Kira read. "That sounds good, don't you think?"

Megan leaned over Kira's shoulder to look at the catalog, but all she could pay attention to was the buzz of Kira's vibrant energy field and the intriguing scent of her skin. She smelled like rain, with a tantalizing hint of feminine musk that drew her in. She had to get closer, had to inhale more deeply, had to fill herself with her scent.

An inch away from her neck, she came to her senses. She pulled back slightly—maybe an inch—and sucked on her bottom lip to keep from touching her. Her lips ached from the deprivation, but this was not the time to be investigating whether Kira's skin tasted as good as it smelled.

"I like the seaweed angle. Kelp, sea rocket—it all fits in with a beach theme. We could put out bowls of potpourri made of dried seaweed and chunks of sea salt." Kira flipped to the next page of the catalog, seemingly unfazed by Megan's proximity.

Megan couldn't quite bring herself to sit back and put a respectable distance between them. "If you're doing a beach theme, you have to offer seashell massage."

"You're kidding. What is that?"

"Have you heard of hot stone massage? You heat up smooth, polished stones and lay them on the client's body? It's the same thing, except with seashells. The shells are supposed to have a more uplifting energy than the stones."

Kira leaned back and Megan should have gotten out of the way, but didn't, and narrowly avoided a collision with her shoulder.

Kira didn't seem to notice. "Have you tried it?"

"No."

"You should try it."

"Me?" Megan loaded the word with a heavy dose of put-upon employee, even though she had nothing against seashells.

Kira grinned and turned back to the catalog. "Do they have shells in here?" She flipped through and abruptly stopped. "Ooh! Mango salt scrub!" She showed her a photo of a flawlessly manicured woman rubbing salt crystals on her bare thigh. "She looks like a salt-encrusted salmon. I always wanted to put that on the menu at my restaurant, but Lizzy…yeah, forget Lizzy. Mm, mm, mm." She sounded like she couldn't decide whether having someone rub salt on her would feel great or make her feel like she'd made an embarrassing mistake. "What's a salt scrub good for, anyway?"

Megan cleared her throat. "You really should try it. If you're this excited just reading about spa treatments, I'm sure you'll enjoy experiencing them."

"Maybe." Kira reached for the notepad in Megan's lap and scrawled *mango salt scrub* before handing it back. "So how much of this salt would I need to order?"

"I have no idea. This is what I meant when I said I don't know how to run a spa."

"You know the important stuff," Kira said, dismissing Megan's concerns. She flipped back to the page featuring body mud.

Kira was going to screw this up if she threw away her common sense. "You sank a lot of money into this—" Megan began.

"It's going to work out great."

Such optimism. Megan reached for her tea, but it was still too hot to drink. Frustrated, she put her mug down and leaned closer to read about the oh-so-fabulous differences between green, pink and black mud.

"Detox," Kira read from the catalog description. "How does that work, exactly? I mean, how does putting mud on yourself—which is basically dirt—detoxify your skin?"

"Um…" They were definitely in each other's personal space, and it felt so good she had a hard time reminding herself she had standards for how to act when discussing business. Standards?

What standards? She slipped her feet out of her sandals and curled her legs underneath her on the couch, crowding Kira even closer.

A pulse fluttered in Kira's neck. Megan watched it for a few beats. So Kira wasn't as unaffected as she seemed. That was… not good.

And Megan knew she wasn't going to do the right thing and move out of range of Kira's aura until Kira made her do it.

Also not good.

When they came in from the rain, she had watched a single drop of water roll down Kira's neck as it traced her dips and curves. She wondered what it would have tasted like to follow that raindrop with her tongue.

Megan caught her breath. She spoke quickly to cover it up. "I'll research spa treatments and write up a brochure for you. But I do think if you'd just *try* going to a spa—and I don't mean hanging out in their accountant's office—you'd have a better sense of what your customers are looking for. At least get a massage."

"I will. Are you sure you don't want to do me the honor?"

No, no, no. Hadn't Kira told Svetlana at the restaurant that she wouldn't ask Megan for a massage? She had said it with such seriousness that Megan was convinced Kira really didn't want her to think of her as a client. Wishful thinking, apparently.

"You don't want to." Kira evidently knew exactly what the look on her face meant.

Megan swallowed apologetically. "There's plenty of other great massage therapists who—"

"Are perfectly safe?"

"Of course they're *safe*…"

"I'm not talking about medical malpractice here, you know," Kira said gently.

Oh.

Megan shifted farther away from her on the couch. Kira closed the catalog and tossed it on the floor. She pulled one knee onto the couch, turning so her whole body faced her, and waited for Megan to say something.

There were many reasons she didn't want to give Kira a massage. Or, at least, one. Because she really did want to, but she shouldn't, and—

"I had a nice time with you at Avalanche," Kira said. "Especially at the end. Up until the part where you said you couldn't kiss me anymore."

Megan opened her mouth but no sound came out.

"So I'm a little confused. You can't kiss me because you gave me a massage, but you can't give me a massage because…?"

Kira had a right to force the issue. Megan had been less than clear. She'd ignored boundaries, she'd gotten too comfortable… and now, to top it all off, she was doing a heck of a job keeping herself in line. She wouldn't give Kira a massage and she wouldn't kiss her, and it was supposed to be one or the other— not both. Maybe Kira was right, and a ten-minute massage in the post-race massage tent didn't exactly constitute a therapeutic relationship. But she knew from experience that lines had to be drawn. It was up to her to draw them.

"I'm sorry, that was rude of me," Kira said. "I'll make an appointment at Peaceful Moments."

Relief loosened the knot in Megan's throat. "For a massage? God, not there. Not for your first time. You'll never want a massage again. Go somewhere good. Call Svetlana. Call *Patrick*. Didn't I already give you Svetlana's number? Geez, I'll give you a list."

"Actually, I was thinking of going to Peaceful Moments for a mud bath. I'll save the massage for later."

"Oh." Did that mean Kira was going to wait for her to change her mind? Megan felt pleased at the thought, then guilty. She *wanted* Kira to get a massage from someone else. It was just that she was jealous of whoever was going to get to do it. "I guess they're good at spa treatments."

"Because anyone can slap mud on a customer, right?"

"Pretty much."

Kira looked like she was hiding a smile. She never seemed to stay mad for long. "Is my spa going to have an anti-spa attitude?"

Megan busied herself making adjustments to their list of

products to order. "I prefer to think of myself as pro-massage. Besides, you're the one who was so determined to hire me for this job. You should have asked about my biases during my job interview."

"Because I'm a professional," Kira said.

"That's right." Megan didn't look up from her list. What kind of businesswoman hired people without interviewing them, anyway?

"Then we'll be the best damn massage-centered spa on the East Coast."

That was nice of her to say. Although it did imply Megan's involvement in the business, which was *not* part of their deal.

"You know," Kira said, "at the restaurant, when you and your friends were figuring out what was wrong with our waitress's shoulder—I got the feeling Patrick doesn't think much of the medical profession."

"Yeah, that's pretty rampant among massage therapists. It's because we see all their failures. The back surgeries that don't help, the knee repairs that go wrong, the chronic pain they can't fix. It's not pretty. I treated a woman last week whose doctor said her severe pelvic pain was all in her head, because weeks of expensive tests had all come out normal. It turned out that the pain was caused by a simple trigger point in her abdominal muscles."

"So we're anti-spa, *and* we're anti-doctor?"

"Can we put that in the brochure?"

Kira laughed. "No."

Megan sat back and crossed her ankle over her knee. "They do save lives, though. If I get in a car accident, for God's sake take me to the hospital, not to a Reiki practitioner."

"Not a problem."

"You think I'm kidding, but some people take the anti-medical thing too far. Doctors know a million times more than we do about the human body, even if it's all disease-focused." Megan uncrossed and recrossed her legs. "I think we get defensive and don't give them enough credit."

"Because doctors don't give *you* enough credit?"

"Exactly. But it's so foreign to everything doctors have ever learned about healing, why *would* they understand the value of what we do?"

"You don't get resentful?"

Megan shrugged. "They deal with life and death. We deal with quality of life, and pain. They're two completely different things."

"I bet you would have made a good doctor, though. Why didn't you go to med school? You're smart enough, and you're interested in how the body works."

Oh, not this. Her parents still had not given up on the idea that she would one day go to medical school. She didn't need anyone else hassling her about it. Megan didn't bother to hide her annoyance. "You're not going to tell me I'm wasting my talents, are you?"

"How can you say that? Your job is perfect for you." Kira reached for her and rubbed her shoulder. To give moral support? Megan fumbled with her list, but didn't pull away. Ninety-nine percent of the time she did not care for back rubs, which were either too intimate or too rough, but Kira's touch was the perfect blend of nonaggressive and respectful, radiating concern without weird sexual overtones. And she broke the contact almost immediately.

"Sometimes I get the sense that people think I'm no better than a high school dropout cleaning hotel rooms, that massage therapists aren't very smart," Megan said.

"Those people are idiots."

Megan's heart thumped at the conviction in Kira's voice. "No they're not."

"Then they're elitist."

"Even my own mother thinks—" Megan broke off, wishing she hadn't said anything. It sounded so childish.

"Your own mother thinks what?" Kira asked gently.

"That I'm not ambitious enough." Megan's throat closed up. She didn't want her mother's respect. She didn't need it.

"You know what? Ruthless ambition is not something we need more of in the world. You care about people and that's a heck of a lot more admirable than having an advanced degree. You've found a job that fits you and you're wildly successful at it. And even if your mother doesn't say so, I bet she's really proud of you."

Megan flushed. "It doesn't matter, anyway."

"So what happened? Why didn't you go to med school?"

How had they managed to turn this into such a big issue? She'd honestly never wanted to be a doctor. The stress would have given her a nervous breakdown. "Doctors are taught to distance themselves emotionally from their patients so they can operate without getting queasy, and I didn't want to do that. I understand why they have to do it, but it seems so cold. I wanted to feel like I was helping a human being, not just a body part."

"So it sounds like you did consider it."

"Not really. I also can't stand the sight of blood."

"Okay, so, not your best career choice."

"You know how some kids have trouble dissecting the frog in high school biology? I didn't even get to the frog. I passed out dissecting the clam."

"The clam? Do clams even have blood?"

Yeah, yeah, it was kind of ridiculous, but she'd better not laugh. It had been pretty traumatic at the time.

"You poor thing," Kira said. "Did your parents have to write you a note to get you out of doing the frog?"

Right, her parents. It might not have been so traumatic if they had understood. "My mother said I had to learn to not be so sensitive."

Kira frowned. "But you said you never did the frog."

"I told the teacher I felt dizzy and she sent me to the nurse to lie down. I think she was afraid I was going to give myself a concussion on her classroom floor if I passed out again."

"Maybe she felt bad for you."

"I doubt it. She did make me dissect the fish."

"How did that go?"

"It went okay at first, because I was used to eating fish—with the heads, even—so it didn't gross me out too much to cut one up, but after twenty minutes the smell of formaldehyde got to be overwhelming and I..." Megan shrugged helplessly.

"You passed out?"

Megan nodded.

"Wow. A fish."

"The clam was worse."

"Really? I would think it would be the other way around. Clams don't have faces."

"Yeah, but they have all this stuff inside you'd never expect. Yucky stuff. Organs."

Kira smiled. "Organs, huh? I guess it's a good thing you didn't try to become a doctor, then."

"Don't laugh."

"I'm not. It's just funny because you obviously know a lot more about anatomy than you're making it sound like."

"I actually do. Massage school gave me the opportunity to learn about anatomy—at least the muscles and bones—without having to cut up a cadaver. But it's not my main focus. What I'm best at is inviting angels to join us in the room. Most of the healing comes from them. I'm just a channel."

Megan braced herself for the scoffing that usually greeted this sort of admission. She didn't even tell half her clients what exactly it was she did that made them walk out of her treatment room feeling peaceful and energized. And her clients tended to be more receptive to talk of angels than someone like Kira, who had called her woo-woo more than once.

But Kira didn't get that disbelieving, dismissive, even angry look she had seen so often on her mother's face, on Amelia's face, on the faces of a long line of others. Instead, her smile turned pensive, like she was trying to figure Megan out, and enjoying the process immensely.

"So when you say angels are in the room with you, that's, like, a metaphor, right? For loving thoughts?"

"No, it means angels are in the room with me." If she was going to tell her, she was going to make sure she understood.

"You mean you can actually see them?"

"Yes."

"Huh."

Huh? That was it? No ridicule?

"You're an interesting person, you know that? You know all this medical stuff, you combine it with the angel stuff, and it all works."

"Except for the anti-spa attitude," Megan joked to cover her reaction to the genuine respect in Kira's voice.

"Now that I know what an expert you are on the clam organ system, it's totally understandable. If we ever have a clam come in for a facial…"

"Clams don't have faces," Megan reminded her.

"That could be a problem." Kira broke into a smile and winked.

Megan huffed.

"You were impressive with that waitress," Kira said, serious again. "I never knew massage therapists could sound so much like doctors."

"We don't. Svetlana and Patrick know Russian medical massage, but a lot of my classmates barely scraped by in anatomy class, and they just do relaxation massage. Or take my friend Gwynnie, for instance. She can treat injuries even though she doesn't give a shit about anatomy. She does it solely through intuition, and her clients adore her because she's great at it. But for me, when I put my hands on someone, I like to know what's under the skin, and what that's connected to, and what massaging it is going to do. My intuition became a lot more effective once I understood anatomy."

"And yet you don't call it medical massage."

"Medical massage, sports massage, deep work—a lot of people respect that more. They want you to make it hurt. It has its place. But until they learn to appreciate how healing it can be to be touched gently by someone whose heart is in the right place, and how wonderful that feels, they'll never really understand what massage is all about."

Okay, maybe she shouldn't have said that last part, because

now Kira looked like she was going to kiss her, and she didn't want to see that. She didn't want to know that Kira felt that way about her.

"I should go," Megan said.

Kira closed her eyes.

That was almost worse—wondering what she would see in her eyes when she opened them. Kira saved her from that by turning away and walking to the balcony's sliding glass door. She pushed aside the curtain and pressed her face to the glass, cupping her hands to block the light from inside. "Looks like it's still raining hard out there."

"I have an umbrella," Megan pointed out.

"The roads—"

"I can handle the roads."

"I know." Kira breathed a sigh of resignation and turned from the window. "That doesn't mean you have to go."

Wow. Megan could hear her pulse pounding in her motionless body. She was sure she was now the one who looked like she was going to kiss someone.

"So we can talk business?" Megan gulped.

"If that's what you want."

"I should go." She had to get out of here before she threw herself into Kira's arms.

CHAPTER TWELVE

That Friday, the phone rang while Megan was in her massage room jotting notes about what muscles she'd worked on with her last client of the day. "Megan McLaren. How can I help you?"

"Next time I get slathered in scented mud, I want you to be the one smearing it on me."

Her heart relaxed at the familiar timbre of Kira's voice. She could almost see Kira's scowl turning into a teasing smile. Good to know that while Megan buried her confused feelings in work—because helping her clients get in touch with their pain was a great way to hide from her own—someone had been busy doing spa research.

"They used scented mud?"

"You would have hated it."

"I would have asked for unscented."

"It was itchy, too. Are they really supposed to leave it on your skin until it dries?"

Megan couldn't tell if Kira was joking or not. "Haven't you ever given yourself a mud mask facial?"

"Seriously?"

"You're not joking." She wondered again what Kira could possibly have been thinking the day she decided to open a spa.

"Never painted my toenails, either," Kira added. "In case you're wondering."

"So you'll be opening a nail salon in the near future?"

"You underestimate me. And I think you were wrong when you said just about anyone could give a mud treatment. It seems to me there's definitely a learning curve involved."

Uh oh. Had some undertrained, indifferent wage slave slapped mud on her in a careless, untherapeutic way and scared her off? "What did they do to you?"

"Maybe not a *big* learning curve..." Kira backpedaled.

Okay, so maybe Kira didn't love the treatment, but mud was not for everyone. "Are you sure it wasn't the whole concept you were uncomfortable with? Maybe it wasn't the esthetician's fault."

"No, I think you definitely would have been much better at it."

"I already told you I can't—"

"I'm not asking you to. I'm really not. I'm just..."

Just what? Just calling me and being charming and pretending I didn't run out on you the other night? And then convincing me to give you a massage?

"Can I come over?" Kira asked.

Kira didn't scare easily? Well, neither did she. "Okay."

"I've got to warn you, I took a shower, but I still smell like that mud."

"I'll keep my distance."

"I can't promise the same thing, myself."

* * *

"You want me to what?" Megan turned away from her kitchen windowsill where she was watering the healthiest aloe plants Kira had ever seen. She set the watering can on the counter with a thunk.

"Teach me to do massage. I'm not asking you to give me a massage." Kira hovered outside the kitchen, wanting to come closer but afraid to, despite the words that had slipped out over the phone. She didn't want to mess this up. Something had spooked Megan the last time they were together—her conscience, no doubt—so Kira wasn't too sure of her welcome.

Megan joined her in the living room. "It's going to be a little difficult to teach you how to give a massage without demonstrating."

"You don't have to touch me. Just tell me what to do."

Megan plopped onto her couch and draped her arms over the suede upholstered back. "That's something we professionals like to call B.S."

Kira remained standing. "You think I'm trying to get you to touch me?"

"Aren't you?"

Well, yeah, but that wasn't the *only* reason. It really wasn't. "Of course not," she said mildly. She settled into one of the overstuffed chairs. She could live without Megan's touch. Probably.

"Then why?"

"Why?" Kira hesitated, unsure whether it was a real question or if that was Megan's way of saying no.

"Why do you want me to teach you to give a massage?" Megan clarified. "I can't even get you to receive one."

"I've been meaning to, but…" Kira really *had* been meaning to. But some stupid part of her still wanted her first real, hour-long massage to be with Megan, so even though she knew it wasn't very nice to hope that her favorite massage therapist would change her mind, she kept procrastinating. And now Megan was mad. "I'm not crazy about letting a stranger touch me. I thought maybe it would feel less awkward if I knew what to expect."

Megan didn't look completely convinced.

Smart woman.

"Tell me again why you wanted to invest in the massage industry?" Megan said.

It wasn't a real question, but Kira answered anyway. "I researched the market and this is where the numbers pointed me."

"Uh-huh."

"I realize you might not want me practicing on you when I don't know what I'm doing," Kira ventured.

"Your competence is not what's holding me back. I went to massage school, remember? Practicing on each other before we knew what we were doing was a major part of the curriculum. You can ask Patrick sometime. We were classmates."

"You practiced on each other?" Patrick seemed like a nice guy, but the thought of his hands on Megan's body did not make her happy.

"Occasionally. Mostly I practiced with my friend Gwynne."

And what do you know, the thought of a woman's hands on Megan's body was not any better. "That's how you know she's bad at anatomy."

"You remember me saying that?"

Well, yeah. Did she think Kira wasn't paying attention? She'd memorized every word Megan had ever said to her.

"So my lack of skill isn't the problem because Gwynne was a terrible practice buddy, too?"

"Actually, no, she was great. Just not at anatomy. But she knew medical massage wasn't going to be the focus of her career. She's mostly an energy healer."

"How come you trade with Svetlana now?" Kira asked. "Seems like you'd prefer that energy jazz that Gwynne does, pulling demons out of people's bodies, etcetera."

"Gwynne is a wonderful, wonderful healer, but I wouldn't dream of working with her. I guess you don't know she's my ex."

Gwynne Abernathy was Megan's *ex*? Shit, if that was the type of woman Megan liked, she was screwed. She'd suspected it, hadn't she? Watching them work together to exorcise that hitchhiker thing, she could tell they had a history. And Gwynne was into all that energy healing stuff that Kira didn't even believe in. Not to mention she was a professional massage therapist, who no doubt knew exactly what to do with her hands.

"It would be awkward," Megan continued, unaware of the explosion she had just set off in Kira's brain. "Even though it was a long time ago. We did a lot of crazy stuff together in massage school, and dating just made it that much crazier. Once in a while someone will still remark on how similar our massage technique is. They don't usually guess the reason."

"Why didn't it work out? I mean, it sounds like you two have a lot in common."

"Too much in common. She's even more of a flake than I am."

"You're not a flake."

"Hmm." Megan looked at her appraisingly. "Angels? Metaphor?"

Kira flushed. So her definition of "flake" was not the same as it had been a few weeks ago. It was all right with her if Megan knew it. "Try not to hurt yourself with that grin."

Megan's smile got even bigger. "So, you sure about this?"

"That you're not a flake?"

Megan gestured with her hands, encouraging her to guess again.

Kira looked at her blankly.

Megan swept her hands through the air, making a squeezing motion that anyone else would have felt self-conscious about.

Right. The massage lesson. That Megan didn't want to give her.

"Am I sure it'll help? No." Kira wasn't sure of anything right now. She personally didn't think it was essential for her to know much about massage in order to open a spa. Her motives for being here in Megan's living room late in the evening were definitely suspect, even to herself.

"I meant are you sure you want to learn?"

Was Megan about to say yes? She hadn't really believed she would. "It's okay if you don't want to teach me."

"Backing down so soon? I do still have my work clothes on." The white camisole and white linen pants with a wide flared leg, accented with an artsy, multicolored silk belt, were a far cry from a medical uniform. Megan kicked off her sandals, removed her wristwatch, and pushed up off the couch. She dangled her wristwatch between her fingers, waiting for a response. "I'm up for it if you are."

Kira gaped. Really, all she'd wanted was an excuse to come over here and be in the same room with her. She'd been sure Megan would say no, and then they could sit and talk for a while, or go out for a late-night power snack.

"You are?"

"Absolutely." Megan clasped her hands overhead and stretched. "Ready to strip?"

Kira's mouth went dry. "I see we're going to be professional about this," she choked out.

"This way," Megan said, leading her to the stairs that went up to the second floor.

"This isn't like you."

Megan paused on the stairs and turned around and gave her a smug look that meant she could tell Kira was wondering what she'd talked herself into. God, even when Megan was feeling superior and letting her squirm, she was gorgeous. Too bad nothing was going to happen. Like it or not, Kira was going to learn how to give a massage, and somehow she was not—*not*—going to melt at the feeling of Megan's hands on her skin. Or at the privilege of putting her hands on Megan's body.

God, who was she kidding?

Megan jutted her chin out and looked down her nose at her with a completely irresistible sparkle in her eyes.

Kira moved up to the next step, getting closer. "Aren't you going to let me borrow a bathing suit?"

Megan pivoted out of reach and continued up the stairs. "If you wanted to do this in a bathing suit, you should have thought of that before you came over."

* * *

Megan knew this was a bad idea.

She was pretty sure Kira did too.

Funny how you could see the potential roadkill from way down the highway and not slow down.

"I must be insane," Megan muttered to herself.

Touching Kira after the charity race had been wonderful. More wonderful than it should have been. As a professional, she shouldn't care what her clients looked like. She shouldn't even notice. She certainly shouldn't let it affect her. She shouldn't still remember, weeks later, how it had felt to run her hands up the back of Kira's taut, muscular legs. The flare of her calf, the soft vulnerability of the back of her knee, the firmness of her hamstrings. Kira's body covered in massage oil was a beautiful, dangerous thing.

She ached to touch her again, and this time with more than just her hands. This time she wouldn't stop where she was supposed to. She wanted to taste the soft skin of her neck and feel her sharp hip bones dig into her. She wanted—

Megan paused at the top of the stairs. A minute ago, she had convinced herself she was making way too big a deal out of this professionalism thing, because being around Kira made her want to do just about anything to keep her from leaving the room, including rationalizing. Besides, teaching her something about the job she loved would be a pleasure.

But she wasn't naïve. She knew exactly what could go wrong.

Kira bounded up the stairs and Megan turned to watch. As if she needed any reminders that yes, Kira did have the powerful legs of an athlete. She needed to get herself under control before they crossed the short hallway and entered the massage room.

As she squeezed past Megan on the landing, Kira took her hand and pulled her through the open doorway to their right. Into her bedroom. Megan stumbled on the rug. "This isn't the massage room," she said. Kira had never been up here before, so maybe she'd made a mistake. Although it was pretty obvious there was a bed in here, not a massage table. More than obvious.

Kira steadied her and Megan straightened, but she didn't pull her hand away, even though it was crazy not to. It felt too good. Kira's nervous, excited energy coursed through their clasped hands, merging with Megan's own jittery excitement, keying her up even more.

She was so screwed.

She squeezed Kira's hand and Kira squeezed back, their interlaced fingers locking more firmly together. Megan bent her elbow to raise their clasped hands to chest level. Kira's nails were cut short, almost as short as her own.

Without thinking, she raised her other hand to touch Kira's wrist, first with just her fingertips, then with her whole hand wrapped around the joint. Unable to resist the warmth of her skin, she skimmed her fingers along Kira's bare forearm and continued to her biceps, fitting the curve of her hand to the shape of the muscle, exploring. Yay for summer and short sleeves.

"I'm having second thoughts about that lesson," Kira said.

"Scared?"

"Not of what you're scared of."

Oh, yeah? With the way their energy fields were aligned, she had a hard time believing their emotions at this moment weren't exactly the same. "What am I scared of?"

"Why don't I just stick with what *I'm* scared of."

Megan was so beyond tact. "You are not backing out of that comment."

Kira squeezed her hand again. "I'm afraid if I go into that room I'm going to have to follow a bunch of rules I don't want to follow."

Megan raised an eyebrow.

"You know, rules about keeping our boundaries clear."

"I know what rules you're talking about." Damn it.

"No dating clients, no kissing, no—"

"What makes you think the rules don't apply in *this* room?" When she'd led Kira up the stairs, it wasn't to bring her here.

Kira glanced pointedly at what Megan was doing with her hands.

Megan yanked away. She took a step back, out into the hallway.

"Don't," Kira murmured.

"It's my fault," Megan apologized. She never should have done this when they were both so full of wanting each other. She knew better.

"Shh." Kira took a step closer. "Let's not ruin the moment."

"There was no moment to ruin."

"Don't say that."

Megan's heart hammered. Kira was so sweet, trying to salvage this disaster when it was Megan's fault. "This was a bad idea."

"No."

"Kira," she pleaded. She could feel the air between them vibrating, stretching like a rubber band about to break. Kira was going to have to help her, because she, personally, did not have the strength to keep her at arm's length for much longer. Because it wasn't only her hands that had a mind of their own at this point. Her whole body was on the verge of mutiny.

CHAPTER THIRTEEN

"What a fantastic massage last week," Barbara Fenhurst gushed as Megan massaged her feet. "I felt all these good vibes coming from you. You knew exactly what I needed. When you put your hands on my heart, right here…" Barbara threw the sheet off her chest to demonstrate. "I sensed it. How you understood me perfectly."

"I'm glad you liked the massage," Megan said, refraining from any comments about nudity as she settled the sheet back into place and returned to the other end of the table. She pushed her thumbs into the sole of Barbara's foot, finding all the crunchy, painful places with a pressure that was deep, but wouldn't make her twitch and pull away.

"I'd come every day if I could afford it."

Megan ignored the squirm of guilt in her stomach. Her fees were not outrageous. Besides, Barbara had meant it as a compliment.

"I have an idea. Next week is my birthday, so I'll come for a massage every day. That will be amazing. Why don't we set that up after we're done?" Barbara was so giddy with the excitement of her plan that she didn't pick up on Megan's dismay. "It would be like a birthday present for you, too, getting that extra income, right?"

Megan studied the shape of Barbara's foot, afraid to look up and give herself away. It was hard to watch Barbara's enthusiasm and feel her own heart sink at the prospect of five days in a row of Barbara Fenhurst. Why did someone she wasn't crazy about have to love her so much? It was sad, really. Barbara felt good when she came to Megan's house, so she wanted to see her as often as she could. And what was the harm in it? Except that Barbara should be out dating, rather than paying Megan for the human contact she was starved for.

"I know you said you don't give discounts, but do you sell packages? You know, like buy four, get one free?"

"Sorry." She could jack up the price to make it look like she was offering a discount, but she hated that method of doing business, manipulating people, luring them with a bargain. Besides, she already had more work than she could handle.

"How about buy ten, get one free?"

She smiled at Barbara's persistence. This was good, actually. It distracted her from thinking about how delicious it would have been to ignore her rules and get involved with Kira. She had almost thrown her training out the window and flung herself at Kira. She'd wanted to. She still did. She wanted to run her hands up Kira's arms again on that wonderful, smooth skin, and this time, she wouldn't stop at her shoulders. She would slide her hands down her back and pull her into her arms and get under her shirt and loosen her bra and find the swell of her breasts. It was going to feel so right to feel the weight of them in her cupped palms and learn their exact shape. She'd worship them with her hands, then her mouth, reveling in her softness and breathing in her addictive scent.

And this kind of thinking—*now*—was so inappropriate. What if she communicated what she was thinking about through her hands? Rubbed Barbara's foot with a caress instead of a strictly therapeutic effleurage? This was exactly what she had been trying to avoid when she stopped Kira from…from what? Kissing her? Pulling her onto her own bed?

Barbara groaned with pleasure.

Megan tensed. Damn it. Were the sound effects her fault, or was Barbara just being her usual borderline inappropriate self? She did not want to be the highlight of Barbara's week. But she shouldn't complain, because happy clients were, after all, her goal. She poked her thumbs into the soles of her client's feet a bit harder than she should.

She never should have taken Kira upstairs. She'd known it was going to end badly. There was no other way for it to end. Kira thought it was massage school where she'd learned to be overly careful about maintaining professional boundaries—that it was a case of Extreme Ethics 101—but she was wrong. It wasn't massage school that taught her boundaries…not that her teachers didn't try. It was Gwynnie. Gwynnie on all fours, trying to find a spot to wedge her knees on the narrow table, tipping the massage table over in a tangle of bodies and laughing screams.

Never could use those sheets again. Every time she put them on her massage table she felt Gwynne's hands on her, violating all their classroom rules, both of them aware she was going to write it up in her practice log to hand in as homework. With a few key omissions, of course.

She didn't have the money to keep driving to the outlet mall for new sheets.

* * *

Shayna leaned back on her beach towel, resting her weight on her elbows. "Real."

Kira looked up absentmindedly from the sand she was mounding and sculpting into the shape of a hand. Shayna nodded in the direction of a woman walking along the tide's edge in a barely-there, leopard-print bikini.

"No way," Kira said. Anyone who bought swimwear five sizes too small cared more about appearance than function, and that ought to tell you something. Besides, the woman had no taste. And fake boobs were, in her opinion, the epitome of poor taste.

Shayna leaned forward, squinting against the sun to get a better look. "Yes way."

"Dream on."

"You know I'm right on this one."

"You'll never know for sure," Kira scoffed.

Shayna leaned back on her hands. "Neither will you."

"Which is fine with me." Kira returned to working on her sand sculpture.

Shayna moved on to the next woman strolling by. "Now *those* are real."

"The one in shorts? Really?" Kira poured on the doubt, even though she was pretty sure Shayna was right. Not that she was looking too hard. Even if no one could tell whether she was or was not looking from behind her sunglasses, she wasn't going to stare like some sexist pig. Besides, the fun part wasn't the scenery, it was riling Shayna up and watching her get all competitive.

"Hard to tell on the brunette in the black tankini," Shayna said.

Kira didn't even look. "I say fake."

"Fake it is. And her friend?"

"Fake."

When Megan had called in the morning to say she wanted to meet on the beach during a break between clients, Kira had given up any hope of focusing on work and had changed out of her work boots and jeans into shorts and clogs and a T-shirt whose constricting sleeves had long ago met with a deliberately unfortunate accident with a pair of scissors, leaving two ripped armholes. On her way to the beach, she'd happened to run into Shayna on the boardwalk, and gladly accepted her invitation to keep her company while she sunbathed, figuring that having someone to talk to would keep her from worrying too much about what to say when Megan showed up.

"You're distracted," Shayna accused.

"Just thinking."

"Thinking about Megan?"

"Trying to figure out what she saw in her ex. If you ask me, the ex doesn't even have curb appeal."

"Good personality?"

"Not really."

Kira built up a second mound of sand and shaped it into another hand, making the fingers of both hands touch but not quite clasp. She cleaned up the edges with a broken shell. Was this her subconscious's way of telling her Megan was out of her reach? She held the shell above one of the hands, poised to draw the downstroke of the letter "M", then realized what she was about to do and tossed the shell aside with a snort of irritation.

"Better to focus on the important things," Shayna advised, "such as learning to not suck at Real versus Fake."

"I do not suck," Kira protested, laughing at the absurdity of it all.

"You do if you think those are fake."

Those would be the ones she hadn't even glanced at. "Whose did I say were fake?" Kira asked, just as a shadow approached from behind, entering her space. Crap.

"What are you two ladies up to?"

Yup, it was Megan. She had to have heard them talking. What she thought of what she overheard remained to be seen.

"Just watching the world go by?" Kira ventured.

Megan loomed in front of her in a white camisole and stylish white linen pants that were identical to those she'd worn the other night, belted this time with a lavender scarf. Her closet seemed to be full of white, and with good reason—she looked great in it. She was born to wear white.

Megan glanced up and down the beach, then back at Kira. "Watching the world go by. Uh-huh."

Kira laughed. Megan did the suspicious mother thing quite well. "Actually, we're—"

"Practicing some important skills," Shayna cut in.

"Unless you're into dating straight women, I seriously doubt this is a skill you'll ever need," Megan said.

"Hmm." Shayna pretended to consider it. "You might be right about that. But I like to be prepared."

"For what?" Kira said.

"You don't have to be straight to get plastic surgery," Shayna pointed out.

"Only willing to risk your life on an unnecessary elective procedure," Megan said as she settled cross-legged on the edge of Kira's towel, awfully close for someone who claimed she didn't want to get close to her. "You both obviously spent too much time hanging out with your brothers when you were growing up."

"Don't have a brother," Shayna said. She turned to Kira. "Is that where you learned to play this game?"

"Shayna, you taught me this game."

Shayna clutched her heart, acting like she was shocked. That was Shayna for you—innocent until proven guilty.

"You teach it to everyone you know," Kira reminded her.

Shayna shrugged. "Nothing to teach, really. It's an inborn skill."

Kira scooted away from Megan and lowered herself onto her back, careful not to bump into her guest or kick her sand sculpture. Positioned with her shoulders toward Megan, she reached her arms overhead and brushed her fingers under the wide hem of Megan's pants to clasp her ankles. She held her breath, hyper-aware that she was touching Megan's body and Megan hadn't flinched. "You want to join us? You'd be good at this."

"I'll pass."

She wished she knew what went wrong in Megan's bedroom. Oh hell, she knew what went wrong. Maybe it was good that Shayna was here—so they wouldn't be alone. Why else would Megan specifically ask that they meet on the beach instead of at the hotel?

When Megan had called, she'd hinted that she wanted to apologize for the other night, but what did that mean? It *might* mean that Megan was sorry she'd pushed her away—and Kira sincerely hoped it did. But she knew it didn't. Because what it probably meant was that she wished she hadn't led her upstairs, or touched her arm and stared at her like she wanted to undress her, or gotten up off the couch to begin with, or dared her to follow through on her supposed reason for coming over.

It could mean anything.

All she knew was that Megan felt responsible for part of this mess. And that she wanted to meet in a public place. As soon as that thought hit her, Kira let go of Megan's ankles. She'd never made a woman afraid to be alone with her.

But she was wrong, because Megan purposefully placed both hands on her shoulders and began to massage her.

Kira's gut tightened. Now she wasn't sure *what* to think, because Megan wasn't acting skittish at all. Not even conflicted. Kira closed her eyes and crossed "upset that they sort of touched" off her mental list of what Megan wanted to discuss with her.

Then, as if having her hands on a safe, socially acceptable part of her body wasn't enough, Megan slid her hands down the slope of her shoulders and gripped her biceps. Kira forced herself to breathe normally. Yeah, Megan was willing to touch her because she was confident nothing was going to happen. She knew she could trust Kira not to try anything until she put up a life-size 150-watt green light.

Which was good, right? She trusted her.

"I'm sorry I was unclear with you the other night," Megan said.

Shayna scrambled to her feet. "I'm going for a swim. Anyone want to join me?" She didn't wait for an answer.

Kira hardly noticed. She was too busy absorbing the shock of Megan's hands on her, warm and electric.

Megan brushed sand off her arms and continued rubbing. "I got a little freaked out."

"That's okay," Kira said.

"It is? Because I'm picking up on some tension here."

You think?

Kira struggled to act relaxed as Megan explored the shape of her arm muscles with gentle, kneading strokes. Did she honestly believe she could touch her like that and *not* make her tense up?

"I wish I hadn't asked you to leave," Megan said softly. "I overreacted."

"We could try again. Do you want to come over tonight after you're done with your clients? I'll make you dinner."

Megan stilled. "I'm not sure that's a good idea."

Kira shot straight up to a sitting position and twisted around. No. They had come this far, they were not going back to *I'm not sure that's a good idea.*

"Why isn't it a good idea? If it's more than a question of professionalism…"

Megan dug her hands into the sand. "What else would it be?"

Do you like me, Megan? Do you like me enough to break your rules? Kira watched Megan draw her hands out of the soft sand and push them back in, fingers first. She'd break her own rules for Megan in an instant. Surely there was some chance she could raise her blood pressure—in the best possible way—without making her run.

"I'm sorry I made you freak out," Kira said.

"Not your fault."

Kira took off her sunglasses and squinted at her in the bright sunlight. "I'd kind of like it to be."

* * *

"Look who I found," Shayna said, returning to her beach towel with police officer Tammi Baldini, saving Megan from having to respond to the seductiveness behind Kira's quiet words or from melting on the spot from the simmering heat in her eyes.

Kira, however, seemed to be in no hurry to turn her attention away. She gazed at her for several long seconds before glancing up at the new arrivals.

It took Megan several seconds more to recover before she, too, could acknowledge there were other people around—people who wanted to talk. "I thought you were swimming," she told Shayna, taking in Tammi's police uniform. No way had Shayna found her in the water.

"Nah. You didn't see me?" Shayna said. "I turned back and went up to the boardwalk instead."

Megan's glance dropped to the police officer's belt and fixated on her gun. She'd be a nervous wreck if she had to carry one of those around.

Tammi gave her a cocky tilt of her head that said *Don't you worry honey, I know how to handle this gun.*

Oh, puh-lease. She bet she could make Tammi yelp if she got her hands on her quadratus lumborum. That swayback was a doozy.

"How's Svetlana?" Tammi asked. She always asked.

"Still straight," Megan said.

"That won't last."

Megan coughed. She never could tell if Tammi was serious.

"I read about you in the paper," Tammi said.

"What?"

"Didn't you see it? Your client, Barbara Fenhurst, was the victim of a suspected arson. When we went over to do the police report, she kept yammering on about how she needed to get a massage to deal with the stress. She must have said the same thing to the reporter, because your name made it into the article. I'm surprised she didn't say anything to you about it."

"I have an appointment with her in a few days." A shiver ran down Megan's spine. Was it more than a coincidence that the victim was one of her clients? Her karmic curse wasn't going to start harming other people, was it? The very people she was trying to help?

The beach receded from her field of vision.

She was caught in a tug-of-war between two men who pulled at her from behind and a woman who gripped her hands from the front, screaming with rage at the men. The men ripped her away and dragged her down a cobblestone street to the center of the town square, where a crowd gathered around a stake set in a mound of kindling. They yanked her arms behind her back and dislocated her shoulder.

"Megan?"

She blinked. It was the same shoulder that had been giving her so much trouble before the angels used the ley lines to heal her.

Kira peered at her with concern. "Your eyes glazed over. You look like you're going to pass out."

"Ms. Fenhurst got out of the house in time," Tammi reassured her. "She's okay."

Megan blinked rapidly to clear her head. "She wasn't hurt?"

"No, she was lucky," Tammi said. "She told us she's a light sleeper and heard a noise. She went to check it out and discovered her porch was on fire. The porch sustained a lot of damage, but the guys at the fire department got there before the fire spread to the residence itself. Are you real close to her?"

"No. She's just a client."

Tammi glanced at her watch.

"You're sure the fire wasn't an accident?" Megan asked.

"I'm not authorized to say too much about it, but as you'll read in the paper, we did find an accelerant on Ms. Fenhurst's porch, so yes, we're pretty sure it wasn't an accident."

"Arsonists don't usually strike only once, right? There's a good chance whoever it is will set more fires?"

"It's a strong possibility, yes. But we'll be doing our best to make sure that doesn't happen."

CHAPTER FOURTEEN

Kira jogged along the edge of the water, enjoying the sea breeze and dodging the waves that washed away webbed bird prints and lapped at her feet. It was a nice time of day for a run. The lifeguards had gone home for the day and the sunbathers had left to have dinner or cruise the boardwalk, leaving the beach relatively abandoned. She zigzagged around a couple doing the romantic walk-on-the-beach thing, holding hands, and noticed there was someone still out there swimming. Was that…

"Megan?" Kira stopped in surprise, then sped along the shoreline toward her.

"Megan!" she called again, waving both arms overhead.

Megan waved and swam toward shore, standing when she reached the breakers. Water glistened on her bare shoulders above a purple bikini top, making her look like a goddess rising from the sea.

"Coming in?" Megan called.

Kira glanced down at her own running shoes, shorts and sleeveless T-shirt. "I'm not wearing a bathing suit."

"You never have one when you want one, do you?" Megan teased.

"I—"

"So come in anyway."

Kira laughed at herself. What was she doing, turning her down? She pulled off her shoes and socks and left them in dry sand higher up the beach, then returned to the water's edge. She ran into the surf, ignoring the cold, and dove under a column of breaking waves.

Shit, it was cold. She waded the rest of the way to where Megan stood chest-high in the water, not quite sure whether her heart was racing from the shock of the water temperature or from watching Megan curl her fingers under the edge of her bikini top and tug to adjust it.

"For payback, you're going to let me feed you dinner," Kira said, catching her breath. She rubbed her arms and bounced up and down. "I'll cook."

Megan joined in with a leisurely, companionable bounce that didn't seem to have anything to do with the need to stay warm. "Payback for what?"

"The cold," Kira gasped. "Aren't you cold?"

"You didn't have to race in here. You're allowed to get used to the water first." Megan ducked underwater and surfaced a few feet away.

Kira rubbed her arms harder. "Where's the fun in that?"

"It might not feel so cold."

"I doubt it."

"Should have left your T-shirt on the beach so it would be nice and dry and warm when you got out." She made a show of staring at Kira's chest. "You're wearing a sports bra under there, aren't you?"

"Yeah." Kira stopped bouncing.

"Am I embarrassing you?" Megan smiled evilly—or as evilly as an innocent happy puppy face like hers could manage, which wasn't much. "You look good in a wet T-shirt."

It wasn't like her. "Are you trying to get back at me for overhearing me playing Shayna's sexist game?"

Megan's smile broadened. "I ought to, but no."

"I have a hard time believing that. A wet T-shirt isn't that flattering over a sports bra—at least not this sports bra."

"Hmm." Megan looked far too smug.

"I look better without it."

"I'm sure you do." Megan sank into the water and leaned back, letting her arms drift out to the sides as her perfect, tempting breasts crested the surface of the murky water.

Kira's breathing turned harsh. She didn't know how any part of her could possibly be warm in this freezing ocean, but she was definitely warming up. And it sure as hell was not because of the bouncing.

"How come you're not cold?" Kira ground out.

"Because it's summer."

"Doesn't feel like it."

"You'll get used to it."

Kira doubted it. "You do this often?"

"Yeah." Megan dove under an incoming wave, moving farther from shore. She wiped the water from her eyes and pushed back her wet hair. "I like to come here to relax after I've had a tough client. It washes away the negative energy."

Crap. What happened to her today? She looked so vulnerable with her hair plastered to her head and her eyes red from the salt water.

Megan flipped onto her back again and floated. "I'm not exactly allergic to perfume, but I have a really good sense of smell. Sometimes I'll get a client who wears way too much, and I get a massive headache afterward."

"Can't you ask them not to wear perfume?"

"I do. It's also in my brochure. But people don't always remember, and I'm not going to turn them away at the door."

The lengths Megan went to for her customers—they had no idea. Why did she do this to herself? She wanted to help others and make the world a better place, but if she wore herself down, how was that an improvement? It didn't result in a net gain in global happiness. Back in the spring there'd been that massage therapist she'd talked to who made it sound like Megan was ready for burnout—something about it only being a matter of time before Megan snapped those scrawny little wrists of hers and started to hate her clients. At the time, she'd chalked it up to professional jealousy. Now she wondered if maybe there wasn't some truth to it.

"I'm guessing you have a headache."

"The fresh air helps."

Kira jumped to avoid getting hit by a random wave that shouldn't have broken this far out. Megan floated gracefully over it, but Kira, who so far had managed to keep her head and neck out of the water after her initial dive, didn't quite make it, and protested the shock of cold water on her head. Man, there were easier ways to get fresh air. "Is there anything I can do to help? Rub your head?"

Megan ducked under the next wave.

Kira waited for her to reappear. "Feel free to say no. Because I obviously have no skills."

"I should say yes just to prove to you that you have more massage skills than you think you do."

* * *

Megan dunked her head again and tasted the familiar comfort of briny seawater. There was something about the cold, turbulent ocean that worked miracles when it came to getting rid of client-induced headaches.

A massage would be nice, though. Kira might think she had no skills because she had no training, but training wasn't everything. Kira had already proven herself the night she'd driven her to her apartment. At one point when they were talking, Kira had rubbed her shoulder, and the way she'd touched her, with her heart open and compassion flowing through her hands, was more healing than half the professionals out there, who were too burned out to care, or in the wrong field to begin with. She would love to feel Kira's attentive presence again, feel her fingers massage away her pain.

And let's face it—Kira's screech when she ran into the cold

water was more than a little suggestive. A bit out of breath, because that's what happened when sudden cold shocked your lungs. As well as in other situations... Kira had looked a little guilty and embarrassed after that outburst, then laughed when she realized that of course Megan had noticed.

She should let her massage her head. Her reasons for keeping her at arm's length hardly made sense to her anymore.

They swam out past the breakers, where the water came to Kira's shoulders and Megan's neck. Kira reached tentatively for her and Megan swung around so she was floating with her head toward her. Kira swept her hands through her hair and kept her from floating away with the slight pressure of her fingertips on her scalp, massaging gently. Megan stared up at the gray sky, breathing in the smell of seaweed and salt. It was so nice to be out here with someone who didn't drain her.

"You work too hard," Kira said.

"My clients don't seem to think so."

"They think you have a natural talent for massage, so it must be easy for you." Kira cupped one hand at the base of her skull and caressed her brow.

"They're right. It's not *hard*. I don't know why it's so exhausting." Her forehead relaxed under Kira's touch and she closed her eyes. "Everyone thinks it's so wonderful that I can intuitively find exactly where it hurts, and I know that makes me a good massage therapist, but some days I don't *want* to feel other people's pain."

"How do you do that, anyway? How do you know where it hurts?"

"I sense it. I sink my awareness into the other person's body. I get quiet and one hundred percent focused and then my hands just know what to do. Some massage therapists can do that and keep themselves separate, but I can't. I get lost in there. Lost in the heartbeat of another person I may not even like."

"That sounds pretty intimate." Kira's fingertips circled at her temples. Speaking of intimate...

"It is. It's...too much, sometimes. I'm too sensitive."

"Don't say that."

"It's true."

"You're not too sensitive," Kira said.

On days like today, when a whiff of perfume could ruin her whole day, she *was* too sensitive. But she wasn't going to argue.

Kira traced the line of her eyebrows, smoothing away the tension in her face. "Can I invite you over for dinner at my place on Saturday?"

"Sure," Megan answered without thinking. Kira's touch felt so good.

"I wasn't sure you'd say yes. You didn't, last time."

"This is so relaxing. Don't stop what you're doing to my head or I might change my mind." She shouldn't have freaked out when Kira had come over for a massage lesson—they could have been doing this for hours.

"I'm glad you have a place to go to de-stress," Kira said.

"The ocean? Yeah. But the ley lines would be an even better place." Thinking about that made the pressure inside Megan's skull increase. She couldn't let her traitorous feelings for Kira make her forget what she really wanted from her. She wanted her to save the angels' gathering place. That was important. "I wish you wouldn't build there."

Kira let go of Megan's head. "How can you say that after what happened to your friend Svetlana? She was throwing up. Now, I'm not convinced the puking wasn't psychosomatic, but maybe I *should* cover up that site if it's going to make people sick."

Megan let her feet drop to the sandy bottom. "It's not dangerous."

"I'm not sure Svetlana would agree with you."

"Svetlana's *fine*. She's completely back to normal."

"You seemed pretty worried about that whatchamacallit."

"Hitchhiker," Megan said. "But they're everywhere. Blocking access to the leys isn't going to do anything to stop them."

"Then why was this hitchhiker there? Why did this one wait for Svetlana to sit by that rock before it jumped her? If they're everywhere, and this rock has nothing to do with it, then it could just as easily have gotten her on the way to the drugstore, or at her office, or anywhere. Except it didn't."

Okay, so maybe Kira had a point. Megan did suspect that hitchhiker had not been there entirely by accident. It might have been a gatekeeper. When she saw the angels glowing above the ley lines, that had only happened *after* she had passed through some kind of spell—a spell manifesting as the shadowy fears that had almost scared her into turning back. It was a spell of ward, most likely, and explained why no one had ever noticed this site and written it up in a New Age tourist guidebook. Svetlana was oblivious when she stepped into it, and wasn't sensitive enough to have picked up on the scary vibes that should have warned her away. If she had done what was expected of her and left, she would have been fine. But when she attempted to astral travel, she left herself completely unprotected, and one of the hitchhikers who were there to scare people off had spotted lunch and grabbed her.

But that didn't mean the leys were dangerous. It just meant Kira shouldn't turn the site into a tourist attraction. The people who were meant to discover the site would discover it on their own. Others, like Kira, would wander through without noticing anything out of the ordinary, protected by their personality's natural shield against psychic phenomena. And wizard wannabes who thought they knew what they were doing, but didn't, wouldn't attempt to meditate—or astral travel, for God's sake— while leaning against the standing stone.

Megan pushed a strand of wet hair from her face. She wondered if the story of the murdered woman was even true. "I changed my mind about advertising it to your customers and making it a tourist draw."

"I think that's a good call," Kira said.

"But I'm not changing my mind about preserving the site. The leys are a valuable tool. I'm convinced they were instrumental in healing my injury. They… Don't blame them for what happened to Svetlana. It wasn't their fault." Megan clasped her hands together underwater in private entreaty. "It's such a beautiful energy. Angels use it as a crossroads when they travel through. If you knew how beautiful it was, you'd never dream of—"

"I can't just abandon my plans. I need to build a spa."

"Then put the spa inside the hotel. Convert a few rooms. Or build an addition. Or add another level. There's got to be some way you can have your spa without destroying the leys."

"Megan…" Helplessness filled Kira's voice.

Megan felt a little sorry for her. She knew how it felt when clients begged her to do something she didn't want to do. She hated it when clients did that. But she had to try. She'd promised the angels she'd protect their grove, and she wasn't going to let her feelings for Kira get in the way. She *promised*. She might not have much time left before Kira started construction and did something that couldn't be undone, but she wasn't going to let them down.

CHAPTER FIFTEEN

That Saturday, Kira made good on her promise of dinner. There was barely enough space for two people at the tiny dining room table in Kira's apartment, let alone for two sets of dishes, and what was even better news, Megan realized as soon as she sat down, was that the living room was in her direct line of vision, making it impossible to escape her vivid memories of crowding Kira on the couch.

She swallowed the last spoonful of yummy homemade tomato and basil soup, conscious that Kira was watching her. She dropped her spoon into her empty bowl and jumped up from the table to clear the dishes, stacking one into the other with an unintended clatter.

Kira reached up and stopped her, taking the bowls from her hands. Their fingertips brushed. "I'll take the dishes."

Megan let go and dropped back into her chair, too unnerved by her own reaction to argue. Every time she touched her— even accidentally—something in her did *not* want to let go.

"You should offer your staff free housing inside the hotel,"

Megan said inanely. "That's why no one answered your out-of-town ads for a spa manager. They can't afford to live here. It would help you attract good people."

"Free housing is a great idea." Kira carried the dishes to the kitchen and returned with two plates of baked trout. "I love the idea of the staff living together. It would be a real community. And it means I wouldn't have to poach the local talent and make the other spa owners hate me more than they do already."

"They don't hate you." Megan squeezed some lemon on the fish and took a bite. It was melt-in-your-mouth good. "This food is delicious."

"The secret is in the salt. I had so many free samples of salt body scrub that I figured…" Kira's eyes twinkled as Megan tried not to choke on her food.

"You really are trying to eliminate the competition."

"Of course," Kira joked, but her smile was weak and her mood seemed to have already sobered. "Nobody loves their competitors, Megan. If I didn't know you better I'd suspect you made up this whole ley line thing to try to stop me from opening a spa."

Megan stiffened, and Kira reached across the table and lightly touched the back of her hand to take the sting out of her words. Megan let herself enjoy Kira's touch for several long seconds before she pulled her hand away. "You don't really think that, do you? That I'm lying?"

"Not you, my little pistachio."

Her little *what*? Megan's heart warmed at the odd endearment. For all her tough business talk, Kira always seemed to have a soft spot for one particular competitor—her.

"But that doesn't mean," Kira continued, "that there aren't other spa owners who would be happy to see me fail before I ever open my doors."

"They might worry about losing business, but they wouldn't hate you. As I said before, we support each other."

"If you say so."

Kira was humoring her, which meant it was time to stop thinking candy-heart thoughts and press her advantage. "So when are you going to decide I'm right about the ley lines, too?"

Kira chewed thoughtfully. "Let me ask you something. Your clients really wear you out, right?"

Where was Kira going with this? Megan savored another bite of the awesome fish before answering. "Not always."

"You looked exhausted the last time I saw you. Fragile."

Kira's concern wedged a crack into her already weakened defenses. Megan pushed the fish skin into a small pile in the corner of her plate. "I was," she admitted. "That's not uncommon in a caretaking-type job."

"And the ley lines give you your energy back?"

Was Kira changing her mind about the leys? Megan's eyes widened. "Yes."

"Isn't there some way you could avoid the need for that and instead protect yourself from getting drained?"

Megan slumped in disappointment. So Kira wanted to find a way to help her without having to change her own plans. Did she think she hadn't spent years trying to figure out a better way to do her job, one that wouldn't leave her so worn out? She ground her teeth. "Distance myself and care less."

"Which would be impossible for you," Kira acknowledged. "I mean something like drawing a circle of protection around yourself."

Megan looked at her blankly. "How do you even know this stuff?"

"I watch movies," Kira said defensively.

"I'm not a witch. Those rituals are used by Wiccans. Witches," she explained.

"Maybe they're on to something. Maybe drawing a circle would help keep you safe."

This was bizarre, hearing those words come out of Kira's mouth. "Drawing a circle is actually a way to build up your power and contain it. It doesn't protect you in the way you mean. And since my client would be in the circle with me, it certainly wouldn't protect me from the client."

"But it would give you more power, right?"

"Not *more* power. More control."

"Sounds useful. Have you tried it?"

"I don't need to," Megan retorted. "I'm in control of my power."

"Are you?"

"Look, I know you're trying to be helpful, but my skill level is way beyond the crap you see in movies." Finished with her food, Megan scraped the fish scraps from her plate onto Kira's and stacked the empty plates together, daring her to stop her. "Besides, I don't do magic. I communicate with angels and work with them to heal people. It's completely different."

"So instead you swim in the ocean." Kira got up and paced, bouncing on her heels as if she could barely restrain herself from racing around the room. "How often do you do that, anyway?"

"Almost every day," Megan said.

"Hard to do in winter."

"If it's cold I take my shoes off and go wading. Or I dip my hands in. Or I watch the waves. It's peaceful when there's no one there."

Kira paused behind Megan and drew in a breath as if she were about to say something. Something she couldn't look her in the eye to say.

"If you're going to feel sorry for me," Megan said, "don't."

Kira exhaled. "Okay. We'll try it your way."

Megan swiveled in her seat. Was Kira actually saying…

"I can't feel the ley lines and I'm not completely convinced they exist, but I am convinced they matter to you. So I'm going to put the spa inside the hotel. I'll convert most of the ground floor."

Megan jumped up and threw her arms around Kira's neck. Her chair crashed to the floor.

Kira laughed, sharing in her elation. "It'll probably be more cost-effective in the long run, anyway."

"Thank you!"

Kira gave her a squeeze around her waist, then disentangled herself from her arms and gripped her shoulders instead. She looked steadily into her eyes. "Next time you hug me like that I want it to be because you want me, not because I did what you wanted me to."

Megan's stomach did a slow flip. Kira adjusted her hands, changing her grip on her shoulders to a gentle caress. In the space between them, Megan could feel the pressure of Kira's energy field touching hers, asking to be let in. Often with her clients she had to shield herself because they sucked her life force right out of her with their neediness and their demands and their pain. But Kira wasn't like that. Her energy was strong and nurturing and vibrant. And exciting. Allowing that energy through would be a high.

Kira shifted her gaze to Megan's mouth. The magnetic pull was inexorable. Megan's lips parted.

Kira bent infinitesimally closer.

If she could only come just a bit closer...

Megan couldn't remember anymore why she was supposed to resist. She raised her face to close the space between them.

"You said no kissing," Kira murmured, stopping her with the slightest flex of her fingers on her shoulders. "So...no kissing."

"Did I say that?"

Kira did not look up from Megan's lips. "Mm hmm."

"I don't remember saying that." It was hard to be sure of much of anything with Kira standing so close, the wonderful scent of her clouding her brain. She knew one thing, though. Where to build Kira's spa wasn't their biggest problem anymore. *This* was. And she was about to fix it.

She didn't believe for one second that Kira meant what she'd said about no kissing, not when the grip that held them apart also kept them firmly inside each other's personal space. Plus she could feel the woman's skin heating up with what was obviously desire. You didn't have to have to be an expert to detect that kind of change in body temperature, nor to sense the emotions smoldering in her aura. So Kira thought she was strong enough to hold her back? Well, there was more than one way to deal with that. Megan snaked her arms up to cup the back of her neck. At her touch, Kira's grip weakened.

"At Avalanche," Kira said. "Dancing. That's when you said it."

Remembering the dance floor made her want to kiss her even more. One kiss had so not been enough. She pushed her fingers into Kira's hair. "I had a nice time with you that night."

Kira let her pull her closer. "It was a mixed bag for me."

Yeah, because of her. "Sorry about that," Megan said.

"What was Amelia's problem, anyway? At Avalanche. She said something about…I don't remember exactly. She sounded patronizing."

"You mean when she said I wouldn't follow her advice?"

"Maybe that was it."

"Seeing me out dancing must have triggered some of our old arguments. She always wanted us to go out more. She thought I was antisocial." Megan massaged the back of Kira's neck, searching for a spot that would make her forget her train of thought. She really did not want to talk about Amelia right now.

"A person can be outgoing without having a bad attitude about it," Kira said.

"It wasn't exactly that she had a bad attitude—it was more that partying was such a big thing with her. A huge thing. She said she couldn't live with someone who hated people as much as I did. I embarrassed her." Megan couldn't believe the lump in her throat. At the time, she'd been so focused on Amelia's good qualities it had been easy to overlook the bad. It was only now, looking back, that she realized how much her criticisms had hurt.

Kira scowled. "You don't hate people. Why does everyone think extroverts love people, anyway? When I have a great time at a party with a big group of people, it's not because I love people, it's because I like the excitement of having a lot going on. If anyone loves people, it's you. You can spend a whole hour listening to a stranger talk your ear off on your massage table and make them feel cared for. And you're not just doing your job—you actually do care about them. Even if they're annoying and they reek of bad perfume. *That's* loving people. Your ex didn't know what she was talking about."

Kira was so sweet. Megan moved both hands to her lower back, to the waistband of her fraying denim shorts, and tried to draw her closer—except Kira kept her at bay by pressing harder against her shoulders. Was she honestly resisting her? There was no reason for that.

"I'm ready to concede a ten-minute massage at a charity event doesn't count," Megan said. Just in case that was what was holding her back. She slipped her hands under Kira's shirt and pressed them against her flat stomach.

"You're changing your mind? You won't change it back?" Kira shook her a little by the shoulders to emphasize her point.

Megan was not letting this standoff continue. Not because of her own confused thinking and certainly not because Kira was trying to be polite. She moved her palms upward, sliding them flat between her breasts, then slowly out to the sides, directly into the danger zone. Kira sucked in her breath.

"Stop being so honorable," Megan mumbled against her neck. The subtle musky, female scent of her skin was intoxicating.

"That will not be a problem." With a ferociousness she wasn't expecting, Kira captured her mouth and stepped one leg between hers. Megan half-stumbled from the impact. Kira steadied her, settling her so she straddled her thigh, the whole time never breaking the kiss. Her tongue was in her mouth like it belonged there, insistent and sure.

If this kept up, she was going to pass out.

It kept up for an eternity, and when they finally stopped, Megan was panting.

"I feel dizzy," Megan said.

"Maybe you need to lie down," Kira teased. "I think it'll help."

"I'll just bet you do." Megan was still sucking in air. "I'll stand."

"Don't think there's anything I can do to you lying down that I can't do to you standing up," Kira warned.

"Is that so?" Megan draped her arms around the back of Kira's neck and caressed her soft puppy fuzz.

Kira kissed her again with a growl that went straight to her ego, and this time when they came up for air, Kira tangled her legs with hers, purposely pulling her off-balance, and helped her stumble into the bedroom.

Kira lowered her onto her bed. "Maybe your blood sugar's low," she said solicitously. "I could go make you a snack."

"Don't you dare." Megan trapped her with one leg and licked her jaw. She tasted like salt.

"Feeling better already?"

"Mmm."

"Maybe I can get you dizzy again."

"Good idea."

Kira touched her lips to hers in a gentle kiss that made Megan shiver. "You sure?"

Megan answered by kicking off her sandals and sending them flying across the room. She, for one, did not plan to do any more thinking tonight.

Kira propped herself up on one elbow and reached for Megan's blouse to undo the top button. Her hand trembled as she touched her fingertips to Megan's bare skin and moved downward, slowly, into the V of her shirt, parting the fabric until she reached the next button.

Was she nervous? Or did that slight tremble mean something much, much better?

She popped the next button, and lust simmered in her eyes. Megan's breath quickened as she watched her drop deeper into the V of her blouse. Her bra was definitely showing. And her cleavage.

Okay, so Kira wasn't afraid to touch her. Good to know. She wondered how many buttons she had left and whether she was going to survive letting Kira do this to her at this languid pace, or whether she was going to break down and yank her blouse over her head.

"Guess you're not one to rip a woman's shirt open, are you?"

"And tear the buttons off, you mean?"

Megan nodded.

Kira slowly undid the next button, exposing her lower ribs. "It seems so destructive—ripping a perfectly good shirt."

"You're not supposed to worry about the condition of the shirt when you're caught up in the throes of passion."

"The *throes* of passion?"

"Are you laughing at me?" There was something going on with the corners of her mouth that looked suspiciously like a laugh trying to escape. Her eyes were twinkling too. "Because I have better things to do with my time than—"

Kira fondled the next button, slipping it halfway out the buttonhole, then pushing it back in. The motion made Megan's shirt rub against her skin in interesting ways that she was sure never happened when she unbuttoned it herself. Megan pushed her chest forward involuntarily.

"Better things than—"

Gasping kind of ruined the effect of what she was saying.

She sat up and tried again. "Than letting myself be undressed...by...someone who..." Who...what? Who wasn't going to feel passion? That tremble in Kira's hand showed more passion than a thousand torn-off buttons.

Kira hooked her fingers under both bra straps and used them to pull her toward her. It was startlingly possessive. Her open shirt started to slide off one shoulder, and Megan did nothing to stop it. With the back of her fingers, Kira caressed underneath her bra straps. It wasn't nearly far enough. Kira really needed to learn how to read her mind, because if she did, she'd be sliding her hands down those straps right now and slipping under the satin of her bra and touching her where she ached.

"We haven't gotten to that part yet," Kira said.

"What?" Megan was having trouble keeping track of the conversation.

"The throes. We haven't gotten to that part yet."

"We haven't?"

"Not yet." Kira brushed over her tight nipples.

Megan's body jerked as a fire sparked deep inside her. "You..." She caught her breath as Kira did it again, and again, more deliberately each time. "...liar." Her blouse and her bra landed on the floor. The rest of her clothes followed. "You said..." Megan stretched, reveling in the feel of Kira's touch. "You said not yet."

Kira hovered over her, supporting herself on her forearms. "Is there a problem?"

Megan placed her hand on her thigh and firmly caressed her along the inseam of her denim shorts. Kira tensed, then weakened and parted her legs. Megan did it again, this time lingering where the denim was hottest. Damp, even. She wanted in there. "A problem? Not for me, no."

She rolled Kira over onto her back and pulled off her shorts, then slid down between her legs and kneaded her inner thighs, working her way up. Kira's hips lifted, trying to show her what she wanted. Megan stroked the crease of her thighs and pressed harder with her thumbs around her glistening entrance, closer to where Kira wanted her, encouraging her.

Kira shook spasmodically. "I wasn't done with you."

"Really." Megan paused and considered ceding control back to her.

Nah.

She went back to making Kira crazy, circling even closer.

Kira rocked faster, panting, shaking. Sweat sheened between her breasts. "If you say 'not yet,' I'm going to kill you."

Megan wet her lips. "No you won't."

She wanted to give in. She was rocking mindlessly with her now, Kira's excitement and desperation echoing in her own body. If she didn't give in soon, they were both going to come just from this.

"Please," Kira whispered, gripping her arms and lifting her hips.

Megan captured her with her mouth, tasted her.

"Oh!"

Kira's thighs clenched. She trembled and Megan was right there with her, moving with her, matching her increasingly erratic rhythm, synchronizing with her energy. Instinctually, she pushed her up, up, higher, higher, getting her ready to crest a stronger, more powerful wave than anyone had ever shown her. She sucked on her, no longer controlled. Her awareness filled with the hard, desperate pulsing of Kira's arteries and the answering heat building in her own core. They were both quivering with need.

"Megan…" Kira groaned.

She knew just what to do to trigger her release.

Kira came with a shout.

* * *

God.

Kira clung to her, molding their bodies together, stunned at the fire that had ripped through her.

"How—"

Megan kissed her into silence.

"Oh God," Kira moaned against Megan's mouth. The best sex of her life, and she had no idea what Megan had done to her.

She had a wicked talent. She'd known exactly what to do, almost as if the two of them had done this before. But no, that was *her* dream—not Megan's. Megan hadn't memorized the body of the girl from her dreams and then met her in person fifteen years later. Megan was just good.

Very, very good.

Either that or Kira was so crazy about her it didn't take much to make her lose it.

Certainly possible. Her arms fell limply to the bed and Megan pulled back and smiled down at her.

Dazed, Kira smiled back. "I don't know how I'll ever move again after that, but I absolutely intend to return the favor very soon." She nuzzled a spot between Megan's shoulder and breast, the closest part of her she could reach. Oh, God. So soft. Anything she did to make love to her would be inadequate, but she was going to try her damnedest.

As soon as she could move.

She took a breath and tried to prop herself up on her elbow, but halfway up she collapsed. Not yet, then.

Megan didn't appear to be in any hurry. She raised her fingertips to the side of Kira's face and combed through her hair. It felt great.

"You have the angel's touch," Megan whispered.

"I have what?" Kira mumbled lazily.

"Your gray hair." Megan touched the spray of silver at the center of her forehead, just at the hairline. Only that one spot had gone gray. "In the Middle Ages, black cats were killed unless they had a tuft of white fur, even just a single white hair. They thought the angels branded the ones who refused to work with Satan. The black cats with a scorch of white—the angel's touch—were spared."

Kira raised her hands to her chest, forming paws, and looked up at her, trying to look pitiful. "Meow?"

"Don't start."

Kira rolled onto her side. This could be fun. She ran her short fingernails up her pistachio's back and made her shiver. "So I'm marked?"

"Hmm." Megan pretended to think about it. "No consorting with Satan, I take it?"

"He *is* male, from what I hear. So that would make it a no for me."

"You're worse than Gwynne."

"Hey," Kira protested. "If I have to be a cat, the least you can do is make me a smart lesbian cat who knows better than to consort with that scum."

Megan smoothed Kira's hair and smiled. "I should've known. I'd recognize that attitude anywhere, even if you were a reincarnated cat."

"Reincarnation. You believe in that, don't you?"

Megan nodded.

"Of course you do." Kira kissed her collarbone to show it didn't affect how she felt about her either way. "*Do* you recognize me?" It was suddenly imperative to know. "Am I in any of your past lives?"

Megan's eyes clouded and Kira knew she'd been shut out. Something about that question had scared the shit out of her.

"You don't believe in past lives," Megan said.

"I'm open to the possibility."

"It's not some joke."

"I know." Kira pulled Megan closer and rubbed her back, pouring her heart into the gesture, wanting desperately to soothe away the defensiveness that had crept into Megan's voice. She didn't ever want to see that coldness in her eyes, especially not when they were lying naked together. "That's why I asked. It seems kind of important, don't you think?"

"I guess I'm the one who started it with the cat thing."

Megan mirrored Kira's earlier move and traced her collarbone with the tip of her tongue. If this was her way of distracting her from the question, she'd take it. At least for now. Anything that brought back their closeness—*anything*—was good.

Megan tasted her way up her neck and mumbled something against her jaw.

"Say what?" Kira said indulgently, not understanding a word.

"No past lives with you."

"What?" Kira was so taken aback by Megan's answer that she pulled away before she could think better of it.

"Past life? No," Megan repeated.

Like that explained anything. Kira pressed for more clarification. "No, you can't remember? Or no, no way?"

"I don't get that feeling about you."

Kira's heart sank. *But I get that feeling about you. Does that count?* She tried to sound casual, or at least not freakily obsessed. "Does that mean you're going to leave me one day and go searching for your soul mate?"

"You think I'm meant to be with someone else?"

"Well, yeah, isn't that what past life people are always talking about? Being reborn to be with each other again? The love that transcends time?" *The face that you recognize from your dreams, even though you know you've never met before?* She had hoped so much that Megan recognized her too, that day they first met. Guess not.

"I don't believe in that One Right Person stuff," Megan said.

Great. Leave it to her to fall for someone who wasn't a romantic. "Aren't you worried that one day maybe there *is* someone you're going to recognize from a past life? Some woman you were best, best friends with while you were both married to men, and now's your chance to finally be together?"

"Best, *best* friends?" Megan smiled like she could not believe Kira's G-rated word choice. She swung one leg over Kira's hips to straddle her and bent to kiss her neck again. She ran her tongue over her skin toward her next quarry. "What is that, exactly?" She captured one of Kira's nipples in her mouth.

Kira closed her eyes from the shock of it. Megan played with her gently, sweetly, until she was so tight she could barely breathe.

Megan was the One Right Person for her. Warm and gentle and unbelievably sexy, able to melt into the tight places in her heart and break her open. If Megan didn't believe they should be together... She did not want to think about what would happen then.

She writhed under another flick of Megan's tongue. The dream was...a dream. If even Megan, who believed in past lives, didn't think they had a past-life connection, then why was she herself—a lifetime member of the seeing-is-believing club—so fixated on needing more?

"I can't believe there was no karmic explosion for you when we met," Kira said. "Are you *sure*?"

Megan lifted her head to reply and Kira's body protested her own stupidity. The next time Megan's mouth was anywhere near her naked body—which ideally would be in the next few seconds—she would be sure not to ask her any questions.

She didn't expect that would be a problem.

"I wish I could give you a romantic answer," Megan said.

"You're not going to make something up?"

Megan sat all the way up, still straddling Kira's body. "I'm actually glad I don't recognize you from a previous life."

"Come on." If that was supposed to make her feel better, it wasn't working.

"Why are you so stuck on this? You don't even believe in past lives." Megan bent her head with more distraction in mind. "Who cares if this is the first time we've met, or the tenth, or the hundredth?"

Kira cared. Because she thought Megan would care. Because despite what Megan said, she was afraid that if Megan's soul mate did show up one of these days, Kira wouldn't stand a chance.

She pressed one hand against the center of Megan's chest to stop her from kissing her. God, she'd promised herself not to do that, like, less than a minute ago. But she needed this to be more than a one-night stand or even a short-term affair. "Touching me isn't going to reassure me." *Although I'm sure it would feel fantastic, and I must be an idiot to stop you.* Kira cleared her throat and tried unsuccessfully to stop fantasizing about what Megan had been about to do. "Nothing's going to reassure me except you telling me where I fit in with those past-life women in your life—because I know there must be some—and why you won't even pretend that I'm your soul mate."

Megan sat more firmly on Kira's hips, pressing her slick heat into her. She gazed at her intently with her head slightly tilted and her hair falling across her shoulders. "I like you. Can't that be enough? No explosive past-life connection?"

"No." Kira tugged on Megan's arms and pulled her down. Megan caught herself with her forearms on either side of Kira's face, their noses an inch apart.

"How about if I tell you I think we have an explosive present-life connection?" Megan suggested.

"That's something, I guess."

"I offer you a compromise and that's all you can say?"

"That was a compromise?"

"Yes."

Kira flipped her over and reached between her legs. Megan was so wet.

"If a present-life connection is all you'll give me, okay, but that means we're going to make it count. Starting right now."

Megan moved her knee up Kira's side and locked their bodies together and shook.

Kira's voice dropped lower. "I'm going to make you explode when you're with me. I'm making that my mission in life. And it doesn't rule out future lives. I'm going to be here inside you for this life and the next life and the next…"

Megan got wetter.

"Just like this," Kira promised.

CHAPTER SIXTEEN

The screaming was the worst part of the dream.

Megan never saw the woman's face, only her hands, which clutched at her with a desperation that echoed in her own gut. She really didn't want to see the anguish in her face. Feeling it and hearing it were bad enough. Because as bad as it was to know something terrifying was about to happen, it was worse knowing she wasn't the only one who would be hurt.

She loved her. And the woman must have loved her too, loved her enough to defy those men, to grab her hands and order them to let her go. But the men were stronger, and her hands slipped free. As they dragged her away, the woman's angry, combative shouts mixed with sobs of fear and despair.

Her vision tunneled, blocking out the townspeople. The last thing she saw was the woman's face.

Kira's face.

Megan sat straight up and screamed.

Kira jolted awake and reached for her, her face full of worry. "Are you all right? What's wrong?"

Megan's heart pounded with a combination of residual adrenaline from the dream and a new rush of adrenaline that came with the realization of who Kira was. She was *not* doing this again. She was not going to date someone she'd been in a past life with. She'd made that mistake with Amelia and she was not making it again.

"You're hyperventilating," Kira said sharply.

"Nightmare," Megan explained. She forced herself to take a deep breath. "Sorry I woke you." She hadn't woken up screaming like that since she'd been a kid. Not that she didn't still have the dream. But she was used to it, and the death-by-fire thing didn't scare her the way it once did. At least not usually.

"Want to talk about it?" Kira prompted.

"Must have been all that talk about soul mates," Megan said.

"*That's* what made you scream like someone was trying to kill you? Dreaming about your soul mate?"

Megan sank back and buried her head in the pillow.

"Must have been pretty real to make you scream."

Kira was actually taking this seriously? A sob rose in Megan's chest, but she refused to let it out. "Used to freak my parents out," she mumbled into the pillow.

"What? Waking up screaming? Of course it freaked them out. They were worried about you."

Kira gently rubbed her back with a touch that felt calming and safe—safe enough to talk about it.

"For years my mother wouldn't let me watch TV because she assumed I'd seen a fire on TV and that was why I was having these nightmares about dying in a fire."

Her mother did try. She taught her to crawl on the floor if there was smoke. They practiced Stop, Drop and Roll. They planned escape routes.

"What if there's fire at the front door?" Megan would ask, worried her mother's escape plan was sorely lacking.

"Then run out the back door."

"What if there's fire at the back door?"

"Then run out the front door."

"What if there's a fire and I can't run, Mommy?"

"Sometimes in our dreams it's hard to move our legs, but in the real world that doesn't happen, okay? The fire is just a dream. It's not real. If you're scared and you can't run, tell yourself it's just a dream and wake yourself up."

Megan knew what she meant about not being able to run very fast in your dreams, but that wasn't what she was talking about. She wasn't talking about running in slow motion. She was talking about her legs not being able to move at all. Because they were lashed to a stake.

"Change the dream," her mother said. "Dream that I pick you up and carry you out and you're safe, all right?"

But she couldn't change the dream. She couldn't change the fact that in her dream, she always died. They tied her up and she couldn't escape and the fire was everywhere and she died.

"You're still having the same dream?" Kira said, her hand warm and solid on her back, somehow managing to reach through time to comfort her child self.

"Yeah. They took me to an allergist to find out why I was waking up coughing and gasping for breath. They didn't believe me when I told them it was the smoke from my dream that was making me choke." Megan rolled over and gripped the edge of the sheet. "I always thought it was something I remembered from a past life."

Kira stroked her hair. "I wish I could have been there to save you."

You tried. She twisted the sheet in her hands. "The dream was different this time."

"Tell me."

"I never saw the other woman's face before—I only ever saw her hands. This time I saw her face."

"And this woman...she was your soul mate?" Kira asked cautiously.

Megan twisted the sheet even harder. "She was you."

Kira's hand stilled. "You've been dreaming of me since you were a kid and you think we're not soul mates?"

She hesitated. Why was it so hard to say she didn't know? She tried it out in her head: *I don't know, I don't know, I don't know...* "Maybe."

"Maybe?"

Kira was being patient, but really, she deserved more than a one-word explanation. "Maybe not," Megan said. Because two words were so much more clear.

"What do you mean, maybe not?"

Megan wanted to scream. Kira was amazing—the most amazing soul that fate could have conjured—but Amelia had seemed nice at first, too. Not as nice as Kira, of course, but...

She'd assumed Amelia was her soul mate.

She'd been wrong.

"Just because I was with you in a past life doesn't mean we're meant to be together," Megan explained.

"Of course it does."

She tried again. "Look at ex-lovers. It's easy to get back in bed with an ex, because you've done it before and you already know how to get into her pants. But the next morning she's hogging your side of the bed, the things that annoyed you about her haven't changed, and you're running out the door before anyone sees your car in her driveway." Megan clenched her fists. "Just because someone's *familiar*"—she punched her pillow to emphasize her point—"doesn't mean they're *right* for you."

"But neither one of us is running out the door," Kira said. "Unless *you're* about to run?" She said it like it was a joke, like none of what Megan had said applied to *them*, because *they* were perfect together.

Something twisted in Megan's chest. It was already too late, wasn't it? Fate had already caught up with them. They were both trapped by the pull of karma, acting out roles that had already been decided. She looked at the wistful, happy smile on Kira's face and wondered if crying was an option.

I'm sorry, she mouthed silently, her throat too tight to get the words out. She couldn't believe what she was about to do. But she had to do it. She had to be strong and do the right thing. When she met Amelia she had jumped in, naïvely assuming it was the right thing to do. She wasn't making that mistake again. She was not going to waste this life being pushed around by karmic forces, pushed into repeating what she'd done hundreds of times before. She had a chance to break her pattern. She had a chance to break free of that fiery death. And the only way that was going to happen was if she did something differently, even if it meant pushing Kira away.

"I don't want to break up with you," Megan burst out, on the verge of tears. She liked Kira. "But now that I know we shared a past life together—"

"Wait a minute. You're *upset* that we were together in a past life?" Kira said incredulously. "That's supposed to be a *good* thing!"

"I don't want to repeat my mistakes. Before I die young again, I want to learn from my past—my past lives and what I've learned in this life—and get off the karmic hamster wheel."

"So I was a mistake?"

Kira's anger hit Megan like a fist to the chest. She tried to breathe in and couldn't.

"Was I?" Kira insisted.

Megan couldn't meet her gaze. "I don't know," she admitted as air finally rushed in. Why *did* she assume that everything— and everyone—in her past lives had been a mistake? Just because Amelia was a mistake, didn't mean they all were. There were probably some things she'd done right.

Hesitantly, Kira put her arm around Megan's shoulders. "I didn't mean to get mad at you." She rubbed Megan's arm up and down. "You surprised me, that's all."

Kira was apologizing? For hurting *her*. When Megan was the one dropping bombs.

"Can you tell me more about your dream? What exactly do you remember about me?"

"I remember we loved each other," Megan said quietly, a little surprised at how easy it was to use the word *love* and not feel she was giving away too much. "And you tried to save me."

"And loving you wasn't enough," Kira said bitterly. "You think loving me was a mistake."

"I—"

Kira moved her arm away and shifted her weight so they were no longer touching. The rejection hurt. And she deserved every bit of it.

Kira sighed. "You know, the first time I met you, I thought it was fate. You looked just like a girl I used to dream about when I was a teenager, and I thought…" She jerked her head angrily. "Who knows what I thought."

"You dreamed—" Megan stopped breathing.

"Who am I kidding? I'll tell you what I thought—I thought it was fate. I never imagined that being right about that was going to make you break up with me."

Megan snatched at Kira's hands. "You knew?" Her voice jumped an octave with an unintended screech.

The sand sculpture. Damn it. Kira had made a sand sculpture of two clasped hands. Megan had been startled by it without quite knowing why. It was so obvious now. The hands had been pulling away from each other, just like in her nightmare.

"You knew we'd been together in a past life and you didn't tell me?"

"It was just a dream," Kira groused.

"A dream about me."

"It might not be you," Kira said. "She looked like you, but that doesn't mean she was you."

Oh, puh-lease. "You knew they killed me! You saw them do it."

"What? No. Different dream. No one kills anyone."

Megan stared at her. A different dream? Was it different parts of the same life, or had they shared more than one life together? Of course they had. They were sharing one right now, drawn to each other as if they had no free will at all. "Why didn't you tell me? If I had known about this sooner…"

* * *

Kira did not like what Megan's ominous tone implied. If she had known about this sooner, then…what? She would have broken up with her sooner?

"Turns out I was right not to tell you," Kira said. "You'd never have given me the time of day."

Megan stormed out of bed and began yanking on her clothes, jamming her arms into the sleeves of her blouse.

No, no, no. Kira propelled herself to the edge of the bed. "It was just a dream! I don't believe in past-life memories. I don't believe in ley lines. I don't believe in any of this. I didn't tell you about my dream because I didn't think it was important, not because I was holding out on you. And then *you* said you didn't believe in The One, in that One Right Person being out there, waiting for you…"

"You didn't think it was important? You told me you thought it was fate."

"I don't believe in fate!"

Megan gave her a look of disbelief.

"I thought it was fate and then I talked myself out of it," Kira admitted. "I decided it was a coincidence. I thought my mind was playing tricks on me, that the resemblance was an illusion."

Megan returned to the bed and flipped up the covers. "Have you seen my underwear?"

"Don't leave," Kira pleaded.

"I have to go."

"It's the middle of the night. You take the bed, and I'll take the couch." She was starting to wish she had waited until morning to discuss this. Her brain didn't function well on three hours of sleep, and it wasn't coming up with words that would help.

"No, thank you."

"I *said*, I can take the couch." Kira grabbed her pillow and stomped out of the bedroom.

"You go right ahead." Megan followed her into the living room and continued past her out the front door.

"Wait!" Kira went after her, still hugging her pillow, just barely remembering to grab her keys from the hook on the way out so she wouldn't lock herself out.

Megan stopped in the open stairwell and turned to look at her. "Are you crazy?"

"I don't understand what just happened." God, that was putting it mildly.

"That is not what I'm talking about." Megan gestured uselessly, her voice strangled. "I'm talking about the fact that we're outside and you're..."

Kira glanced down at herself. Oh. Her pillow was covering most of the important parts, more or less.

"Let me take you inside," Megan said.

"Only if you stay."

Megan extended her arm as if she were going to come closer and take Kira's hand, then let it drop helplessly at her side. She looked at the stairwell, then back at Kira, not bothering to hide the detour her gaze took before returning to my-eyes-are-up-here level. She sighed. "Why is it so hard for me to stay mad at you?"

* * *

Kira knew about one of her past lives. One that Megan didn't know about. It shouldn't have been a shock, but it was.

And not just one past life, but two. First there was the one where Megan got burned at the stake. Kira claimed she didn't consciously remember that one, but she'd made that sand sculpture. Then there was the one Kira had dreamed about as a teenager. She might insist it was just a dream, but it was obvious from all her pointed questions about soul mates that deep down, she suspected it meant something more.

Why hadn't she recognized Kira the first day they met? She'd recognized Amelia, after all. Had she been so busy feeling attracted to Kira—and telling herself not to be—that she failed to notice there was something familiar about her?

Megan sat on Kira's bed and leaned back against the headboard while Kira threw on some clothes. This was not the way she had imagined their first night together would go. If only Kira had told her sooner... But, of course, she hadn't told her. Even though Kira had agreed to protect the ley lines, she still didn't believe they existed. Why would this be any different?

Maybe she *wanted* to believe in past lives, but she didn't—not really.

Once she was dressed, Kira settled between her legs, her back to Megan's chest. It should have been nice, except they were both completely tense. Wary. It was clear Kira didn't want to tell her what she knew, not after the way Megan had reacted. If she could get her to stay without having to tell her about her dream, Megan had no doubt she would. She wrapped her arms around Kira's waist and Kira didn't resist, but she didn't relax, either.

Megan shifted uncomfortably. "Tell me about your dream?"

"Are you going to run out on me again if I do?"

"I'll try not to." She pressed her lips against the back of Kira's head and breathed in the faded scent of her shampoo. "I want to understand what we're up against. I want us to figure this out together." She slid her hands underneath Kira's shirt and moved them up the sides of her body, feeling the rise and fall of each rib, skimming close to the sides of her breasts where—hmm, no bra—her skin became even softer and more dangerous.

"Does this mean you're not dumping me?" Kira made herself more comfortable, fitting her spine against the curve of Megan's body.

Megan tried not to enjoy it too much, but she felt so perfect against her and God, she smelled good. She couldn't get enough of the way she smelled, of that warm, subtle musk beneath the lingering trace of that morning's shampoo. She was completely addicted.

"You can't dump me if you're going to kiss my hair. Don't think I can't tell what's going on back there."

"Let's not make any decisions right now."

"Are you going to leave after I tell you my dream?"

She pressed her forehead to the back of Kira's head. "No," she whispered, surprising herself with her answer. She hoped she wasn't making a huge mistake.

"My very first girlfriend laughed at me when I told her. That's partly why I was in no hurry to tell you about it."

"Why did you tell *her*?" Megan asked, curious. "Was she in it, too?"

Kira paused for such a long time that Megan started to wonder if there was any way she could take back what she had said. She was usually so good at keeping her mouth shut—at least with her clients. Why couldn't she take that talent out of her massage room and apply it to situations like this? The problem was she let her guard down around Kira. Put her arms around the waist of an attractive woman without a bra—especially when that woman was carrying tons of karmic baggage—and she lost all her social skills.

Kira inhaled as if she was about to speak, but didn't.

"That's not the important part," Megan said. "You don't have to tell me."

"No, I want to." Kira took another deep breath and blew it out. "We were so young—not that I thought so at the time—but she didn't believe I'd never gone out with anyone before. She asked me how I knew what to do. In bed."

"That was rude."

"That was just the way she was—an 'F' for effort when it came to tact. She didn't mean any harm. So I told her I'd been having this dream. This amazingly vivid dream. She thought I was lying to avoid telling her who I'd had sex with."

Megan pressed her lips to the back of her neck and ventured a few tiny, reassuring kisses.

"Why would I lie about that? Why would I make up some story about a stupid dream?"

It had to be hard for her to trust anyone with her secret again after that first bad experience, and Megan had gone and yelled at her for it. "I didn't realize—"

Kira cut her off. "It's not the same thing. She didn't believe me. You actually do."

"Of course I do." Which was why she'd been upset. Was still upset.

"That means a lot to me."

Megan nuzzled the back of her neck. "Why was the dream so important?"

"I was in high school. All my friends were dating, and I didn't know anyone gay, and I didn't think I'd ever, ever meet anybody. Ever." Kira spoke so quietly that Megan stilled so she could hear. "The only thing that kept me going was that dream. It gave me hope that maybe I was wrong and someday I'd meet someone wonderful."

Megan hugged her more tightly.

"Thank you for not leaving," Kira said.

"I promised I wouldn't."

"You promised you wouldn't leave if I told you what the dream was about. Which I haven't actually done yet."

"I won't leave." Megan let her hands stray upward from Kira's waist. Her breasts fit perfectly in her hands. Kira moaned in approval and wedged herself more firmly between her legs. Megan reinforced her hold, taking full advantage of her position, and moved her thumbs over Kira's already hard nipples.

Kira's head lolled back, relaxing against her shoulder. "Hold that thought."

Megan did. But as much as she'd like to continue for hours, they were definitely getting sidetracked. "What was the dream about?"

Kira spoke haltingly. "There was a round pit—a bowl sunk into the floor that had turned black with soot. The fire in the pit supposedly rose from molten lava at the center of the earth through some sort of volcanic vent under the temple, although I have a hard time believing that was true, since we had to feed it constantly with wood."

Megan flashed back to her own brief memory of falling to the floor of a Greek temple during an earthquake. "Your job was to feed the fire?"

"Feed it. Guard it. Keep it alive. That vent was important— it wasn't for cooking or warmth, it was the city's connection to the goddess's womb at the center of the earth."

That sounded familiar. "And that was my job, too?"

"I think so."

"Any sense of the time period?"

"No."

"We were keeping the fire going inside a temple. So we were priestesses?" Megan prompted her.

"I guess so."

"What was the name of the goddess we were priestesses of?"

"I have no idea. It was a dream," Kira reminded her.

"I'm not so sure about that."

"So you said."

"I need to know what happened."

Kira gripped Megan's thighs on either side of her. Her touch burned through the fabric of her pants. "So you can break up with me?"

"Kira—" Megan's voice cracked as her thighs clenched. Walking away from this attraction was going to be extremely hard. Maybe too hard. They were in this together no matter what she did, and the thought of leaving was killing her. "I'm pretty sure I'm not going to break up with you."

"You'd better be."

"I want the name." The more they knew, the better chance they had of figuring out which direction her karma was pushing her—pushing them both.

"I'm telling you, that was not one of the details that was burned into my brain. I was far more interested in remembering what you looked like—well, what the girl in my dream looked like, but she *was* you—maybe a younger you—and remembering what you made me feel—than remembering some goddess's…" A strange expression came over Kira's face, as if she were trying to catch a word that was on the tip of her tongue. Megan sat perfectly still, afraid to distract her and make her lose track of the memory.

Kira shook her head.

Megan bit back her disappointment. "What did this goddess look like? Was there a statue of her?"

"No statue."

Huh. Weren't statues typical inside ancient temples? "Why not?"

"She didn't take mortal form. She was more of an essence than a solid being. Closer to pure energy. Light. Consciousness."

Megan could almost see her, the spirit of the fire, dangerously white-hot. There was no way Kira's dream was just a dream. It fit in too perfectly with her own past-life memories.

"You think it was real?" Kira tightened her grip on Megan's legs.

Megan caressed Kira's fingers, trying to reassure her, trying to ignore the jolts of lightning shooting up her thighs. "We'll find out."

CHAPTER SEVENTEEN

"The priestesses of the ancient Greek goddess, Hestia," Megan read aloud from the computer in Kira's bedroom, "later known as Vesta by the Romans, were virgins. As in many religions, it was believed that chastity allowed these individuals' sexual energy to be transmuted into spiritual fervor and allowed them to devote themselves completely to their goddess."

Kira stood beside her, reading over her shoulder. "It's not her," she said. "There was definitely no chastity going on in my dream."

Megan reached under Kira's shirt and caressed the small of her back. "That's not the part we're trying to focus on here."

"It is if you're going to stick your hand up my shirt." Kira covered her fingers on the mouse and clicked on a link to another ancient goddess.

"Hey!" Megan protested.

Keeping her right hand exactly where it was, Kira planted her left hand on the other side of the desk beside the keyboard, trapping her. Her chest brushed against Megan's back. It was quite clear it was deliberate.

A small sound of satisfaction escaped from the back of Megan's throat. Damn reflexes. "Trying to get me to let go of the mouse?"

"Just trying to see over your shoulder," Kira replied innocently.

"Are you sure you can see from so far back?"

Kira laughed. "Just read."

Megan returned to the previous screen. "Hestia's priestesses were charged with guarding her sacred fire," she read. "Every home had a hearth honoring the goddess, and every city had a public hearth that was kindled from the perpetual flame kept at the temple at Delphi, which was a shrine to the goddess before it was assumed by the god Apollo. It is believed this 'forgotten' goddess was served by several priestesses serving in rotation to keep the flame alive day and night, for it was believed that the city's fate was tied to Hestia's fire, and if the fire went out, the city would suffer. The temple was destroyed several times by fire or earthquake."

Megan clicked on a photo of limestone ruins and pulled up an illustration of what the temple had originally looked like—a round, open structure supported by stone columns that looked very, very familiar. "Temple look like this?" She swiveled to look over her shoulder and see Kira's reaction.

Kira blinked at the screen. "How did you do that?"

So she was right. It *was* Hestia. "I told you not to take the mouse away from me."

"You have control issues." Kira put her hands on Megan's shoulders and turned her to face the computer like she was daring her to prove her right.

"You're just figuring that out now?" Megan tried to swivel back, but Kira's fingers tightened against her shoulders, resisting with a pressure that shouldn't have felt so electric. The strength of her, the aliveness of her, all concentrated in that one small touch...

She'd told her she was pretty sure she wasn't going to break up with her, and she'd meant it. But pretty sure wasn't completely sure, and they'd both be happier in the long run if they kept that in mind.

"It's her, isn't it?" Megan said.

Kira released her. "I'll admit there are some similarities."

Some? Kira didn't want to make this easy, did she. "So what's different? You're hung up on the sex thing?"

"What I'm hung up on is matching up real history with reincarnation. But since you brought it up, how *do* they know they were virgins?"

"Who knows? I guess one of the Greek poets must have written about them," Megan said offhandedly. As far as she was concerned, virgins or no, they had found the location of Kira's dream. And past life. "He could have been misinformed."

"I'll bet there were mysteries they didn't tell outsiders."

"Mysteries. Right." Megan smirked.

"You know I'm right. If those priestesses were having sex with each other as part of their rituals, they weren't about to tell the townfolk."

"Is this the only part of the dream you feel like talking about?"

"It's not *part* of the dream—it *is* the dream." Kira's face scrunched up in thought. "Maybe sex wasn't even supposed to be part of it."

No...wait. If sex wasn't supposed to be part of it, then... "God, you're probably right. It would explain the situation we're in now. In this lifetime."

"Ah, yes, screwing a client."

She said that so casually. As if it wasn't a big deal. Screwing your co-priestess wasn't exactly the same thing as screwing a client, but there was something about it that felt familiar, and Kira seemed to feel it too.

Megan said what she figured they were both thinking. "I want you now because thousands of years ago it wasn't supposed to happen and it did anyway."

I want you. She watched that admission hit Kira in the gut, her body crumpling ever so slightly before she caught herself. An echoing desire ricocheted inside her own body. She shouldn't be saying things like that—not until she was sure.

"Or because it *was* supposed to happen, so now it feels natural," Kira countered. "Could go either way, don't you think?"

She had a point. They still didn't have any answers about what any of this meant for their future. How was she supposed to figure out what to do when their visions were so frustratingly vague? "You don't remember if what we did was supposed to be part of the worship?"

"Let's reenact the ritual," Kira suggested. "You want more information about who we were in our past lives together. Maybe this will help me remember more details."

The fire-watching ritual? A knot started in Megan's stomach. "True…"

"And you get a chance to deal with your fear of fire."

"Not to mention you get to have sex with me."

Kira grinned. "Definitely a plus."

Megan rolled her eyes.

"No, seriously, we don't have to take it that far."

"Good, because we're not going to. We're not together," Megan reminded her.

"We could be," Kira said gently.

Megan shivered.

"I'll bet you look beautiful in the firelight." Kira wasn't smiling anymore. She looked wistful, her eyes out of focus.

Megan had no clue whether this was a good idea or not. But she did know firelight was not her thing.

* * *

"Ready to play with fire?" Kira asked cheerfully.

"You and your magic circles." Megan knelt barefoot on Kira's carpeted living room floor inside a ring of pillar candles. "I feel like I should cast a spell."

"Go right ahead, my witchy friend."

"I'm not a witch." People burned witches. Megan edged closer to the center of the circle to keep as much distance as possible between herself and the lit candles.

"Still not sure what the difference is."

"Not important. Where did you get all these candles, anyway?" Kira didn't strike her as a dinner-by-candlelight kind of person.

"I needed a few in case of a power outage, and I was buying in bulk, so..." Kira stepped inside the ring. "Move over," she said, lowering herself to the floor to kneel opposite her.

Megan's heart beat faster as she checked behind her and scooted back slightly to give her space. It would be so easy for one of them to accidentally knock over one of the candles, for a spark to land on the carpet, for their clothes to catch fire.

"We need a bonfire if we're going to do this right," she said, trying to convince herself she meant it. "If we're really trying to reenact your dream..."

"I'd rather start small until we know whether you're going to freak out."

Too late. All this talk about fire, and now the candles, made it hard to stay calm. Or maybe it was Kira's proximity that made her jittery.

"Although it would be nice to build a firepit behind the hotel," Kira continued. "It would be a great place for the guests to hang out, roast marshmallows, relax."

"Not for me." Megan shuddered.

"You might surprise yourself one day."

Megan reached for one of the burning candles and placed it in the center of the circle. "The fire's between us, right?"

"Right. It's burning in a pit in the floor."

Megan shut her eyes, folded her hands in her lap, and ordered herself not to panic. Fire was safety in Hestia's day. Fire was protection. It meant you weren't going to die come winter. When did she start thinking of it as a weapon instead of a tool?

Probably after it killed her a few too many times. That would probably do it.

"Want me to move the fire extinguisher closer?" Apparently Kira didn't think she looked unpanicked enough.

"I'm fine."

"I can move it if you want me to."

"No thanks." Megan imagined floating in the ocean, thinking calm thoughts.

"If you're nervous about this, we don't have to do this."

Megan opened one eye to glare at her. "It was my idea."

"As a matter of fact," Kira said, "it was *my* idea."

"But I'm the one who wants to know more about what you remember. I won't freak out. Just tell me what to do, what I do in the dream."

* * *

"We both kneel, facing each other…" Kira trailed off, struck by the way Megan had positioned herself within the circle.

Megan was already kneeling. She had her hands in her lap with her palms facing up, one hand on top of the other, thumbs touching. It wasn't a normal way to rest your hands. It was, in fact, the exact position she was about to describe.

"How did you know how to sit like that?"

Megan shrugged. "It seemed like the priestess-like thing to do. What's next?"

Okay, so maybe it was coincidence. "We stare into the flame."

"That's it? Doesn't it start with just one of us watching the perpetual flame? I thought the part where both of us watched together was some kind of changing of the guard."

"How did you know that?"

Megan looked puzzled. "You told me."

"No, I didn't."

"Are you sure?"

"I…" Kira shook off her confusion. "So…okay." She focused on the candle flame, trying to recall the details of her dream. "I stare into the fire until I see the goddess in there and enter a trance. I watch the flame and I wait for you. The goddess waits for you. I'm thinking about you while I'm praying and then at last it's time, and you walk in, barefoot, and kneel on the other side of the fire."

It wasn't the same, staring into a weak candle flame instead of a big, blazing fire, and they weren't wearing sleeveless white dresses—basically linen sheets draped around the body, held together by a belt tied high beneath the breasts—but the hum of Megan's presence—of her kneeling across from her, all serious and attentive, waiting for something to happen—felt utterly familiar.

"We were supposed to be looking for the goddess, opening ourselves to her spirit," Kira continued. "Watching, waiting, praying...and then at some point, instead of staring *into* the fire, we stared *through* the fire, and into each other's eyes, with the flames flickering between us. The goddess was in there and she got all mixed in with my feelings for you, and I couldn't tell anymore who was who. The heat was inside me and it was you and it was her and I was burning, sweating..." Kira took a ragged breath. "And all I could think about was untying that belt of yours and how the fabric would fall open...and then you were on top of me, making me feel things I'd never imagined."

Megan looked up from the candle and locked eyes with her.

Kira couldn't remember whether they had agreed to reenact that part or not. She was guessing not. She swallowed. "That website said the priestesses were transmuting their sexual energy. I guess that's what celibacy is supposed to do for men who are monks and priests, right?"

"Yeah. The theory is you block one channel so the energy is forced to move through another channel. I don't think it works that well, though. You set up this huge pattern of resistance, and the energy just ends up getting stuck."

"So either the historians are wrong about the virgin priestesses, or my dream is just a dream, because that's not what we were doing. We weren't suppressing our sexual energy."

"We let the energy build up," Megan agreed. "We watched it the same way we watched the sacred fire, and we let it rush through us, burn us, consume us…until the only thing that made sense was…"

Megan didn't complete her thought, but she didn't need to. They both knew what came next.

Megan stood and pulled Kira to her feet and led her outside the ring of candles. "Then we performed the sacred dance." Megan swayed forward and back, executing a pattern of steps that came straight from Kira's dream.

Kira mirrored the familiar steps perfectly for a few seconds, then came to an incredulous halt. "Are you reading my mind?"

Megan's lips quirked with amusement. "No." She resumed the dance as if it were perfectly natural to know the strange pattern, as if she and every other kid in the state had learned it in third grade along with the steps to the Virginia frickin' Reel.

"How could you possibly know how to do that?" Kira demanded.

Megan hesitated, and Kira knew she wasn't going to like her answer.

"I think I've had this dream, too."

Yup, she did not like that answer.

"How could we both have had the same dream?"

Megan drew her eyebrows together in pity.

Kira fought the gorge rising in her throat. She didn't want to be one of those people who believed in reincarnation. Telepathy was almost preferable. "It's not a dream, is it?"

Megan's eyes flicked right, left, down, as if it were too painful to look at her and see whatever it was she saw in her eyes. "It's the best explanation."

Well, hell. It would take some getting used to, but she didn't *feel* like she was losing her mind. She'd always wondered about that dream—wondered why it felt so real, so much more vivid than any other dream she'd ever had.

It wasn't a dream.

And on the bright side…it looked like Megan really *was* her soul mate.

* * *

Megan perched on a stool in Kira's kitchen and watched her slice a banana over a bowl. She loved fruit salad for breakfast. Kira had also promised French toast, and if it was anywhere near as good as dinner was last night… Megan opened her mouth and Kira fed her a slice of banana. She could get used to this.

Kira peeled an apple, starting near the stem and rotating the apple in her hand. When she reached the bottom, she held up the intact spiral of apple peel between her thumb and forefinger and stared at it as if there was something worrisome about it. "Do you know what this is?"

Apparently Kira wasn't completely functional after a night of almost no sleep. "A weird party trick?"

"Never mind."

"You're not going to tell me? What is it? A garnish?"

Kira lowered the peel to the countertop, guiding it into some semblance of its original shape. "When you were a kid," she said carefully, focusing on her task, "did you ever do that thing where you throw an apple peel over your shoulder to predict who you're going to marry?"

"Like a bride throwing her bouquet? You hit the lucky boy with an apple peel?"

"That, I would have enjoyed. But no."

Megan fished a slice of banana out of the bowl. Mmm—not too green and not too ripe. "Never heard of it."

"I can see that."

"So how does it work?"

"You stand at the top of the stairs with your back turned and you throw the peel over your shoulder. Then you race down the stairs and see what letter it made."

"Which is the initial of the person you're going to marry," Megan concluded.

Kira nodded. "It's right up your alley."

"Never tried it."

"I did."

"And?"

Spreading the apple peel on the countertop, Kira arranged the breaking loops into a string of notched humps. "You'd think a curly thing like an apple peel would be incapable of forming anything but the letter C. Maybe a J or a G. I remember telling myself that—that the whole thing was bogus, that even if I tried a million times and it finally made a J, it was only coincidence, even though I really did want it to make a J because I had a crush on Jackie Jurgens at the time."

"How old were you?"

"Nine, I think."

So even when she was nine years old, Kira was trying to talk herself out of believing in magic. And also kept tossing those apple peels over her shoulder and barreling down the stairs to discover whether the alluring Jackie was meant to be.

"The peel kept folding back on itself at the creases and making these damn letter M's." Kira pushed at the apple peel, fine-tuning the shape of her M. "Maybe it was a sign."

"You don't believe in signs." Kira didn't believe in ley lines, she didn't believe in angels, but she did believe in fortune-telling fruit?

Her eyes downcast, Kira gathered up the parings she'd been so interested in and walked them to the trash. Megan instantly regretted opening her mouth.

"I didn't mean—"

Kira cut her off, her voice full of resignation. "Now you're going to decide we can't be together, right? Because you have to cheat fate?"

Megan snapped her head in her direction. "Wait a minute. *This* is why you think we should be together? Because of an apple peel when you were nine?"

A faint smile played across Kira's lips. "Not exactly."

"Then why?"

Kira's eyes filled with warmth. "Because I love you." She shrugged, as if it should be obvious. "I can't seem to get enough of you."

Megan's heart squeezed. It was hard to stay logical when

Kira said things like that. But that was fate's blueprint tugging at her heartstrings, and she believed in free will. Kira didn't know what she was saying.

"You think it's fate," Megan said accusingly.

"Yes, I think it's fate." Exasperation crept into Kira's voice. "Why are you so determined to avoid anyone you've lived a past life with? How can you be so sure it would be a bad idea?"

"Amelia," Megan admitted. "That didn't work out too well." She'd given their relationship a second chance—and a third and a fourth chance—because she was sure there was a reason they were meant to be together again. She'd never found one.

"Amelia—" Kira choked on the name and tried again. "Amelia was in a past life with you?" She whacked a lemon in half and crushed it over the cut fruit. "That explains a lot. No wonder you... I can't believe you didn't tell me. Were you even lovers in your past life? Maybe she was your no-good neighbor. Or your abusive husband. She clearly wasn't your soul mate."

"Easy to say in hindsight," Megan grumbled. Did *everyone* think she was blind for trying to see the good in Amelia?

"So give me a chance," Kira suggested. "And a year from now you can look back and see if I was right about us or not."

Her logic was tempting.

"You don't know for certain that I was a mistake," Kira insisted.

"I'm sorry I said that earlier. I didn't mean you were a mistake. I mean, I did, but..."

Kira laughed good-naturedly. "I see you're not going to quit while you're ahead."

"What I meant was, you don't feel like a mistake, but it's so hard to know, and I want to be sure." Megan reached into the bowl to pick out the lemon pits. She couldn't look at her. She didn't want to look at her and see she was hurting her.

"Don't look so worried." Kira intercepted her hand over the bowl and intertwined their lemony fingers. "You believe in reincarnation. You'll get another shot at it in your next life."

Her grip felt perfect—and reminded her of her nightmares. "Another shot at making the same mistakes all over again."

"Awesome. You can make it up to me the next time around."

Megan smiled despite herself. Kira didn't sound hurt—she sounded *happy*. "You're willing to wait that long?"

"Hey, you said you always die young. It won't be *that* long."

Megan's jaw dropped and laughter bubbled up. "Can you at least pretend to take me seriously?"

Kira grinned. "Nope. I'm too happy that you're not breaking up with me."

"We're not together."

"I think we kind of are."

Yeah, okay, maybe. She squeezed their clasped hands and let herself imagine what it would be like to have a future with her—to forget her visions and just be happy. Could she do that? Would it be fair to either of them? Regretfully, Megan let go. "I wish I knew if it was the right thing to do. If I can be with you and still avoid my fate."

Kira sighed. "Why are you trying so hard to avoid your fate?"

"Because it's a painful, early death by fire, and I think this time I have a chance to change that."

The lines around Kira's eyes tightened. "Even if that's true, I don't see how being with me would affect that."

"Because it's all part of the pattern." Especially now that she knew Kira was the woman in her old nightmare. "I'm tired of living it over and over again. If you are entangled in my destiny, I should avoid you. Which technically would include not sleeping with you."

Kira's mouth pressed into a hard line. She turned to the sink and washed her hands, then straightened the dish towel that hung from the oven door. "Is it even possible to change your fate?"

She did wonder that sometimes. And now, when fate meant a woman who made her feel alive and safe, a woman she looked forward to seeing so much that she sometimes trembled with it—a woman she could barely face now because everything inside her was screaming at her to change her mind before she pushed her away for good—did it really matter how she died? What if she did escape her fate? She'd die some other way instead. She'd suffer some other form of pain.

But that felt like giving up, and she couldn't give up, because she might never get this chance again. Yes, she'd have other lives, but she couldn't be sure that next time she'd have the ability to remember her past lives and be able to learn from them.

"You can't control everything that happens to you," Kira said.

"I can try. I can make smart choices."

"You can make all the right choices in the world and it doesn't guarantee things won't go wrong."

"That doesn't mean I shouldn't keep trying." She might have bent her no-dating-clients rule for Kira, and she might be on the verge of breaking her recent no-dating-women-I-recognize-from-past-lives rule, but she refused to say the hell with it and let some ancient karmic blueprint call the shots.

Kira leaned against the kitchen counter. "Maybe you're trying so hard to avoid your pattern that you're getting stuck there instead. Like the priests you said were stuck in their sexual energy because they won't allow it to flow through. You're obsessing about fire instead of letting go of it."

She *was* trying to let go. But Kira was right—it wasn't working. Apparently part of her thought letting go sounded too much like failure.

"I'm not telling you to give up," Kira said. "Just…find a way to do it that doesn't involve pushing me away."

She wished she could, but it didn't seem possible, it didn't seem… Megan bit her lip. She really was stuck, wasn't she?

If you can't change the dream… Her mother's voice echoed in her head. *If you're trying and it's not working… If you can't change the dream then wake yourself up, Megan. Tell yourself it's just a dream and wake yourself up.* Her mother hadn't been talking about jumping off the karmic wheel, she had been trying to talk her out of her nightmares. But maybe she hadn't been as hopelessly unhelpful as Megan had always thought.

Because if you couldn't change the dream, there was another way out. The only way out. To wake up. Which meant the only way out was not to change her karma, but to stop believing it could hurt her. To stop letting it scare her. To stop trying so hard to change things.

If you're trying, and it's not working...

It wasn't free will if you only allowed yourself one choice.

CHAPTER EIGHTEEN

"Found a buyer yet?" Kira's dad folded his arms across his chest. His shirtsleeves were rolled to the elbows, his ropy forearms deeply tanned.

Kira shook her head in response to his favorite question and led him into the hotel's west wing, where she was converting most of the ground level into her new spa. "Haven't even finished renovating it yet."

Her crew was busy knocking down walls and tearing up the floor to create a spacious sunken lounge as well as several soundproofed treatment rooms and a couple of private changing rooms. She was excited about how well it was all coming along, as well as her solution to where to put the swimming pool—the architect was finalizing the design for a gorgeous rooftop hangout.

"What do you think?" she asked as they reached the site of her future lounge. She knew her dad liked watching the rip-it-apart stage—the finished product was boring to him—so this was where she'd taken him, to the area that was currently under the most construction. Unfortunately, it didn't distract him from his obsession over how soon she could sell.

"Never too early to plan ahead," he said. "I told you there wasn't a market for this sort of thing. Spas are luxury destinations. People who want the spa experience want to stay at a classy resort, not a dime-a-dozen roadside hotel."

"An affordable, yet fun and classy, hotel," Kira corrected him.

He patted her on the back with a well-meaning fatherly gesture that made her feel ten years old. "That's my girl. Always had a knack with the PR. I'll see if any of my contacts know anyone interested in taking it off your hands. We'll get your deal made."

"I appreciate the offer, but I'd like to handle this myself."

"You get the place finished, honey. I'll find you a buyer." His posture radiated confidence as he surveyed the exposed walls.

Kira bristled. "No need."

"Tell you what. I'll hold off a couple months, you see what you can do, then we'll talk."

"Really, Dad. It's sweet of you to want to help. But I'm perfectly capable of finding a buyer on my own."

Or deciding not to sell. Her whole life, she'd been doing what he expected of her. She'd gone to work for him at sixteen, starting businesses and selling them. She was good at it. She'd never stopped to think about whether it was what she really wanted to do.

Buying this hotel had started as an investment—just another business to set up and then get rid of. But now she wasn't sure she wanted to leave Piper Beach once this baby was up and running. It might be fun to stick around and try her hand at keeping a business for once. Her priorities were starting to shift, and she wasn't even sure when that had happened. But Megan probably had something to do with it. Megan was making her rethink a lot of things.

"Maybe if you put in some tennis courts..." Her dad still had that calculating look in his eye, damn him.

Kira's jaw tightened. How could he possibly think this

looked like a boring place to stay? It was well on its way to being the most beautiful building she'd ever worked on. "I think women will like it just the way it is," she ground out.

"I almost forgot about your women-only plan."

"Why am I not surprised?" She'd known all along that her father thought a lesbian hotel was an unprofitable idea, but she didn't work for him anymore and he couldn't stop her from investing in projects she cared about.

"Be reasonable. You're going to be managing the hotel for six months, tops. What do you care who the customers are? Whoever takes this property off your hands is going to do whatever the hell they want with it anyway. You want to offer a turnkey operation, make it a normal hotel. Besides, you know as well as I do there are laws against discrimination in public accommodations."

He was as stubborn as she was. It wasn't even worth arguing about, not if he was just going to lecture her. Kira changed the subject and showed him the gorgeous new ductwork instead. He might not like her spa idea, but Megan did. And Megan's opinion mattered more.

* * *

"Ever had a mud bath?" Kira asked the awkward-looking job applicant who stood stiffly in her dress-to-impress interview suit while Kira hunted through her office for her list of spa treatments. She'd cleaned off her desk for this interview, and now she couldn't find anything, including this poor thing's résumé. What was her name again? Trish something?

"I love mud baths," Trish-something said.

She looked sincere. And why not? According to Kira's research, mud baths were popular. Even though she personally had not been impressed. She spotted her list—and Trish's résumé—on top of a file cabinet. Trish Martin—that was it.

"Here are the services we plan to offer." She handed her the printout. "As you can see, it's heavy on the massage options."

"Does the staff get free spa treatments?"

"Half-price. Or negotiate on your own with the other staff." Kira gave her a few minutes to look over the list while she reviewed her résumé. "Are you familiar with what all these things are?"

"Of course."

That was a good sign. And she seemed enthusiastic, too. The staff and the guests would like her.

"If a guest showed up at the desk and had never had a massage before, what type of massage would you recommend she sign up for?"

"Gentle Swedish," Trish answered without hesitation.

Megan would have wanted to know more specifics about the guest before she fired off a recommendation, wouldn't she? She'd want to know what the guest was looking for, and tailor it to her tastes.

So, newsflash, she wasn't Megan.

Who had assured her that the professional grapevine said Trish Martin was a decent massage therapist, and anyone who could put up with a boss like chiropractor Dan Bristow would be able to handle difficult hotel guests. She needed to give her a chance.

"If a guest had a sunburn, what would you steer her toward?"

Trish studied the list. "When I get a sunburn I don't want anyone to touch me, so I'd suggest Reiki."

Okay, so she didn't pick the hydrating aloe wrap, which Megan insisted was a must for any reputable seaside spa. Kira watched herself twist her pen between her thumb and fingers. Was this her way of giving Trish a chance? There was nothing wrong with her answer. A year ago Kira wouldn't even have known there were different types of massage, and here she was, trying to trip up someone who knew way more about all this than she did. It made her feel like her father, ferreting out posers and bullshitters for sport.

She looked up and saw Trish's doe eyes filled with panic, aware that her potential boss wasn't happy with her answer. Kira swore under her breath. Trish couldn't be that bad if she had that kind of ability to read body language.

She hadn't interviewed a promising candidate in weeks, and holding out for the perfect candidate was getting her nowhere. Trish was certainly better than the waitress who had insisted that although she didn't have the requested national certification and had no formal training, all her friends said she gave great massages. So why was she feeling so reluctant about her?

Maybe because part of her was holding out for Megan. Because deep down, she hoped that if she couldn't find a spa manager, her favorite massage therapist would step in and take the job. And that wasn't fair to Megan, who'd already given her a ton of advice and hours of her time. Besides, Megan had made it clear she had no intention of officially working for her, ever.

"You do understand the job involves hiring and supervising the massage therapists. I'm concerned about your lack of managerial experience."

"I'm good with people. I know I'd be a great manager."

Maybe she would, maybe she wouldn't. You had to admire her confidence, though. It took guts to ask to be shot down.

"Why haven't you started your own business?"

"I really like being part of a team, which I got to do working for a chiropractor."

"Meaning you don't like being in charge."

"Meaning I don't have the capital to hire my own staff," Trish shot back.

Kira gave her an appraising glance. Trish was starting to win her over. "You sure you want to be responsible for taking care of everything? Finding someone to cover for anyone who gets sick, ordering supplies, keeping the massage therapists happy, appeasing angry clients…"

"I can do that," Trish insisted. "And you'd be my boss?"

"Yes," Kira said uncomfortably. "At first. But I plan to sell once this place gets off the ground." She didn't want to be reminded of that right now, or of what it might mean to her relationship with Megan. She needed to go for a long run and get that sorted out in her head—soon. But not now.

Trish leaned forward earnestly. "I can handle it. Don't worry about a thing."

Thoughtfully, Kira twisted her pen. "How would you decide if you needed to fire a massage therapist?"

"Uh…"

As Trish struggled to come up with an answer, Kira squeezed her pen, telepathically trying to help. Her father would hassle her if he knew what she was thinking. He'd accuse her of being a lightweight. And he wouldn't have averted his eyes, either, when he heard Trish Martin dig herself into a hole. He would have enjoyed feeling superior.

Turned out, he didn't teach her everything she knew.

She gave Trish a reassuring grin, because personnel decisions were something she could teach her how to make. "I'd like to offer you a job."

* * *

Megan handed Barbara Fenhurst a glass of water after her massage.

"How do you feel?"

"Great," Barbara said in between gulps of water. "You're a great masseuse. Always know right where to find the knots." Far from being upset about the fire on her porch Officer Baldini had mentioned, Barbara had spent most of their session telling her how exciting it had been to see her name in the paper. Whatever stress she had complained about to the police seemed to have worn off before her appointment.

"The water at your house always tastes better than at my house. Can you get me a refill?" Barbara handed her the empty glass, picked up her purse, and followed her into the kitchen. Megan refilled her glass from the filtered tap. When she turned back to offer her the water, Barbara was across the kitchen helping herself to a handful of cherries from a bowl on the breakfast table. "I'm starving," she said, nibbling away. "Can I have some of these?"

"Um…" Megan gave Barbara the glass of water and hoped it would distract her from the cherries. She was happy to share, but she didn't like having her personal space turned into a hotel's all-you-can-eat continental breakfast buffet behind her back. Clients weren't even supposed to be in her kitchen.

Barbara's hand hovered near her mouth. "I can pay you back."

"Don't worry about it." Megan edged toward the doorway, hoping Barbara would get the hint that it was time to leave.

Barbara held out a fistful of cherry pits and stems. Megan showed her where the compost bucket was, and her wayward client scooped another bunch of cherries from the bowl. "Mmm." Instead of following Megan to the front door, she wandered into the living room with her prize and slowly turned around to take it all in. "I love your house."

"Thanks." Megan followed, wondering what was coming next.

"It's so big for one person. Are you looking for a roommate? I'd love to live here. I could have your extra bedroom, and I have this great futon we could set up in the living room for guests."

Huh? "It's only two bedrooms. One's the massage room and one's my bedroom. There's no extra bedroom."

"Oh. So we could put up a wall in the living room. That should give me enough space."

Was Barbara insane? "I'm not looking for a housemate," Megan stammered.

"With this big empty townhouse? And you live here all by yourself?"

How did she know that? Was she assuming she lived alone because she'd never seen anyone here, or had she actually researched this? Megan knew she'd never told Barbara anything remotely bordering on her housemate and/or relationship status. Looked like she'd trained herself too well. She could turn a conversation around as well as any self-respecting psychotherapist, keeping the focus on the client the way a good therapist should, never burdening the client with details about her own personal life. Now look what had come of it. Left free to imagine whatever she wanted about Megan's private life, Barbara had gone wild.

"Don't you like your own place?" Megan said. Or... "Is it the fire? Are you afraid the arsonist might come back?" If she didn't feel safe at home, that would explain her sudden interest in moving in with her. That had to be it.

"Fire's no big deal for me," Barbara said. "Didn't I ever tell you my dad was a fireman?"

"You didn't. But that doesn't mean you—"

Barbara snorted. "I'm not scared."

Okay, well, good. Discard that understandable explanation and that left a great big blank for why she wanted to convert Megan's living room into a guest suite. Megan hated being judgmental, but unfortunately she had no trouble filling in the blank with words like *self-centered* and *needy* and *desperately lonely*. Just what she needed in a housemate.

"He took my brother for visits to the firehouse all the time, but he never took me. He said it was no place for a girl. My brother got to do all the fun stuff—ride the fire truck, learn how to hook up the water hose, watch them burn down old houses for practice..." She popped more cherries into her mouth and spit the pits into her palm with so much force that slobber went flying.

"That sounds unfair," Megan said.

"That's exactly what it was. Unfair." Barbara went back to the kitchen and dropped more cherry pits into the compost bucket. "How much do you want for rent?"

"I don't have room," Megan said firmly.

"I'm good about helping with housework and all that. You'd hardly notice I was here."

Right. She'd hardly notice an extra person in the house, not to mention a *wall* in her living room? "Sorry."

Barbara turned on the kitchen sink to wash her hands. "Think about it."

Megan shook her head in disbelief. Talk about persistent. She showed her to the door.

With Barbara safely outside, Megan rushed to the bathroom and ran her hands under cold water to wash off the experience.

Her body was shaking, even though Barbara really wasn't a threat. She was lonely, that was all, and she didn't understand that professional nurturers were there to care, but not to be your best friend. She had probably offered to split the rent with her acupuncturist, too. And her physical therapist. And God knew who else. There could be quite a list.

* * *

"She wants to move in with you?" As if the jolt to Kira's lungs from chasing Megan into the cold ocean wasn't enough of a shock to her system, now there was this delightful news.

"I'm not taking her up on that, obviously."

Megan sounded like the voice of reason, as usual. Kira didn't understand why she herself was the only one ready to burst an artery over this. She would have been happy if Megan never saw Barbara Fenhurst again, but apparently Megan didn't think there was a problem. Just another harmless looney tune who helped pay the bills. "She has a crush on you."

"She says she's straight."

"She *says* she's straight? What does *that* mean?"

Megan slipped her arms under Kira's clinging wet T-shirt and Kira's already-racing pulse picked up speed. Megan moved her hands up her back with expert skill and Kira tried not to think of her amazing touch being wasted on grabby Barbara Fenhurst, because thinking about it was not helping.

"Barbara Fenhurst is the last person on earth you need to be jealous of," Megan said.

"Sorry," Kira said. "It's not you I'm mad at."

"Maybe it's my fault. Maybe I shouldn't work out of my home. I know it's not the most professional setting."

"It is *not* your fault."

"If I drew the line more clearly…"

Kira gripped her wet arms, feeling the steel underneath the softness, hating that anyone could make Megan doubt herself. "Will you get upset if I tell you I want to beat her up?"

"You wouldn't do that."

"Probably not," Kira admitted. "But keep in mind she'd be just as bad in a real office. And it is *not your fault*."

"I don't know." Megan chewed on her lip. "If you were at someone's place of business and you saw food lying around, how would you know it wasn't fair game?"

"*She eats your food?*" What a piece of work. "What is she doing in your kitchen?"

"She forgets it's not a social call."

Megan was the most generous, forgiving person she'd ever met. Forgiving enough for both of them, really. If there was anything Kira could do to protect her from people who took advantage of her, she'd do it. And there *was* something she could do. "Do you want office space at my spa? I'd love to have you there. There's plenty of room."

"Thanks, but I don't want to work for you."

Yes, she remembered that quite clearly, and it wasn't what she meant. "Not working *for* me. Completely independent. I have Trish Martin working for me now, and I will *not* let her ask you to step in and help."

Megan considered it for a moment. "I don't know if I can afford it. Anyway, you'll need all those treatment rooms for your guests."

She could afford to rent Megan one of those rooms for free. Was there a way to give her a room without insulting her pride or making her feel beholden? There had to be a way.

Megan rubbed her hands down Kira's back and around her waist. "Maybe there's something I can do to hide my living space from my clients. Folding screens around the living room or something. A door blocking the kitchen." Her hands kept moving around her waist, gently at first, then with increasing frustration. When Kira started wondering whether Megan was actually going to hurt her, she abruptly stopped. "I can't believe that woman had the nerve to suggest building a wall in my living room so she could move in."

Kira whistled in disbelief. "That's what that freak wanted you to do?"

"I guess I should be glad she didn't suggest taking over my bedroom." Megan gave a high-pitched giggle that sounded like she was on the verge of hysterics. "I wouldn't put it past her." She hid her face in Kira's shoulder and started shaking. "It's my house. It's my space."

"Oh, honey, don't cry," Kira whispered into her hair. She held her tightly and stroked her wet head. Megan felt so tiny and vulnerable. "Tell her you can't see her anymore."

"I can't."

"Sure you can."

"I'd like to, but I…I can't bring myself to do it."

* * *

Monday evening Kira sat on the steps in front of Megan's townhouse doing some paperwork while she waited for Megan to finish up with her last client of the day. Their plan was to walk down to the beach, eat dinner on a blanket on the sand and swim, because after working with Barbara Fenhurst, Megan was definitely going to need to unwind.

When the door finally opened, Barbara did not look pleased to see Kira there.

"Is she one of your clients?" Barbara demanded. "I thought six thirty to seven thirty was your last appointment of the day. Do you have a seven forty-five? Because I can come later."

"No, she's…"

Kira tightened her grip on her papers as it suddenly occurred to her that by arriving a few minutes early she'd put Megan in a tough spot. She hadn't intended to do that. Would Megan say she was her girlfriend? A friend? A neighbor? She knew Megan liked to keep her personal life private. She knew about Megan and her rules.

"…just visiting," Megan said easily. That seemed to satisfy Barbara because she went back to chattering with Megan as if Kira weren't there.

"If we lived together, I could make you breakfast," Barbara said. "I make a great omelet. People beg me for my omelets."

Wow. Megan wasn't kidding when she said Barbara wanted to move in with her.

Barbara kept it up. "I'm very easy to live with. You'll see."

Kira rolled her eyes. Barbara could talk all she wanted, but she was never going to get a chance to prove her qualifications as a housemate.

"First I'll need to repaint. I can't live in a place that's not moss green. That's the color my old masseuse in California used. You'll love it."

What do you know, disproved herself already.

"I'm not interested in a housemate," Megan said. "I don't have room." She actually sounded sorry that she had to let Barbara down.

Kira put away her paperwork, impatient for Barbara to finish up with the bullshit. The fried chicken and sweet potato fries in the take-out bag at her feet were going to get cold if they didn't get a move on.

At last Megan and Barbara hugged goodbye. Kira's fingers dug into her palms. If it were anyone else, she wouldn't have minded. Sure, there wasn't a lot of hugging going on in most businesses, but massage wasn't most businesses. It was more like kindergarten, where the teacher hugged the kids and it was all very nurturing. What got to her was that it was Barbara. I-have-a-crush-on-my-massage-therapist Barbara. With Barbara, things were not all warm and fuzzy and innocent. She didn't deserve one of Megan's hugs.

Kindergarten, she reminded herself. Nurturing. She looked to see what was taking so long and saw Megan was engulfed, her arms pinned at her sides, her face stoic as Barbara squeezed the life out of her.

"Can't wait till next week," Barbara said cheerfully, keeping a suspicious eye on Kira as she made her way past her down the steps. "I'll bring a measuring tape so we can figure out where to put that wall for my room." She was so busy glaring over her shoulder at Kira and giving her the evil eye that she stumbled on the last step.

As she struggled for balance, Kira leapt up and caught her arm to make sure she didn't bash her face on the concrete sidewalk and then need to make even *more* appointments with Megan to speed the healing process. Barbara needed to stay away from Megan. And work on her listening skills.

Barbara shook off Kira's restraining grasp and scowled. "Watch what you're doing, you idiot!"

"Are you all right?" Megan rushed down the steps to Barbara's other side.

"Did she trip me?" Barbara accused.

"Of course not. Why would you think that?" Megan gave her a look that might have passed for concern if Kira didn't know her so well. The eyebrows were right, but her eyes were distant and cold. She hadn't appreciated that claustrophobic hug.

Devoid of support for her accusations, Barbara changed tack. "I think I twisted my ankle."

Kira didn't believe that, not for one minute. "Do you need help getting to your car?" she offered, knowing it would be difficult for Megan to resist her Good Samaritan instincts. Barbara would be only too happy to get herself invited into the house for first aid, and then it would be impossible to get her out.

"We'll both walk you there," Megan said, jumping in before Barbara could respond.

Good call. Kira took hold of Barbara's arm again, this time with both hands. Barbara resisted, but Kira kept a firm grip. Otherwise Barbara would sag her weight against Megan, who had her other arm, and no way was she going to let that happen. Barbara's hour-long appointment was up.

In a few minutes they were helping Barbara into her car, watching her drive off, and walking back through the courtyard to Megan's door.

"There's no way she really twisted her ankle, is there?" When the angry glares in her direction had stopped and the limping continued, Kira had started to wonder.

"I think once she gets home she'll be happy she has an excuse to call her doctor. And her chiropractor. And me. The woman's a hypochondriac."

Megan looked tired, and that made Kira mad again. "You know how I said I wouldn't really beat her up? I changed my mind."

"You're joking, right?"

"Yeah." How could she even ask?

A hint of amusement crept into Megan's voice. "She might deserve it."

"What? Is that an un-Hippocratic attitude I hear coming from your oh-so-professional lips?"

"My lips are *not* professional. Eew."

Kira cringed. She wished she could joke about that aspect of Megan's career's reputation, but she still wasn't used to it. "You know what I mean."

Megan put an arm around her shoulders and gave her an apologetic squeeze. Kira relaxed into it. She had to admit she understood why Barbara craved Megan's company. Barbara might be crazy, but she had good taste.

"Speaking of professional," Kira said, "you really smoothed things over." Megan in action had been impressive. In just the few minutes it took them to walk her client to her car, she had calmed her down to the point that Barbara was thanking her for the wonderful massage and seemed to have forgotten all about their little incident.

"I didn't want either of us to get sued," Megan said. "Amelia taught me to be paranoid about that."

"Barbara wasn't hurt," Kira protested. And Megan's ex was out of her lawyerly mind if she thought Megan would ever get sued for a trip-and-fall outside her townhouse. Her clients loved her. Customers sued because they were angry—they didn't slap lawsuits on people they adored. "She wasn't hurt, right?"

"That might not stop her."

CHAPTER NINETEEN

"I give an awesome massage myself," Barbara said as Megan lifted Barbara's arm in a gentle stretch so she could massage the underside of the arm and all the way down the side of her ribcage. "People tell me I should do it professionally. We should trade sometime."

"I'm sorry, I don't trade with my clients," Megan said absently.

"I could still pay. So you wouldn't be losing me as a paying customer."

"No thanks."

"Why not? I used to massage my boyfriend and he thought I was pretty good. I know I'm not a professional, so I probably wouldn't give you chills the way you do, but it would be fun."

Chills? Now there was a compliment she could do without. Was it Barbara's word choice or the way she said it that made her want to say...eew?

"Sorry." Megan focused on her long effleurage stroke up Barbara's side. When she was in the midst of giving a massage and tapped into the flow of universal love, she could ignore stuff that would normally make her uncomfortable, such as the thought of letting her boundary-impaired client touch her naked body.

She took a deep breath and invited the angels to fill her with their healing light. Barbara had momentarily knocked her out of her zone, but she'd get it back. As the angels appeared and the light began to flow through her, she relaxed and sank into a love space. Compassion bubbled up and she blinked back tears. Underneath all Barbara Fenhurst's crap was a little girl who liked her and wanted to be her friend.

Barbara's voice snapped Megan out of her trance. "I don't have a massage table, but we can use yours, of course. It would give me a chance to practice. Don't want to get rusty."

"You'll get more out of this massage if you don't worry about conversation. Just pay attention to your body."

"Mmm." Barbara purred in appreciation. "You're amazingly gifted at what you do. You have this healing touch that no other masseuse has. You give me the shivers, you know that?"

Megan tried to stop her hands from shaking.

Barbara took Megan's silence as encouragement. "We have such a great connection. It's like you're psychic—you always know exactly where I'm hurting. You understand me."

Megan moved Barbara's arm back down to her side and carefully rested it on the massage table.

"You understand me like no one else," Barbara continued. "I feel like we've known each other forever." Her arm shot out and grabbed Megan's waist under the floating hem of her blouse, fondling her bare skin.

Megan sprang back, her heart racing.

Clients never touched her—not when they were on the table.

When she worked she was always conscious of the fact that she was intruding into her clients' personal space. She leaned over them, she undraped them, and occasionally she got too close and inadvertently breathed on them. But it didn't feel intimate, because *she* touched *them*, and *they* did not touch *her*. That was the rule.

Barbara sat up, not bothering to cover her breasts with the sheet. "I've never dated a woman before, but—"

Oh, no. When had Barbara gotten *this* idea into her head? Megan cut her off before things got completely out of hand. "Any connection I have with you is strictly professional."

It was sad. She did have a connection with her clients—with every single one of them—and she did care about them deeply. It disturbed her that Barbara misunderstood that love.

"The way you touch me…I know that's not true."

"I don't date clients."

"There's a first time for everything."

Not this time, there wasn't. Megan moved to put herself farther from Barbara's breasts and closer to the door.

Her client's jiggling flesh leaned forward pleadingly. "We'd be so good together. You know we would! Just imagine how much better it would be if I was touching you too."

Okay, no. She would rather not imagine that. "I'm going to have to ask you to leave."

"But why?"

Megan's heart pounded. How could a sane person act so bewildered? "I'm going to leave the room so you can get dressed, and I'll be waiting for you by the front door."

"I don't understand. Don't you owe me an hour? I think I should get an hour if that's what I'm paying for."

"You don't have to pay me for today. I just need you to leave."

"Now?"

Megan closed the door and hoped to God Barbara was getting dressed.

She wished Kira hadn't been right about her.

Barbara met her downstairs a few minutes later and flipped open her checkbook. "I'm sorry if I said something that offended you. Can I pay you for the twenty-five minutes?"

"Fine." Anything to get her out of here.

"Do you have a pen?" Barbara was suddenly in her living room, looking around.

Megan dashed into the kitchen, grabbed a pen from her junk drawer, and returned to the front door with it rather than follow

Barbara into the living room. If she was lucky, the pen would lure her to the door without the need for another discussion of wall placement or her supposed need for a roommate.

Her luck held and Barbara returned to write out her check. "Let's hope that bitch who was on your stoop last week isn't here today. She's not your next appointment, is she?"

Megan gritted her teeth. She hoped the expression on her face wasn't as violent as she felt. "No, she's not."

Barbara ripped the check out of her checkbook and handed it to Megan. "If I was a celebrity you could be my personal masseuse and I'd be your only client and you wouldn't have to deal with psychos like her." She put her checkbook back in her purse and pulled out her planner. "Can we set up an appointment for next week?"

Someone should hire this woman for their sales team. She didn't understand the concept of rejection.

"I think it would be better for both of us if you saw a different massage therapist from now on."

"What?" Barbara's shock was palpable.

She should have known Barbara wouldn't make this easy. "I'm not comfortable working with you anymore. Someone else could do a better job."

"What did I do wrong? Tell me what I did wrong. I'll fix it."

It should be obvious what she did wrong. "I'm not interested in a sexual relationship with you, and I'm not comfortable working with you anymore. I'm not the right massage therapist for you."

"All you have to do is say you don't want to date. That's all you have to do. You don't have to stop giving me massages," Barbara explained to Megan like she was a child who didn't understand you were supposed to play nice on the playground. Next she'd be telling her she had to learn to share and let the other kids have a turn on the slide instead of throwing a tantrum.

As if Megan were the one misbehaving here.

"I'm not comfortable working with you anymore," Megan repeated implacably. As much as she couldn't bring herself to believe that Barbara meant any harm, it would be a relief not to have to see her again. She felt a little guilty for feeling that way, but only a little.

Maybe it was about time she took advantage of her popularity and used it to become pickier about whom she chose to work with. She could charge a lot more, work less, refer her difficult clients to a recent grad desperate for work... Except everyone deserved the healing touch of massage, and she didn't feel right overcharging them for it, and she wasn't willing to hasten another massage therapist's descent into burnout. She really hated that Barbara made her think like a jerk.

"You can't do this to me!" Barbara threw her hands up in the air and practically howled with frustration. Her pain filled the house.

Megan wanted to disappear and escape Barbara's terrible need to be near her, but even more, she wanted to see this through and know that Barbara Fenhurst had moved on. A referral would help with that. She couldn't just cut her loose without a referral.

"I could—" Could what? Give Barbara the names of other massage therapists she liked and respected, so Barbara could annoy them, too? Send her to Patrick, who was a man, and therefore immune to her crushes? Except Barbara thought she was straight, and that had to be part of why she was acting so inappropriately around her—her crush on her female massage therapist was throwing her for a loop. Megan thought fast. "I could give you the URL of the National Association's website so you can find someone else." Not the best suggestion in the world, but she was not siccing her on her friends.

"You're the best masseuse ever. I can't go to someone else."

"That's very flattering, but there's lots of good massage therapists out there, especially in Piper Beach."

"Not like you!"

Barbara burst into tears and flung her arms around Megan's rigid body. Megan stood in stunned silence, then patted her on the back as Barbara sniffled against her shoulder. She felt herself relent, felt herself about to offer her another chance. She owed her that, didn't she?

No, she didn't. Barbara had crossed the line too many times. She didn't even understand that her flattery was unwelcome. She had zero ability to pick up on social cues. Megan tried to disentangle herself from her embrace, but Barbara held on tight, crushing her ribs.

"Let up a little. You're holding me too tight," Megan said in a low, irritated voice, pushing her away as she would an over-enthusiastic dog—gently—and being completely ineffective.

"You can't do this!" Barbara sobbed, a note of hysteria entering her voice.

Her desperation rushed into Megan's body, magnified by their physical contact. Megan struggled to block it out. She'd never been any good at throwing an emotional energy barrier around herself, and she wasn't any good at it now. She wanted to be supportive—for God's sake, she wouldn't normally turn her back on someone crying like this—but it was hard to feel sympathy for Barbara when she had her immobilized in such a stubborn grip. She didn't seem to know her own strength.

"Let's sit you down somewhere," Megan said. "If you would just let go…"

Barbara continued to sob. Her flushed face was alarmingly close, and her hot breath blew on Megan's neck.

Megan's shoulders clenched reflexively to protect her neck. "You have to let go of me."

Barbara pressed her wet face into Megan's neck, making her flinch. She squeezed her even closer, suffocating her. Megan's body screamed at her to push her away, but even when she wanted to act unprofessional, she couldn't do it.

Yes, she could. Enough was enough. She was a human being with a right not to be strangled. She wedged her hands between their bodies and pushed Barbara's ribcage, hard. Barbara lost traction but recovered immediately, repositioning her monster grip on Megan's ass.

So now they'd moved on to groping? Megan made an exasperated sound from the back of her throat. She pushed her again, harder, slamming her hands into her chest. Her breasts, actually, which had to have hurt. Barbara stumbled back. Megan took a quick step back in case she tried to grab her again. She raised her forearms subconsciously in a defensive stance and caught up on her breathing.

"Please leave."

"For saying you're a great masseuse?"

Not this again.

"For scaring me!" No, wait, too much honesty. She'd already found out that didn't work. Keeping her eyes on Barbara's hands and trying to stay out of reach in the narrow entryway, Megan opened the front door. Barbara didn't budge. Why wouldn't she leave? If they'd been anywhere else, Megan would have fled. Unfortunately, since Barbara was in her house, that wasn't going to work.

She tried again. "I'm sorry it had to come to this, but I can't see you anymore."

"Can't we talk about this?"

"We already talked about it. You crossed the line. You can't come here anymore."

Her next client would arrive in half an hour, which was not nearly enough time to breathe and get centered and change the sheets. She didn't know how she was going to put on a smile and give a decent massage after this.

Unbelievably, Barbara remained inside the entryway.

Please, please just go.

Megan held the door open with one hand, and, cringing because she really didn't want to touch her again, took Barbara by the arm and guided her in the direction she wanted her to go.

"But—" Barbara's mouth hung open like a fish, then clapped shut. She stepped backward over the threshold.

Megan quickly slammed the door and ran to the bathroom and washed her hands, then her face, then her hands again. She leaned over the sink, shaking.

Pushing her had felt unbelievably wonderful. And made her sick to her stomach.

Who would Barbara try to get a massage from next? Would it be unprofessional to warn everyone in town? Megan looked at herself in the mirror. Unprofessional? She coughed out a harsh bark of laughter at how ridiculous that particular concern sounded, considering what she'd already done. Pushing a client in the chest was about as unprofessional as it got. Not to mention rude. Uncivilized. Inappropriate. Not the recommended course of action when dealing with a difficult client.

And she was not at all sorry.

CHAPTER TWENTY

The doorbell rang downstairs as Megan massaged Matt Larapinta's back. She ignored it. She placed her hands on either side of his spine and glided toward his pelvis. There was something profoundly wrong with the shape of men's bodies. Not that they could help it, but why would you encounter narrow hips under broad shoulders? Honestly, it wasn't normal. Her hands wanted to sweep all the way down his back and then flare out to the sides along the wide bones of the pelvic bowl, sinking the heels of her hands into the lower back, but no matter how many times she did this, she ran into Matt's pelvis sooner than she expected because the hip bones came up higher than they should, and then there was nowhere to flare out to. She hoped she wasn't jabbing him.

She'd forgotten about the doorbell by the time she let Matt out the front door, but there was Barbara Fenhurst, pushing herself up from her perch on the stoop and thrusting a plastic-wrapped baking pan at her.

"I brought brownies," Barbara said cheerfully. "Homemade."

"Thanks," Megan said automatically, accepting the pan while kicking herself for her politeness Tourette's.

"I added chocolate chips for that extra burst of flavor."

"Barbara—"

"I tried to call."

Yeah, like that was the issue here. Barbara had left her dozens of messages in the past week—some pleading, some rational-sounding, and some oblivious, as if by pretending nothing had happened, Megan would have to call her back. She had called Barbara back once to let her feel heard, and a second time to try to reason with her. Neither call had helped. After that, she switched to erasing Barbara's messages without listening to them. She'd thought about blocking Barbara's number, but that wouldn't stop her for longer than it took her to streak to the nearest pay phone. At least this way she knew who was calling.

"I hope you like the brownies," Barbara said. She didn't show any signs of leaving.

It felt rude to slam the door in her face, but Barbara was liable to invite herself inside if she left it open, so Megan joined her outside and pulled the door shut behind her.

"Did you get my other gifts?" Barbara asked.

Uh...no? The aromatherapy candles with embedded seashells, the box of saltwater taffy, the Dalai Lama T-shirt, the second set of aromatherapy candles, this time in a rainbow of colors, the third set of aromatherapy candles, one for each sign of the zodiac—which was good, because it meant Barbara didn't know her birthday—each day something new appeared at her doorstep, complete with a cheerful handwritten card. Why couldn't she leave her alone?

"I can't work with you anymore," Megan said.

Barbara looked confused. "I just want a second chance."

Yes, Megan was well aware of that. "I'm sorry, that's not going to happen."

Barbara waved her hands dismissively. "No, no, don't decide now. We'll talk later."

Not if I have anything to say about it.

Megan locked herself inside and hurried to the kitchen with

the pan of brownies. She hovered over the compost bucket, about to scrape out the pan, but she couldn't bear to contaminate her bucket with the brownies's negative energy, so she changed course and dumped them in the trash instead. She shouldn't have accepted them, because Barbara was going to take that as a sign of encouragement. Good thing she had ended things when she had. She'd had no idea Barbara's obsession with her was this bad. Or maybe rejection had amped up the crazy.

She reopened the lid of the trash can and glared at the brownies. She didn't want those things in her house at all. Did she have time to run to the Dumpsters down in the maintenance yard before Kira arrived for dinner? She'd better call and make sure. If Kira had to wait on her stoop and happened to spot Barbara lurking in the bushes—not that she thought Barbara was deranged enough to do that—she didn't want Kira to worry she had a stalker.

She looked out the peephole in her front door to make sure Barbara had left. No sign of her. She set the trash and its brownie smell outside the door and went back inside to call Kira.

"I need to drive down to the maintenance yard," Megan told her.

"I'm just pulling in now," Kira said. "I'll go with you."

* * *

"I wonder how long it'll take before she gives up and finds another massage therapist," Megan said to Kira as they walked through the courtyard to her reserved parking space.

Kira took the trash bag from her and tied an extra knot in the drawstring handle. "Do you know what kind of car she drives?"

"A gray Taurus. I don't see it." It was sweet of Kira not to complain about the detour. If it weren't for Barbara's dumb brownies, they'd be heading out for a late dinner right now, not scanning the street for suspicious cars.

"I think you should call the police."

"She hasn't actually threatened me. It's not against the law to show up at someone's door and give them food."

Kira eyed the plastic bag, lifting it to eye level. "Maybe we should take these brownies to the police and have them tested for poison."

"She didn't *poison* them. She's trying to get me to spend time with her, which would be kind of hard to do if I were dead."

"You can't know for certain that that's what she wants."

"I just want the brownies out of my house. I don't want to be reminded of her."

"Okay, it's your crazy client."

They reached her car and Megan cleared the passenger seat so Kira could get in. "I wish I could return the pan right now, too, but I want to wait until she's at work so I don't run in to her and have to talk to her."

Kira fastened her seat belt. "You're returning her brownie pan?"

"I'm not keeping it." Megan started the car.

"This is her way of keeping a connection going. If you wash out her pan and return it to her, she'll think you two are friends."

"She already thinks we're friends. I don't think it'll make any difference."

"Throw the pan in the trash."

"It's not disposable," Megan said. "It's a real pan."

"So?"

"I can't throw out a real pan and add it to the landfill."

Kira shook her head like she could not believe what she was hearing. "I hope she doesn't turn it into a shrine of objects you've touched. But I'll return it for you. I'll get it out of your kitchen as soon as we get back."

"You don't have to do that."

"I want to."

Megan pulled up to the gate that secured the maintenance yard and waved her passcard in front of the sensor. The gate opened and she drove through. "Thanks, but it's really no big deal. I'll do it."

"I could go with you if you want."

"It's all right. I'm not scared of her." Barbara's last hug had been claustrophobic, her insistence on being her roommate had been annoying, and grabbing her from the massage table had made her nervous, but... Okay, so she was scared of her.

"She's still filling up your voice mail?"

Megan drove past the communal compost heap and parked by the nearest Dumpster. "I just have to wait it out. She's got to stop eventually with the calls and the gifts."

Kira paused with her hands on her seat belt buckle. "Once Trish hires a receptionist to book spa appointments, you're welcome to have them take your calls as well. Whether or not you move your office to the hotel."

"Wow, that's...thanks, but...that's not necessary."

"I know, I know. You like screening the perverts yourself." Kira unsnapped her seat belt.

"I'm good at it," Megan objected.

"You *are* good at it. I've seen you in action." Kira opened the door and started to get out. "But just because you're good at it doesn't mean you have to do it."

Megan got out and circled to the passenger side to seize the trash bag from Kira's hands. She wanted to be the one to get rid of the brownies and purge herself of Barbara's oppressive energy. She swung the plastic bag back, overhead, and into the Dumpster's unseen depths. It landed with a soft thump.

It was such a muted sound, so unsatisfying. She swung her arm again and slammed her hand into the side of the Dumpster. The impact reverberated up and down her arm. Ow. She whimpered and tried to shake the pain out of her wrist. She didn't know it was going to hurt like that.

"Megan. Honey. Come on." Kira pulled Megan into her arms before she could do herself any more unintentional damage. "We'll take care of this. I won't let her scare you." Kira slid one hand up the back of her neck and stroked her hair upward, sending chills down to her tailbone. Their lips connected and Kira's mouth moved softly against hers, gentle and reassuring.

Megan pulled back, gasping for breath. She sagged on weak legs. Kira was being so careful with her, so kind.

"You're not still worrying about that psycho client of yours, are you?" Kira whispered into her hair. "Don't think about her right now."

"I'm not."

"Glad to hear it."

She kissed her again. Megan relaxed into Kira's body and stopped worrying about anything at all—not Barbara, not soul mates, not fate. Kira was hers, and she was not going to give her up.

Kira must have sensed her surrender because this time, her kiss was different—it wasn't careful and reassuring anymore. Kira was losing control, and Megan was too, driven by the feel of Kira's desperation and a level of need within herself she'd never, ever felt. How had she fought this for so long? When she realized her hand was already inside the front of Kira's jeans and she had not thought twice about unzipping them, even though they were outside in the maintenance yard where anyone could drive in at any moment and see them, she groaned. "We have to stop."

"Why?" Kira chased her lips and recaptured them. It wasn't that hard to do.

Megan's hands shook as she zipped up Kira's jeans and fastened the button, which was a lot harder to do than the reverse, especially when her mouth was busy meeting Kira's onslaught. She pulled away from the kiss so she could concentrate, regretted it immediately, and went back for more. Kira pressed her up against the Dumpster and pushed one thigh between her legs.

The sound of the gate opening on its rattling gears made Megan freeze. Kira muttered a curse. She stepped back with a slow caress down Megan's arm, as if she couldn't bear to stop touching her.

"Your house is closest," Kira suggested, pulling her toward the car.

"Your place isn't that far."

"Yes, it is. Besides, I'm planning to distract you on the way."

Megan batted her eyelashes at her as they got into the car. "In that case, I'm definitely taking the long way."

CHAPTER TWENTY-ONE

Megan grabbed her mail from her mailbox on her way in the door. Bills, pleas from charities, junk and a letter from the National Therapeutic Massage Certification Association that looked interesting. She pulled out the letter and dropped the envelope into the recycling bin.

OFFICIAL SUMMONS, the letter read. Megan's stomach dropped.

Dear Ms. McLaren, certified member no. 270164:

We have been advised of a possible violation of the NTMCA's Code of Ethics, specifically Standard I (Professionalism) and Standard VI, Part d (Sexual Misconduct).

Megan was vaguely aware of the sound of the letter opener clattering to the floor. She checked the name at the top of the letter, certain it had to have been mailed to the wrong person. No, it was her name all right. How could this happen? She was always so careful. The only person she'd ever been less than professional with was Barbara Fenhurst. And Gwynnie, of course, but that was years ago, and Gwynne would never do something like this. She couldn't see Barbara doing this, either, but only because it would never occur to Barbara that massage therapists actually had ethical guidelines they were supposed to follow.

This complaint was filed by Ms. Barbara Fenhurst as a result of events that occurred in June through August of this year.

Barbara? Of course it was Barbara. It all made a sick kind of sense. She couldn't get what she wanted, so she figured out a way to get revenge. A very effective way. Of course she was lying about the sexual misconduct, but how could anyone prove that? And even if Megan could convince the committee it was a lie, Barbara still might be able to get her on a professionalism charge, considering the way she pushed her way out of that last stranglehold of a hug. Fortunately she didn't think she could lose her license over *that*. Could she?

We have scheduled a review of these allegations for September 19 at 9 a.m. at the NTMCA Regional Office in Wilmington, Delaware. Please inform us immediately if you are unable to be present on this date.

* * *

"No way," Kira sputtered, accidentally getting a mouthful of seawater from treading water too vigorously when Megan told her about the letter. "No. Way."

Megan took off in a flurry of arms and legs, speeding away from her and from shore. Kira followed. She'd never seen Megan react like this. One minute she swam like a madwoman, the next she seemed to barely be able to move. Kira kept abreast of her, keeping an eye on her the whole time, afraid to put her head underwater and miss the moment she started to drown. She knew Megan was a good swimmer, but the way her body slowed down and stopped working, like it wasn't worth the effort to stay afloat, scared her. She was much more comfortable when Megan was pounding through the water in fury.

"She won't win," Kira said when Megan slowed down and flipped onto her back and floated. "They'll never take her side."

"I don't have any proof," Megan said, her face to the sky.

"It's obvious she's lying."

"It's my word against hers."

"She's lying!"

"Yeah, I know, but the truth is, I wasn't one hundred percent professional with her. Even if they don't get me for the alleged groping, they might get me for the way I acted with her that last time. For assault."

"For pushing her?" Megan's excessive conscientiousness had better not be what made her lose this fight.

"I pushed her pretty hard. And I shouldn't have yelled at her."

"Your idea of yelling wouldn't be loud enough to scare a mouse."

"Yelling is not always about decibels."

"I'll bet it is to the police." Whatever Megan thought she'd done, it couldn't have been that bad. "Look, if she wanted to get you for assault, she'd have called the cops. She knows she can't pin anything on you."

"I hope you're right."

"They'll believe you. If they have any sense at all, they'll believe you. Of all the people this could happen to, you are the last person who deserves to be accused of having sex with her clients, or of being unprofessional in *any* way. You're so careful about that."

"Turns out that being careful didn't protect me." Megan spun herself in violent circles, kicking up turbulence, but her voice was flat. "Besides, I wasn't careful that last time. I panicked."

"They're not going to take away your license for pushing her."

Megan stopped spinning and rubbed water over her face and out of her eyes. "Just the groping, you think?"

Hearing the vulnerability in her quiet voice as she struggled to keep it light sent Kira into another silent round of swearing. "I'll go to the hearing with you and set them straight."

"No one's allowed inside. Anyway, Svetlana already offered to go."

She told Svetlana about this before telling her? "We can both go. We'll wait for you outside."

"You sure? If you're going, I'll tell Svetlana not to cancel her clients."

"I'm definitely going with you."

Megan disappeared underwater and Kira didn't let herself blink until she saw her re-emerge. Megan ducked under again and grabbed Kira's waist, tangling their legs on her way up. Kira grunted at the impact and hugged her back, even though they were both struggling to keep their heads above water and they were far from shore.

Megan pushed them both to the surface and let go. "I'll try not to grope you in front of the committee," she said, sounding almost normal. "It might look bad."

* * *

Megan stood next to Kira in front of a rack of fashionable business suits she couldn't imagine wearing. She was deathly unexcited about picking one out, but she needed one to face the committee in. "Am I looking for a skirt suit or a pantsuit?"

"I think pantsuits are more businesslike." Kira pulled one off the rack and held it up to Megan's body appraisingly. "But that's only because skirt suits turn me on. All I can think about is getting my hand up that short hemline."

Megan paused in the act of taking the hanger from Kira's grasp. "A skirt suit is not sexy."

"Sure it is."

Megan hung the suit back on the rack. "It's staid and boring."

"That's what's so great about it—knowing that underneath that proper, professional exterior is a woman who wants me."

"Not helping."

"You're worrying about this too much. They're not going to be judging you on your clothes."

No, they weren't. The NTMCA Ethics Committee was going to be judging her on how well she defended herself, and she was not looking forward to that. How did you defend yourself against a lie? Still, she wanted the committee to take her seriously, and dressing professionally wouldn't hurt. "These all look so uncomfortable."

Kira drifted off in hunting mode. She waved Megan over to a rack of suits that were less boxy and more like her typical drapey, flowing clothes. "Here, look at these. These look comfortable, don't they?"

"For a suit, maybe," Megan conceded.

"Feel how soft this one is." Kira caressed the arm of a silky-looking jacket and held it out for Megan to feel.

It did feel soft.

"It comes in both pants and a skirt."

"You think I should get the pants?"

"Whatever you feel more comfortable in. If you happen to pick the skirt, that'll just be a bonus for me."

Megan found her size—in a pantsuit—and handed it to Kira to carry for her. She was too worried about the hearing to be anything but irritated that she had to spend money on something she would never wear again. "How could these hideous skirt suits possibly be a turn-on? Are you making this up to try to make me feel better?"

Kira shook her head, but her broad grin kind of ruined the effect. She walked over to a mannequin, ran her thumb along the hem of the mannequin's skirt, and winked. "I can't believe you dated a lawyer and you don't know what I'm talking about."

"Amelia's business suits did not turn me on," Megan snapped.

"You missed out."

Megan flung another suit at Kira.

"Ah, a skirt." Kira held the suit up to get a good look before draping it over her arm. "Do I get to watch you try this on?"

Megan glared at her.

"Oh, come on, I hate shopping. I ought to get something in return for my fashion advice."

Granted, Megan was grateful to have the advice of someone with a job that did occasionally require business attire, but they both knew Kira was the one who had insisted she take her shopping. "You promised to help me prepare for the questions if I let you come along," Megan reminded her. "There was no mention of fashion advice."

"I'll think of some good questions while you're changing."

"Questions about what happened with Barbara Fenhurst."

"Of course questions about what happened with Barbara Fenhurst. What else would I—"

"Hard questions."

Kira came closer, steely-eyed, ready to prove herself. "Why did you encourage Ms. Lunatic to schedule late-night appointments with you?"

Megan stiffened. She'd been so sure Kira wouldn't behave that the question caught her off-guard. She'd expected a not-quite-under-her-breath question about her underwear, not this. And she was annoyed with how defensive the question made her. She had to get over that if she wanted to give intelligent responses at the hearing. "I don't consider six thirty to be late."

"Why did you encourage her to continue seeing you when you couldn't cure her? When her pain showed no improvement resulting from your treatment? Isn't that unethical?"

No improvement? Did Kira honestly think... Okay, trick question. Kira was better at this than she'd realized. "Misleading, but good. I'll have to think about that one."

"In the meantime..." Kira stopped outside the entrance to the fitting rooms and handed her the clothes she'd been carrying for her. She looked so hopeful.

"You can wait outside."

Kira bent close to her ear and muttered, "Was waiting *inside* the fitting room with you actually an option? Because that's kind of what you made it sound like."

Megan blushed. Of course it was an option. Just...not today, not when she was trying on a suit that needed to give off an aura of unassailable appropriateness. She hugged the clothes to her chest and slipped inside one of the rooms. "Let's just get this over with."

"Take your time," Kira said sweetly, catching the door as it swung shut. She held the door ajar and spoke through the opening in a lowered voice. "You're really not going to ask me in so I can see how they look on you?"

"I don't think so."

"I'm a woman. I'm allowed in here. No one will notice."

Megan hung the suits on a hook. "That's not what's stopping me." She placed the palm of her hand on the center of Kira's chest and gave a gentle yet pointed push. Kira immediately stepped back and let her lock the door. So different from the last time she'd had to push someone out. She loved her for that.

"The saleslady would be more than happy to unlock this door if I asked her to," Kira teased.

"That I'd like to see."

"What *I'd* like to see is—"

"I might need your advice about the length of the hemline," Megan said, raising her voice to be sure Kira would hear her through the closed door. She didn't need to whisper in her ear to pay her back and put her imagination to work. "I'll measure it by hand lengths and you can tell me exactly where you want me to stop."

CHAPTER TWENTY-TWO

Inside the nondescript office building in downtown Wilmington that housed the National Therapeutic Massage Certification Association's regional office, the three members of the Ethics Committee sat at one end of a small, outdated conference room behind a long table on which lay a laptop computer, a voice recorder and several stacks of paper. Megan and Barbara faced the committee from behind two smaller desks. They had both been provided with an official copy of the complaint, a pencil, a glass and a sweating pitcher of ice water—massage therapists did love to encourage everyone to stay hydrated. Megan already had a headache from the buzzing of the overhead fluorescent lighting. She couldn't decide whether pouring herself a glass of water would help, or whether it would make her even more anxious by adding a full bladder to her list of stressors.

The lead investigator—Ms. Ariana Poplin—glanced at her watch and nodded to one of the women next to her, who switched on the voice recorder. "As we all know, Ms. Fenhurst has made some serious accusations against Ms. McLaren," she began. "If we decide that Ms. McLaren did in fact engage in sexual misconduct, we will revoke her national certification. The behavior of which Ms. Fenhurst accuses Ms. McLaren is a violation of Standard VI, Part d, which states that the practitioner shall not touch the client's genitalia at any time. We will also consider whether Ms. McLaren was in violation of Standard I, professionalism."

They had arrived in Wilmington early. Kira had helped her fuss with her appearance in front of the restroom mirror, smoothing the collar of her blouse and the lapels of the chocolate brown jacket they'd picked out together, teasing her about her pantsuit, tucking a flyaway hair into place. Megan had felt prepared. But now, with Kira waiting in the reception area outside the conference room where she'd left her looking calm and gorgeous in her own business clothes, Megan wondered how prepared she really was. Two minutes in and her blouse stuck to her body and she already stank.

"You seem to have received a lot of massages from Ms. McLaren," Ms. Poplin told Barbara. Her voice sounded far away. Megan strained to hear above the roaring in her head. "That would suggest you liked her work. Would you say she was a good massage therapist?"

"Yes, at first," Barbara conceded, patting her hair and touching up her lipstick. "Until she touched me inappropriately."

This couldn't be happening. And since when did Barbara know the meaning of the word "inappropriate"?

"Could you tell us what happened during that last appointment?" Ms. Poplin asked.

Taking her time, Barbara nonchalantly snapped her lipstick shut. "We were about halfway through the massage when she started working on my legs, massaging my inner thighs. She kept going higher and higher up my leg and then, you know, before I hardly even realized what was happening, she was touching my privates, massaging my crotch. I wasn't wearing any underwear, of course—you're supposed to be naked. I never expected her to take advantage of me, her being a woman and all. But that's what she did. Made the moves on me. I couldn't believe it. I jumped off the table and yelled at her to take her hands off me."

"That never happened," Megan protested.

"We'll ask the questions," Ms. Poplin reprimanded her.

Megan shrank back in her seat. Yes, she'd walked in here knowing what Barbara Fenhurst was going to accuse her of, but nevertheless it was a shock to hear her say it out loud. How could she make up such a big, disgusting lie? How could she make up those details? After all the love Megan had poured into her during so many massages? How could anyone—especially Barbara, who always raved about her healing hands—hate her so much?

"Then you got dressed and left?" Ms. Poplin said.

"She begged me to make another appointment," Barbara said smugly.

Megan put her head in her hands.

"And you never returned," Ms. Poplin prompted.

"To tell you the truth I think she kind of fell in love with me, seeing me every week." Barbara looked proud of herself, impressed with her own version of reality. "Monday nights at six thirty, that was our day. Never missed a week. Well, there was that one time—"

"My question was, did you return?" Ms. Poplin said.

"Why would I?"

Sure, lie about that too. She should have saved those damn brownies and brought them as proof. And she should never, ever have torched the stack of handwritten greeting cards begging her to take her back.

"Ms. Fenhurst, back in mid-July, you had a massage with Ms. McLaren every day for five days in a row. Do you remember why you did that?"

"My back was acting up," Barbara said.

"Did Ms. McLaren pressure you to come in every day? Coerce you in some way?"

"It was her idea to schedule five massages that week," Megan interjected. "I think it was her birthday."

Ms. Poplin ignored her. "Ms. *Fenhurst*, did Ms. McLaren encourage you to get several massages a week?"

"I'm sure she wanted my business."

"You must have felt close to her after so many visits. Did you ever suspect she was inebriated during a session?"

"Uh..." Barbara looked like she couldn't decide which answer would be more incriminating, but finally just shrugged. "Uh...not really."

Before that small victory could sink in, it was Megan's turn to talk.

"Ms. McLaren, did you encourage Ms. Fenhurst to schedule frequent appointments with you? Did you suggest that she see you every day?"

"I usually recommend that my clients see me once a week or once a month, depending on their needs. It's up to them what they want to schedule."

Ms. Poplin shuffled some papers on her desk. "Both of you agree on the date the alleged incident occurred, but Ms. McLaren, in your treatment notes we see no mention of this session. Are we missing some of your treatment notes?"

"I think you have everything," Megan said. "I didn't make any notes for that session."

"It certainly would have been incriminating for you to write down what occurred if Ms. Fenhurst's allegations are correct."

"That's not what happened."

"Then why did you not make any notes for this massage, when you were so consistent about making notes for all her other sessions?"

"I was too upset. I should have written something down, I guess—and I wish I had so you could see it—but I was too upset and I forgot."

"So something did happen during that massage," Ms. Poplin suggested.

Megan paled. Barbara had fooled the committee. As the investigator looked at her expectantly, she felt her blood pressure drop and wondered if she was going to faint. The room turned to fog. She saw herself at the stake, flames licking at her feet. In that lifetime, people had killed her to stop her from healing the sick. They knew she was good at it and they killed her anyway. They killed her *because* she was good at it. The same thing was happening again. Barbara Fenhurst, with her stupid play for revenge, could take away her license and stop her from doing the job she loved.

She wasn't going to let her. She was not going to let this happen again. Not this time. She wasn't bound to a stake this time. She could fight. She could win this thing.

Megan rubbed her eyes and the room swam back into focus. "Something did happen," she said. "Barbara asked me out on a date. I immediately terminated the session and told her I couldn't work with her anymore. She didn't take it well. She made up this whole lie about sexual contact to get back at me."

Ms. Poplin's expressionless face never changed. "Did you touch her genitals at any time?"

"Never."

"How about in a therapeutic manner?"

"That's against our code of ethics."

"Glad to know you're familiar with that." Ms. Poplin turned to Barbara. "How did Ms. McLaren drape you? Did you feel securely covered by the sheet at all times?"

"She told me it was better not to lie under the sheet if I didn't want to. I think she wanted to see me naked." Barbara glanced over at Megan and smirked.

Megan gave her an angry, tight-lipped smile in return. The liar thought she could get away with this. She thought she was winning. But she hadn't won yet.

"How did you feel about this optional draping, Ms. Fenhurst?"

"I thought it was inappropriate."

Megan thought back to her notes. She'd looked over them dozens of times in the past week, but she hadn't known what she was looking for—it was all muscles and techniques, reminders to herself about what she had worked on. The committee had requested her notes, but what could the notes tell the committee? Nothing. They couldn't honestly be hoping she wrote down in her treatment notes that she had sex with a client.

But draping—that was another story. Megan's heart flooded with relief. Barbara had just handed her the proof she needed.

"Ms. McLaren," Ms. Poplin said. "Do you deny this allegation that you encouraged Ms. Fenhurst to be undraped?"

They knew. Ms. Poplin and the others knew Barbara was lying. At least about the draping. And since the draping had not been part of Barbara's original complaint, Megan would have had no reason to lie about it in her notes. They had to know.

Megan tried not to show her elation. "Absolutely," she said. "I always drape my clients securely. It's very important to me to be conscientious about that so my clients feel safe."

"There is some leeway—some difference of opinion—as to what constitutes appropriate draping. Ms. Fenhurst, did Ms. McLaren at a minimum cover your pubic region with a small towel?"

Megan waited for Barbara to dig herself in deeper.

"Nope. I was buck naked," Barbara said.

Megan sat up straighter. "Ma'am, I'd like you to look at my notes from her first two visits. I know I made a note to myself to remind Barbara about proper draping procedures during future visits. I had to insist that she stay under the sheet."

Ms. Poplin pointed to something in her files and showed it to the woman seated next to her, who nodded. She looked up from her files and looked sternly at Barbara from over her reading glasses. "We do see that in the notes."

"She could've written those notes last week for all we know," Barbara complained. "She could've lied in there about all kinds of stuff."

"Yes, that is always a possibility," Ms. Poplin said.

Megan tensed. No. They were not going to believe Barbara. They couldn't.

"She did say a few minutes ago that she liked my work up until our last visit," Megan said, thinking fast. "She came back every week, week after week. That's a lot of money to pay someone who's making you uncomfortable. Why would she keep coming back if she didn't like the way I draped her?"

"Ms. Fenhurst?"

"I didn't say being naked made me *uncomfortable*," Barbara groused. "I said I thought it was *inappropriate*."

"So you do know the meaning of the word," Megan snapped.

"Thank you," Ms. Poplin said. "We're going to deliberate on the information you've provided. When we've come to a decision—"

A siren interrupted her—the building's fire alarm. One of the committee members flinched and pressed her hands to her ears.

Ms. Poplin glanced at her colleagues. "What should we do?"

"We should get the hell out of here," Megan said. She grabbed her purse off the floor and hastened out the door without looking back. Fire alarms made her twitchy.

Kira was sitting in the reception area, watching the door to the conference room. Her face lit up when she saw her.

Megan reached for her hand. "Let's go."

"It's probably a false alarm," Kira said, but she followed her out into the hall and toward the stairway, anyway.

"I hope you're right." Her legs wanted to run, but she forced herself to keep to a fast, purposeful walk.

They trotted down the stairs and made it down several flights before a small group entered the stairwell from a lower floor and impeded their progress. Megan's nerves twitched with impatience. People just did not take these things seriously enough. It was a fire alarm, people. Get out!

"Almost there." Kira tightened her grip on her hand.

Megan barely felt her touch. She was too focused on how good the heavy emergency exit door was going to feel beneath her hands when she pushed it open.

The door was already propped open when they reached it. Once she was out, the relief was immediate. They crossed the street and finally looked back. A steady trickle of people flowed out of the building from all sides. Kira led her farther down the street and into the shade of a sheltered alcove in front of a bank.

"You okay?" Angling her body so no one from the street would see, Kira smoothed the hairs on Megan's forearm.

"Yeah."

"How's the hearing going? You winning?"

"God, I hope so." Megan slumped against the support of the building's marble façade. "I didn't expect Barbara to lie so much."

"Lying is the only way she could have convinced them to hold this hearing in the first place."

"I know. When I read that thing in the mail it was obvious she had lied, of course. But I didn't really believe she would go through with it." Megan pounded the back of her shoulders into the wall. "I didn't think she'd be able to lie to my face. All those times she complained about having to stay underneath a sheet. All those times. I fought her on that and *now* she accuses *me* of not wanting to drape her." She would have kept banging herself against the wall if Kira hadn't put her hands on her shoulders and gently pried her away from it.

"How did she even know there was a rule about using a sheet?" Kira asked. "I can't see her figuring out that that would be enough to make you lose your certification."

"I don't think she did. What she actually accused me of was…was inappropriate…t-t-t…" Somehow Barbara had managed to say it in front of a roomful of people, but Megan was having trouble spitting it out to an audience of one. It wasn't this hard when she talked to horny male callers on the phone, when she was the one in charge and had the moral high ground. "Inappropriate…" She still had the moral high ground. The only problem was that not everyone knew that. "…Inappropriate…"

"I know," Kira said, saving her from the need to say more. Her fingers dug into Megan's shoulders. "I wonder how she figured out *that* could make you lose your certification."

Megan freed herself from Kira's death grip. She was sure Kira meant it to be reassuring, but it was starting to be painful. "Good question."

"It's going to be all right."

"I hope so. I hope the committee's on my side."

* * *

Twenty minutes later the firefighters who'd shown up shuffled back to their truck, looking bored that there was no fire. While Kira went in search of coffee, Megan followed the crowd back into the building. She wanted to hang back for a few minutes in case the firefighters missed something, but knew she had to go in.

When she reached the NTMCA office, Barbara was waiting in the reception area.

"They're deciding what to do about you," Barbara informed her. "They said we have to wait here for thirty minutes."

Megan directed a fake smile at the receptionist. "I'm going to wait outside, if you don't mind. I'll be back in half an hour."

"I'll let them know," said the receptionist.

"They said to wait here," Barbara said.

Megan kept her fake smile as she backed away, afraid to turn her back on her former client until she was out the door.

* * *

"Therapeutic massage is a service fraught with the potential for misunderstandings and sexual misconduct," Ms. Poplin pronounced, reading from a sheet of paper. "The onus falls on the practitioner, who is taught ethical standards and boundary-setting, to create a safe environment and to protect the client from any real or imagined violation of boundaries. It is the responsibility of the practitioner to—"

How long was she going to ramble on like this? All her fidgeting outside while the committee made their decision had raised Megan's anxiety level to the point where she could barely process what Ms. Poplin was saying.

"...guard against impropriety..."

"...highest ethical standards..."

Was this directed at her? Did they find her in violation? Did she misread them during the hearing? Megan stared at her hands clasped in her lap, her stubby fingernails digging into the flesh.

"We find Ms. McLaren to be not in violation of NTMCA standards."

Megan slumped in her seat with relief. "Thank God."

* * *

Megan woke with Kira's arm flung across her ribcage, her fingers curled lightly around her arm, holding her even in sleep. She traced lazy patterns with her fingertips on Kira's skin, reveling in how good it felt just to be near her.

"You have clients today?" Kira asked, her eyes still shut.

Megan snuggled closer. "Since I didn't lose my license yesterday, yes." She wished she could keep touching her for the next twenty-four hours. She'd have to get out of bed eventually, but right now all she could think about was here within reach.

"Are you free for lunch? We should celebrate," Kira said.

"I thought last night was our celebration." After Kira had driven her home, Megan had been so worn out from the hearing that she'd slept the rest of the afternoon. Kira had made dinner, and by then Megan was too well-rested to go back to sleep. She didn't have any trouble talking Kira into an extended discussion on when it was appropriate for a vindicated massage therapist to remove someone else's clothing, and how exactly it should be done.

Kira moved so she was on top of her. "I think we need to celebrate more. Don't you?"

She totally agreed, but reality intruded. "Can we make it dinner? I have a couple of clients in the afternoon, but no one after five."

"That long from now?" Kira moved against her enticingly.

"I could stop by at noon for a few minutes, just to say hi."

"As long as stopping by involves this." Kira angled her head to kiss her neck.

Megan's hips started a slow, involuntary undulation. "Why do you think I suggested saying hi in person instead of over the phone?"

* * *

Megan's phone rang a few hours later as she was walking to Kira's hotel. She glanced at the number displayed on her phone and decided she might have to take Kira up on her offer of having the spa's receptionist handle her calls, because why, why, why in the world was Barbara Fenhurst calling her?

Against her better judgment, Megan picked up. And instinctively yanked the phone away from her ear at Barbara's screech of joy before she damaged her eardrum.

"I'm moving to Richmond!" Barbara announced.

Megan glared at the phone. She should hang up on her. But she did want to hear this—it sounded like good news for everyone. Cautiously, she moved the phone closer to her ear.

"I wanted to let you know so you can update your address book," Barbara said.

"Okay." Megan didn't know quite what to say.

"I wish you could meet Derek."

"Derek?"

"My new boyfriend. I'm moving in with him."

"Congratulations. I'm happy for you." She really was. And relieved. Barbara would be hours away, and in love—a combination that should guarantee she'd never hear from her again. She ought to send this guy a thank-you card.

"Isn't it wonderful? And guess what? Derek is a masseur. He's a professional, like you. And he's such a hottie. We gave each other massages last night. Nude massages." Barbara paused expectantly, but Megan really didn't think this information deserved a response. Did Barbara seriously think this would make her jealous? Did she want her to regret what she lost when she turned her away? "He says I could do it professionally. Maybe a four hands kind of deal, where we both massage one person at the same time."

Who was this guy? She was positive she knew all the massage people in Piper Beach, and he wasn't one of them. "How did you meet?" Not on Derek's massage table, she hoped.

"In Wilmington. I ran into him in the lobby yesterday after the hearing."

"He works for the NTMCA?" That actually was more disturbing to her than the idea that Barbara was moving in with a guy she'd only met the day before.

"No, he was there for an ethics hearing, too. Sexual misconduct. It wasn't his fault, though—the woman was out to get him. She won, but he's going to get himself reinstated, and in the meantime he says he can still run his practice as long as he doesn't call it massage."

Megan swallowed the protest lodged in her throat. Sounded like those two deserved each other. She hung up and immediately called Kira.

"Guess what? Barbara's moving to Richmond."

"She called you?" Kira, not surprisingly, did not sound pleased. "She never gives up, does she? You'd think after what she put you through yesterday, she'd stop harassing you."

"I think this may be the last time I hear from her. She can't swing by my house if she's in another state."

"If you ask me, Richmond is not far enough away."

"Richmond is good!" Megan protested.

"She still has a phone."

"She won't use it." She'd be far too busy performing four-hands massage.

"Did I tell you I ran into her in the ladies' room yesterday when we were waiting for the verdict? She thinks I'm the reason you won't talk to her. She doesn't seem to grasp that she did anything wrong."

"She'll forget about me eventually."

"Maybe," Kira said. "What's she doing in Richmond, anyway?"

"She's going to become a massage therapist." Megan giggled, then clapped her hand over her mouth, appalled by her inappropriate reaction.

"I bet she just said that to piss you off. Since she lost at the hearing yesterday."

"Let's hope."

"So when are you coming over?" Kira's voice softened to a caress. "Soon?"

Her legs weakened and her stride faltered and slowed. "I'm already on my way. Is it still okay for me to drop by?"

"My dad's here, actually, but he usually doesn't stay long. Do you want to meet him?"

Fifteen minutes later Megan was inside the hotel lobby shaking hands with Kira's dad, Jason Wagner.

"I was just telling Kira what a great job the two of you did with this property," he said, beaming proudly at them both. "Kira, I'm going to send your mother out here for a massage once you've got the spa operational."

"You should come with her," Kira suggested.

He raised his hands, palms out, and shook his head. "Not me. I know you don't want men setting foot in this place."

"I can make an exception for you."

"No need," he said magnanimously.

"You're just afraid Mom and I are going to talk you into getting a spa treatment."

"Busted." He winked at Megan. "But I'll bet your spa's going to be a hit with the ladies."

Her spa? Megan looked questioningly at Kira, who shook her head helplessly with a smile that said no, she hadn't made her spa manager behind her back.

"Has my daughter talked you into sticking around yet?"

What was he talking about? Megan wanted to make a good impression, but that was hard to do when she felt like she'd missed a huge chunk of the conversation. She wished she'd asked Kira on the phone for details and found out what she'd told him about her—about them. Not that they'd even discussed the direction of their relationship with each other—they'd just fallen into bed together and assumed... Well, what *had* Kira assumed?

Mr. Wagner wasn't done. "Has she talked you into working with her on her next hotel?"

Her next hotel? Megan looked at him stupidly. Was *that* what he meant by "sticking around"? She knew Kira had moved several times in the last few years, searching for the right properties to invest in, but somehow she'd assumed she would stay in Piper Beach for her next project. But that was dumb. There weren't any other dilapidated hotels for Kira to transform in this small town.

Oh, no. Megan had been so trusting, so overconfident in her ability to sense what Kira was feeling, that it hadn't even occurred to her to ask about her plans. When Kira told her she was going to get the hotel up and running before she tried to sell it, why hadn't she thought to ask whether that meant in a couple of years, or in a few short months? Construction would be finished soon. When exactly had Kira planned to tell her she was leaving town for her next job? Megan wasn't sure she could handle a long-distance relationship. Physical touch was so vital to her ability to communicate, to sensing and conveying emotion. And what if she'd moved her massage office into the hotel, only to find herself stuck in a building owned by a stranger who didn't want her there?

So she'd move her office back, and she'd figure out how to have a long-distance relationship. She'd adapt. Unless Kira was counting on having a ready-made excuse for ending things once she lost interest—which she didn't want to believe—they'd find a way to work it out. She just wished Kira had been the one to break this to her, not her dad.

"I don't know if there's going to be a next hotel, Dad." Kira looked straight at Megan as she said it.

We'll talk later, Kira mouthed silently behind her father's back.

Megan's eyes blinked rapidly, erratically.

We'd better, she mouthed back.

* * *

Kira straightened as her dad pivoted to face her. She could not believe he had opened his big mouth, presuming things he had no business presuming. Her employment choices were her own. If she didn't want to continue jumping from one new project to the next, chasing the thrill he was addicted to—the excitement he got from starting over—that was her choice.

Her dad threw his shoulders back and seemed to grow taller. "Why wouldn't there be a next hotel?" It was more an attack than a question. "Don't tell me you're going back to the restaurant business."

"Of course not. I—"

"I know a great property in Philly you could snatch up. It's the perfect location for another hotel/spa combo. You put Megan in charge of designing the spa. She provides the vision; you're in charge of construction. You'll make a great team. You *are* a great team. You've already proven that."

Kira knew from the way Megan was staring at her that she looked as stunned as she felt. It was just like him to think he could tell Megan what to do—to barge in and delegate the job like he was the one in charge—but what was interesting was how much he seemed to instantly like her. He'd never been so openly supportive of the choices Kira had made in her personal life. Tolerant, yes, for the most part. But he'd hated Lizzy for talking her into opening a restaurant. When it came to business, he always said, she had to learn not to think with her dick. How equal opportunity of him. But even though he'd hated the spa idea, too, at first, somehow Megan had managed to win him over.

He couldn't boss Megan around, though. Did he not understand?

Her eyes narrowed. "We are a good team, but it's not *just* a work relationship."

He shoved his hands in his pockets and rocked back on his heels, looking slightly uncomfortable. "I know, pumpkin. You don't have to spell it out for me."

CHAPTER TWENTY-THREE

"I thought I'd find you here."

Megan turned at the sound of Kira's voice just as the sea lifted her feet off the ground. Kira was grinning at the water's edge with her Windbreaker unzipped and her hands in her pockets, and Megan found herself grinning back. It was so easy to forgive her, so easy to push aside her anxieties about their future.

"Come on in," Megan yelled, wading through the surf toward her.

"In my jeans? No, thanks."

"What you wear is totally up to you."

"The water looks cold."

"Are you kidding me? It's really not." Summer might be officially over, but the ocean hadn't gotten the memo yet. It would be another month before the bracing cold returned. "The water's warmer than it was in June."

"The air's not."

Probably true, considering the overcast skies—which

was all the more reason to be in the water. "Other people are swimming."

"Other people are wading. You're the only one in there up to your neck."

Only to her waist, at this point. Megan reversed course and walked backward, hoping to lead Kira into the waves. "So... wade. Put your feet in the water."

"I'd rather put my feet in one of my new hot tubs." Kira pumped her fists in a victory dance. "We hooked up the ones in the woods today."

After Kira had made the decision to build the spa inside the hotel instead of in a separate building, they had brainstormed what to do with the land next door and decided to hide a large gazebo and several small hot tubs among the trees, carefully positioned under Megan's guidance to avoid interfering with the ley lines. Tall shrubs were planted around each tub for privacy.

"Want to test it out?" Kira asked. "The water will be nice and warm."

"Wuss."

"You won't think so when you feel my hands all over you."

Megan's body tightened. A wave smacked into her, pushing her forward. "If that's what you want, you'll have to swim out here," she taunted, swimming farther out, where it was safer. Kira should be in the water with her if she was going to say things like that. That way she could grab her perfectly shaped ass and remind her there were other people around who could hear.

"Not if I can convince you to try out the hot tub," Kira shouted after her.

"And how are you going to do that?"

Kira rubbed her arms as if she were cold inside her jacket. "Nice warm water?"

"I don't think so."

"More private?"

Megan hesitated. The end-of-season sunbathers were starting to pack up and clear out for the day, but the beach was by no means as deserted as she would like it to be.

"It's closer to the ley lines," Kira said.

"Now you're really reaching."

"If that's what I've got to do to tempt you…"

All Kira had to do was say she was going to be there. That was already quite tempting enough.

"Your workers are gone?" Megan said.

"Every last one."

"What about dinner? I thought we were going out."

"Not for another hour. Unless you want to go eat now."

"No, that's all right." Megan waited for the next wave to roll out, timed her exit, and strode to shore. They had to talk, and it would be easier to do that in private. She ran the last few steps to shore and Kira reached for her hand.

"Wait. I need my clothes."

Megan headed for the spot where she'd left her tote bag in the sand. She stepped into her flip-flops and slipped on a hooded cover-up she figured could pass for a dress, although the way Kira was checking out the hemline that skimmed high on her bare thighs, she might have to rethink that assumption.

"Do you have to put that on?" Kira said.

Megan slung her bag over her shoulder. "Why? Because you're going to help me take it off soon anyway?"

Kira flipped Megan's hood onto her head. She smoothed a wet strand of hair away from her face, tucking it under the hood. "You know me so well."

Did she? Megan wasn't so sure about that anymore.

* * *

In the woods next to the hotel, steam rose from a hot tub sunken into the ground to look like a natural spring. Megan took off her cover-up but kept her bathing suit on before she stepped in.

Kira was less modest.

Considerate of her. Megan smiled, taking in the view.

"You like our idea?" Kira asked.

"Genius." A stack of folded white towels on a low wooden bench nearby made it clear that Kira had been confident she'd be able to talk Megan into coming here, which was a little galling, but Megan wasn't going to complain. The hot tub was almost too small for two people, which meant every time she sank lower in the water she inevitably drifted into Kira, bumping into her in a welcome way that wouldn't have happened in a giant communal tub. The evening air was cool, and made the hot water feel good. Middle-of-the-night air—for guests who were so inclined—would feel even better.

She wondered if she'd ever set foot in one of these again after Kira left. If she left. Shit. She really wanted her to stick around. If their souls had already decided that spending two—or more—previous lifetimes together wasn't enough, you'd think this wouldn't be an issue. Kira had always seemed so convinced they were meant to be together. But they'd never actually talked about the future.

"So." Megan sat up so she wouldn't keep brushing against Kira's legs. She took one of Kira's feet and massaged it with her thumbs. "Interesting talk with your dad."

Kira pulled her foot out of Megan's hands, her eyes evasive. "Yeah. About that…"

So Megan wasn't imagining things. She gripped the edge of the underwater bench and swung her hips off the seat and sat farther back. "I put all that time into helping you design this spa just so you could make money off of it and *leave?* You never said anything to me about leaving."

"I'm not leaving," Kira said.

"Then why did your dad say you were?" She wanted Kira to have an explanation. She wanted her to have a really good, really convincing, really hallelujah-now-I-can-relax explanation. She wanted her to want to stay.

Kira's jaw jutted forward and the faint lines around her mouth tightened. "Don't pay attention to him. He means well, but what he said about my leaving Piper Beach…that wasn't true."

"But it used to be true, didn't it? He wouldn't have said something like that if there wasn't some truth to it. You told me yourself about all the times you've moved. You rent apartments month-to-month and keep your stuff in storage because you know it's only temporary."

Kira didn't deny it. "This time is different. This time I have a reason to stay."

Megan narrowed her eyes at her. "What does that mean?"

Kira rubbed the hinge of her jaw as if she were trying to get the muscles to relax. "I don't want to sell the hotel anymore. It was our first big project together, you and me. I seem to have developed a sentimental attachment to it."

"To the hotel," Megan said flatly.

"And to you."

Kira slid her arches up the inside of Megan's legs and tangled their legs together in a slippery, seductive dance. Her breasts glistened through the steam.

Megan softened. And not because Kira was naked. "You're really going to stay?"

"Yes. Not because of the hotel. Because of you. I want to be with you."

Megan felt hot and slightly dizzy. "Me, too," she whispered.

Kira pulled her into her arms and pressed her lips to her tangled, wet hair. "I know I've already asked you, but if you ever want to move your massage room out of your condo, you're more than welcome to set up shop inside the hotel."

"I'll think about it," Megan said, mainly to stop her from launching into a discussion of potential business plans. This was not the time for it.

Kira touched Megan's face, caressing her cheekbones. "I want us to live together."

"That sounds way better than moving my office."

Megan kissed her and Kira moaned. Megan thought she might be moaning, too. She wrapped her legs around Kira's waist as her heart and her throat and her soul melted with desire. She needed to touch her, needed to open to her, needed to know that it was really true. She needed to get as close as she possibly could and never let her go.

* * *

Megan smelled smoke.

She shifted against Kira in the hot tub and trailed her fingers down the length of her wet arms. The smell was faint, she decided, and probably not from nearby. She always overreacted to the smell of smoke. She moved back up Kira's arms, then down her back and down her delicious legs, but as she started back up she slowed, because she was having a hard time blocking that smell from her awareness. Damn it. She wanted to block it out.

"Do you smell something burning?" she asked, giving in to defeat.

"No," Kira said. "Do you?"

"Maybe I'm imagining it."

"Could be someone's having a bonfire."

"It doesn't smell like a bonfire. It smells kind of like the time my mother left an oven mitt too close to the stove and it caught fire. It was one of those plastic polyester materials. Those fumes are toxic. I had to wash my hair a bazillion times before I could get the smell out."

"My hotel's carpeting is made out of polypropylene. The padding's synthetic, too." Kira sniffed the air, looking around worriedly. "Where is the smell coming from?"

"I don't know." Megan rubbed her wet hands over her face, hoping the smell of the hot tub's chlorinated water would distract her from the smoke and help her act like a normal person in front of this woman she didn't want to scare off. "Maybe it's burnt barbeque."

"Maybe it's not."

"You don't have to humor me."

"What makes you think I'm humoring you?"

"Because you're being nice?"

Kira splashed her. "I'm not being nice!"

"You are. You think I'm slightly nuts but you're trying to be nice about it."

"Honey. Didn't we go over this already? I like your take on reality."

"You didn't at first."

"I was a slow learner."

Kira looked so earnest and charming that Megan barely breathed.

"I'm not scaring you off?"

"I've never been scared off by you. You know I haven't."

It was true. The ley lines, the past lives... How many people could have watched her and Gwynne pull that hitchhiker out of Svetlana and not wonder if the two of them weren't a little loose in their grip on reality? Kira had disagreed with her, but she had never made her feel as if she didn't respect her and like her as a person. She had never stopped asking for her input on the spa, even when she didn't like the advice Megan gave her.

"So no matter how crazy the woo-woo factor gets," Megan said, "you accept me?"

Kira took Megan's hands and rubbed her thumbs into her palms. "What are you going to spring on me if I say yes?"

Megan couldn't tell if she was giving her a hard time or if she was honestly worried. "I think you've seen the worst of it."

"That was a joke." Kira shook her head, smiling. "I accept you. No matter what. I'll do everything I can to make you feel like you don't have to hide yourself from me." The movement of her thumbs was both hypnotic and reassuring. "And I'm not the only one who accepts your woo-woo factor, you know. Your clients accept you."

"They only know me in my role as their massage therapist. They have no idea who I am as a person. They don't count."

"Svetlana accepts you."

"Uh...no. She thinks I make up all my stories about angels. As a marketing gimmick."

"Really? Gwynne believes you, though. She accepts you."

"Gwynne dumped me."

Kira interlaced her fingers with hers. "Thank God for that."

"Maybe we'd better go make sure your hotel's not on fire," Megan suggested.

Kira gave her a swift kiss, hard and approving. "Good idea."

* * *

Megan hustled after Kira through the hotel parking lot, wringing out her wet hair and trying not to stumble in her slippery flip-flops. However much she'd loved Kira before, she loved her more now, because wasting time tracking down harmless smoke was no one's idea of a good time. Megan had done it often enough to know.

Kira stopped when they were close enough to see the front entrance of the hotel. "It looks fine from here. Which direction is the smell coming from?"

"I can't tell," Megan said anxiously. The smoke didn't have to be coming from the hotel—it could be coming from anywhere.

"We'll check inside, just to be sure."

"Thank you for being so nice about this."

"I'm not being nice. I'm worried something might be on fire."

Kira was so full of shit. "But you don't smell anything. And besides, the fire alarms aren't going off."

Kira checked her pocket for her keys. "They're not going to. They're not in service."

Megan's stomach dropped. "What? Why not?"

"We always take them out of service during a job. Otherwise the dust from the construction would constantly set them off. They're a nuisance."

"But what if something catches fire?"

"Yeah. That could be a problem."

"At least the sprinklers would go off, right?" She was pretty sure hotels were required to have those in every room.

"We don't fill the sprinklers until we're mostly done with everything else. It's too easy to break the sprinkler heads, and then you've got a big, soggy mess on your hands."

"But that's dangerous!"

"Not really. The hotel's not cleared for occupancy. It's not like we have guests smoking in there. And most of the electricity's cut off, so there's not much danger of an electrical fire."

"I'm starting to see why you're willing to believe that I smell something." The whole setup sounded like a disaster waiting to happen. Did she really have no fire protection at all? "What about those fire alarms that detect heat, not smoke?"

Kira looked pained. "Megan. It's just you and that nose of yours, okay?"

"Do you really believe me, or are you just afraid of what might happen if I'm right?"

Kira planted her hands on her hips in exasperation. "Do you want me to not believe you?"

"Of course not," Megan said meekly. Kira was going out of her way to take her seriously. The least she could do was stop fighting her.

"Good."

"I'm just not used to it," Megan added.

"You'll get used to it," Kira said matter-of-factly. "Now let's go."

CHAPTER TWENTY-FOUR

There was an angel at the hotel's front door. Guarding? Welcoming? A random coincidence? Megan couldn't tell. Kira's key ring jingled as she searched for the key she wanted. The angel unfurled her wings and splayed herself against the door.

Okay, thanks for the clarification.

"Kira?" Megan said hesitantly.

Kira stuck the key in the lock, her arm passing through the angel's transparent form.

"No!" Megan threw herself at Kira, gripping her arm to stop her from opening the door.

"What is it?"

"There's an angel here. She doesn't want us to go inside."

"Okay…" Kira sounded doubtful, but she pulled the key out of the lock and let Megan lead her a few steps away from the door. "Does that mean I need to call the fire department? I still don't smell anything, but if you do…"

"I still smell it."

"Let's go around and check the back. Maybe we'll see something from there."

The angel floated contentedly beside them, so Megan figured they were on the right track. When they rounded the corner of the building, their companion whooshed ahead and stopped by one of the ground-floor windows of the section that was not being turned into the spa, but would remain hotel rooms.

"She's waiting for us," Megan said.

Kira spotted the broken window before Megan did. "If someone broke in here and stole the copper pipes again…" Her voice trailed off. "Shit. I smell it now." She stomped right up to the window, heedless of the shrubbery, and peered inside.

Megan hung back. The smell of something burning was definitely stronger here. "Do you see anything?"

"Yeah." Kira sounded strangely calm.

Megan took a few halting steps closer. "What do you see?"

"Stand back."

"Why do *I* have to stand back?" Kira had better not do anything stupid, like crawl in through the broken window. "What's going on in there?"

Kira pulled out her phone and started punching in numbers. "That carpet was supposed to be nonflammable."

A jolt of fear hit Megan in the solar plexus. It was happening again—her karma playing itself out. Again. Her legs were frozen in place, paralyzed, pulling her back into her old dream where she couldn't run because her legs were tied.

But this wasn't a dream. Megan snapped herself out of her paralysis and ran toward Kira. She could see smoke now. Kira was standing too close, watching through the window, mesmerized, holding the phone to her ear. She had to get her away from that window. Megan took her arm and tugged. "What are you doing? Get back."

"Hang on." Kira pointed to her phone.

"We need to get out of here." She didn't want to interrupt her conversation with the 911 operator, but Kira was going to have to continue her call from a safer distance.

The floor-to-ceiling drapes burst into a wall of flame and they both jumped back.

"Come on." Megan dragged Kira away from the building. The angel was drifting through the parking lot toward the woods, so Megan headed that way too, adrenaline fueling her legs.

"I think we're far enough back now." Kira slowed to a stop, forcing Megan to stop too.

While Kira finished her call, the angel flew straight to one of the trees at the edge of the parking lot and circled it at high speed, around and around, like it was caught in an invisible tornado.

Megan pointed. "Something's going on by that tree."

Kira was still staring at her burning hotel. "Like what?"

"I don't know. But that angel is…acting weird."

"She's playing a bad game of charades with you again?"

"How did you—"

The angel stopped whirling.

"I think she heard you," Megan said.

"Why? What's she doing now?"

The angel hovered in front of the tree, leaning sideways like she was peeking behind it.

"I think something's behind that tree."

"The arsonist?" Kira hissed, fury garbling her attempt to whisper. "Which tree?"

"Follow me."

They quieted their footsteps and came closer, angling off to the right so they could see if there really was someone back there.

And there was.

Barbara Fenhurst was standing with her back as close to the trunk of the tree as she could get. In her hand was a can of gasoline.

The angel vanished, her message delivered.

"What are you doing?" Megan cried, the words flying out of her mouth before she could stop them. Barbara was the one who had set fire to the hotel? Barbara was capable of this?

Her former client turned tail and ran.

Megan chased her into the woods, clenching her toes in her flip-flops, praying she didn't trip. Kira was faster. She quickly overtook Barbara and caught her around the waist from behind and tried to push her to the ground, but although Kira was a fast runner, she unfortunately wasn't going to win any tackling awards. Barbara bucked like a rodeo horse, trying to throw her off. Kira held on, but Barbara was much bigger and heavier, easily outweighing her two-to-one, and Kira's wiry strength was not enough to overpower her.

"I could use some help here," Kira called.

Megan caught up and tried to catch hold of Barbara's arms.

"Let go." Barbara windmilled her arms, not about to cooperate. "Stop or I'll throw gas on you."

Megan glanced at the can of gasoline that had miraculously remained upright in Barbara's hand. It didn't have a cap. No wonder she could smell it. She hated the smell of gas almost as much as she hated the smell of smoke.

"Megan has this funny idea that you don't want to kill her," Kira said, holding on tight. "Don't prove her wrong."

"Not her. You."

A cry of outrage escaped Megan's throat. "You are *not* throwing gas on Kira."

Megan grabbed for the gas can. Barbara evaded her, moving the container quickly in one direction, then another. She never thought she'd see the day she'd find herself wishing an arsonist had thrown more gas on a fire, but honestly, why was there any gas left in that can? There clearly wasn't much in there—otherwise she'd hear it sloshing—but it wouldn't take much. Just a few splashes of gasoline would be more than enough to burn someone if they got near a heat source. She didn't know if Barbara had a lighter, but she didn't want to take the risk. She had to have started the fire with something.

Why hadn't they just called the police instead of running after her? They didn't need to stop Barbara themselves.

"Get away from her, Kira," Megan pleaded.

"I'm not leaving you alone with her," Kira said.

Barbara growled. She kicked backward and got Kira in

the shin. Kira rammed her foot into the back of Barbara's Achilles tendon. Megan didn't want to get anywhere near, but she grabbed for the gas container again. Kira hooked one leg around Barbara's, trying to trip her.

"Help me get her to the ground," Kira said, breathing hard.

Barbara jerked the gas can in the direction of Kira's leg.

Nothing came out.

Barbara banged on the can and tried again to shake it out. It was empty.

Kira's fancy footwork was not having much effect, but she kept trying. "Don't scare Megan like that."

"Fuck you." Barbara dropped the gas can and pulled something out of her pocket. It looked sort of like a gun. Megan wasn't sure what it was, but if Barbara was threatening them with it, she'd better try to get it away from her.

Kira recognized it, though. "A soldering torch?" She sounded incredulous. "That's how you started the fire? What… you couldn't just use a match?"

"That's right. Hot enough to melt metal. Now let go of me." Barbara pointed the torch over her shoulder at Kira's head.

Kira ducked so she was hidden behind Barbara's back and marginally out of range. "I've got her," she told Megan. "Go. Call the police."

"Like that'll do you any good," Barbara mocked.

But the good thing was that in pointing her torch, Barbara had abandoned her evasive maneuvers. It was just the opportunity Megan needed. She dove for Barbara's wrist, skidding on the sandy ground, and tried to uncurl Barbara's clenched fingers. But brute force had never been her strong suit, and Barbara was impossible to overpower. She just couldn't do it.

Brute force wasn't the only way to get her to drop that torch, though. She had a client once whose hand went numb because the nerves were compressed. If she could re-create that… She squeezed the underside of Barbara's wrist, with no effect.

"My brother told me I'd never be a fireman. He said I'd be too scared to enter a burning building. He thought because he was older, he could boss me. But he couldn't boss me. No one can boss me."

Megan moved up Barbara's arm and grabbed her elbow and dug her fingers into the groove where the ulnar nerve ran close to the surface. Maybe that would weaken her grip.

"Ow," Barbara complained, no more annoyed than if she'd accidentally hit her elbow getting onto the massage table.

Damn, the nerves weren't enough. She could really use some martial arts training right about now. "Drop. It."

"No." Barbara twisted suddenly, breaking Megan's hold. Flame shot out.

Megan screamed.

"Get away from her, Megan." Kira's voice was tight.

Shit. Was Barbara going to kill her? Was this the memory she was about to carry with her into her next life? All the elements were there: Fire. Smoke. And Kira. She'd tried to avoid all three of those, and failed.

Next time I'll do better. Next life I'll figure out a way to not get myself killed. Megan launched herself at the soldering torch with everything she had.

"Let go!" she screamed, forcing Barbara's thumb away from the ignition button.

Barbara pivoted, trying to dislodge her attackers. She turned the muzzle of the torch toward Kira's forearm, which was wrapped around her waist. Megan knocked her off her trajectory. Barbara grazed her own body with the hot tip and screamed.

"Shoot that at me and it's going to get you too," Kira warned.

Megan's heart pounded. There had to be something she could do to stop her. She was not going to let Barbara burn Kira with that horrible thing. She just wasn't.

Her arms clumsy with fear, she kept fighting for control of the torch with one hand and jabbed the fingers and thumb of her other hand into the front of Barbara's neck on either side of the throat, high up in the carotid triangle. She might not be strong enough to strangle her, but this way she didn't have to actually squeeze her throat shut to cut off the flow of oxygen to the brain. All she had to do was find the carotid arteries. Easy. And pray her teachers in massage school were right when they'd warned her to stay away from that part of the neck because it could have dire consequences.

Dire consequences would be great right about now.

Barbara was so busy trying to keep her from grabbing the torch that she didn't even seem to notice what she was doing with her other hand. Shouldn't something be happening? It looked so easy in the movies—just press under the jaw and the bad guy instantly blacks out. It had to work. It had to work *now*. How long did it take for lack of oxygen to make someone pass out? Maybe she wasn't in the right spot. Crap. If Barbara could just stand still... Megan adjusted the angle of her fingers.

At least Barbara wasn't trying to stop her. Of course, that was going to be a problem if the carotid thing didn't work and Barbara gained the upper hand. Why wasn't it working? It shouldn't take much pressure to occlude a blood vessel. Megan pressed harder, jamming her fingers deep into Barbara's neck, violating every caution she'd ever been taught.

It worked.

Barbara slumped unconscious, dropping the torch as Kira slammed her to the ground. Megan snatched up the torch. Kira readjusted her hold, and Megan just stood there, watching to see if Barbara would wake up. Now that blood was flowing to Barbara's brain again, she might regain consciousness, although thanks to Kira's added momentum when she fell, she'd also hit her head pretty hard.

"I think you can let go now," Megan said cautiously.

"She could be faking." Kira disengaged slowly, ready to pounce if Barbara moved. "What did you do to her? Is she really knocked out?" She stood and nudged Barbara's limp form with her foot. Barbara didn't react. Her stillness was almost a shock after all that struggle.

Sirens wailed in the distance. "The fire truck's coming," Kira said.

"Finally. We need the police here too."

"I'll call nine-one-one again to make sure they're coming. They need to know where we are so they can arrest her."

CHAPTER TWENTY-FIVE

"The air still smells like smoke," Kira told Megan in the parking lot after the last of the firefighters and police had left. "How come you're not freaking out?"

Good question. Megan could still feel the adrenaline coursing through her veins, but she wasn't scared. "I'm okay."

"You're really not nervous?" Kira said.

"Nope. How come *you're* not freaking out?"

"About the hotel, you mean? I have insurance."

"But all your hard work! Your renovations were almost done." Even in the dark, the back of the hotel did not look good. And the water damage inside had to be extensive.

"It's not as bad as it looks. It would have been worse if you hadn't caught it so early." Kira positioned her hands appreciatively on Megan's waist. "I owe you."

"You really don't. If it weren't for me, none of this would have happened." It was Barbara's fixation on her that had led to this.

"Oh, come on. It's not your fault. You saved our butts." Kira moved her hands down Megan's hips and over the part of her anatomy in question, drawing her closer with a gentle, insistent hold. "I have some ideas for how to thank you, and I can tell you Miss Manners would so not approve."

Megan blushed in the darkness. "We should get home. It's late."

"I'm too wired to sleep."

"Me too," Megan admitted, melting into her. Kira had the best touch.

"Hungry?"

Her stomach rumbled. She hadn't thought of food in hours, but now that the fire was out and Barbara was under arrest and it was just the two of them, she realized she was starving.

"I have food in my car," Kira said.

"Melted protein bars from the glove compartment?"

"O ye of little faith." Kira started across the parking lot and Megan hurried after her. "I have real food." She opened her trunk and pulled out a plastic serving platter loaded with baby carrots and triangles of pita bread arranged around a giant bowl of hummus. It looked fresh, too.

"Where did you get that?" Megan said.

"Eucalyptus. I had it delivered."

"When?" Megan asked incredulously.

"While you were busy talking to the police."

So while Kira's property was burning thanks to one of Megan's clients, Kira had had the presence of mind to order food. With all the commotion of the firefighters and the police, Megan hadn't even noticed.

"I didn't know they deliver," Megan said weakly.

"And you call yourself a local." Kira balanced the platter with one hand, found a flashlight in the recesses of the trunk, and handed her the flashlight so she could shut the car. "Let's eat in the gazebo."

* * *

Their oversized hotel-issue towels were still by the hot tub where they had left them hours earlier. Kira retrieved them and spread them on the floor of the nearby gazebo as a kind of picnic blanket. She loved this gazebo. She loved the trail through the woods that led here, and the layout of the hot tubs, and the design of the spa—all products of her and Megan's combined vision.

Megan sat down on the towels and started in on the pita and hummus with huge, wolfing bites. "I can't believe Barbara was so jealous of you she'd try to destroy your hotel," she said between mouthfuls. "I mean, yes, she asked me out, but I honestly don't think she's even gay."

"Maybe she's repressed," Kira said.

"I guess."

"Being naked in a small room with you for an hour every week, knowing she wanted something from you—"

"And knowing she wasn't going to get it—" Megan pointed a triangle of pita at her in warning.

"And not knowing what it was, because she was so repressed—that would have made *me* crazy." Kira stole a bite of Megan's pita from her outstretched hand. "Although in Barbara's case, I think she was already crazy before she met you."

"After the ethics accusation didn't work out, she must have decided she'd have to get at me some other way. And we'd just had that fire alarm at the hearing. She must have seen my reaction when the alarm went off and known this would scare me."

"Didn't Tammi Baldini tell us a few weeks ago that Barbara's porch caught fire? I doubt your reaction at the hearing had anything to do with this."

"You think she set her own porch on fire?"

Hell, yes. Would Megan never stop giving people the benefit of the doubt? She ought to call her on it, but she knew she never would. The world could use more of Megan's brand of forgiveness. "It's possible."

"I guess it's a good thing we caught her."

"You were awesome. And so was that angel of yours." She

wasn't sure why the angel had wanted to help them, but she was grateful. Guess that meant she might have to start believing in their existence. Maybe. Kira leaned back on her elbows. "I'm glad Barbara didn't get a chance to try setting your place on fire."

Megan stopped with a carrot halfway to her mouth. "You don't think…"

"No," Kira said decisively before Megan could start worrying about whether Barbara had visited her house before vandalizing the hotel. "Tammi or one of the other cops would have told us. They would have known if there was another fire in town tonight."

"You're right."

"They were impressed you were able to knock Barbara out. How did you do that?"

"I didn't really know what I was doing."

"You never took a self-defense class?"

Megan crunched down on her carrot and gave a little self-satisfied smile. "Turns out that knowing human anatomy has more uses than I realized."

Kira loved that smile, loved seeing her happy. She had worried about Megan while they were talking to the cops, waiting for the firefighters to put out the fire—worried she was putting up a good front for the professionals while she panicked underneath about the smoke and the fire. But instead she seemed genuinely happy. Happy and relieved.

If anything had happened to her… It hurt too much to think about. Thank God Megan was safe, not burned or injured or dead.

"You saved my life, karma girl. You and that sensitive nose of yours. Thanks."

"Happy to help."

Kira really wanted to see more of those relaxed, life-is-good-now smiles. Like, every day for the next million years. She cleared her throat. "So about those thank-you ideas of mine…"

* * *

Oh, God—Kira was looking at her in that way that always made her melt. How had they gotten distracted by food and talking inside the gazebo when they could have been...

But that didn't mean she didn't get another chance. Kira had thank-you ideas, and Megan was feeling pretty darn grateful herself.

"I'm worried you might have gasoline on your jeans," Megan said. "So whatever you're thinking about, if it'll get you out of those jeans, I'm all for it."

"There was nothing in that gas container," Kira said.

"There might have been a few drops."

"If you insist." Kira must have known Megan was honestly worried, because instead of giving her a hard time about her ulterior motives—not that she didn't have a ton of ulterior motives—she lay back without saying another word and wriggled out of her jeans.

Great legs.

Great everything.

Megan folded Kira's jeans and wrapped them in the towel Kira had been sitting on, then carefully tucked the whole bundle into a corner. She sat back down on her own towel, making room at one end. "You can share my towel if you want."

"Thanks. Wouldn't want to get a splinter." Kira crawled over and straddled Megan's lap, her bare legs brushing against her with a seductive heat. She pulled Megan's beach dress over her head in one efficient movement and before she knew it, her bikini was off too.

Megan grabbed for her bikini top in Kira's hands. "Some people think a potted plant makes a nice thank-you gift."

"I don't." Tossing the bikini aside, Kira anchored one knee against Megan's side and lowered her to the ground and lay on top of her.

The weight of her made Megan desperate. She clutched Kira's backside and ground her hips into her. "Decorative soap?"

"That crap is usually scented. I'd never get you that."

"Smart woman."

They rolled together, touching everywhere, pulling off the rest of their clothes. Rain started to fall, pelting the roof of the gazebo and sheeting off its perimeter, turning it into their own private shelter. Then Kira was on top of her again, stroking into her wetness. It felt unbelievable. She found the place where Megan's nerve endings were going to lose it and slowed, becoming more deliberate, more forceful, more inescapable, more sure.

"Maybe we should get out of the rain and go to your place," Kira said, maintaining her rhythm. She slid down and sucked one of Megan's nipples into her mouth. God, that felt good.

"Don't you dare stop what you're doing." She didn't care about the rain—she didn't care about anything—as long as Kira kept touching her like that. She needed her in the worst way. "Don't you like the rain? You're the one who...wanted to...walk home in that storm, remember?"

Kira raised her head. "I didn't want to walk home in that storm. What I wanted was you."

"Oh." The ache and the need and the tightness grew. She couldn't really concentrate. At all. "This might be better than decorative soap."

"*Might* be?"

Megan giggled helplessly, then screamed—laughing and screaming at the same time—as Kira nudged her into unbearable hardness.

Oh God oh God oh God.

Screeching need built, peaked, past the point of endurance. Megan shuddered and lost control of several crucial muscles. Kira thrust inside her, chasing her contractions, drawing them out. Then she pulled out and started up again, casually brushing her desperate, already reawakened nerve endings with a light, inescapable touch that Megan both yearned for and tightened against. Kira wasn't going to stop—not until Megan had nothing left in her.

Each time she made contact was an exquisite new shock; each lull left her panting with anticipation. She wanted her. She wanted this. She wanted Kira to move against her again, faster, and Kira kept giving it to her, kept making it better, kept making the shocks come stronger and stronger and closer and closer together, until there was no way out but to climax.

Megan's final release crashed through her and flung her through time. She was making love with Kira inside Hestia's temple. In a prehistoric cave. On a pitching boat. In a moss-covered cottage with chickens running loose outside and a fire blazing in the hearth under an abandoned cooking pot. Dozens of realities played out simultaneously, and in each one Kira was everywhere, life after life, smiling at her with her soul in her eyes, making her come again and again and again.

* * *

"Don't ever leave me." Megan ran her fingers through Kira's hair, her heart still pounding even though the rest of her body could barely move.

"I won't." Kira pushed herself up and smiled down at her as she straddled her hips. "So don't die on me, okay? A few centuries here, a few millennia there—who has that kind of time to wait around?"

"I love you," Megan said.

That summed it all up right there. A woman who was easy to love and who could joke about fate was the perfect combination.

Kira's aura blinded her with joy. "I love you, too. Always." She took her hands. "And we'll find a way around this fire destiny problem."

"You know what? I don't think we need to." Ever since Barbara had been taken into police custody, something had changed.

"Now that I believe you, you're telling me not to?"

Megan let go of her hands and gripped Kira's waist, then slid her palms down her hips to her thighs. "All these years I've been terrified of fire, terrified something like this would happen and it would kill me. But it didn't kill me. There was a bad fire, and it didn't kill me. And I realized that what scared me even more than dying was losing you. When I thought Barbara was going to throw gas on you and set you on fire, I was ready to jump on you to smother the flames. Even when she pulled out that torch, all I could think about was making sure she didn't point it at you."

"Yeah, that was surprising. Next time we wrestle a psycho with a butane torch I think you probably should run."

"There won't be a next time." There was no need for a next time. The freedom of it was palpable. She could easily have been burned, but she wasn't. She'd been spared because she'd learned what fate wanted her to learn.

Kira raised herself slightly on her knees, her quadriceps contracting under Megan's hands. "You're saying we broke the pattern? It's over?"

Megan's heart strained against her ribcage. "I'm going to miss hearing you tell me I'm deluded, but yeah."

"I never thought you were deluded."

Megan waggled her fingers at her like a demented witch casting a spell. "Yes, you did."

It actually meant more to her that Kira *hadn't* believed all of it, yet respected her anyway. And loved her. And didn't try to change her. Because it was easy to love someone who agreed with you. Loving someone who didn't, and not trying to change her—that took real love.

Kira leaned forward and nuzzled her neck until she made her laugh. "I thought you were charming."

"And nuts."

"Maybe a little."

"Gee, thanks." Megan rolled her eyes.

"Before you know it I'll be talking angel talk and we can be nuts together."

EPILOGUE

Megan smiled at how excited Kira was to be showing Gwynne around the new spa. Orbs of colored glass of all sizes glowed from the ceilings. In the lounge, a mural of a mermaid sunbathing on a rock managed to not actually show anything R-rated and yet still be risqué. Kira was truly happy with the way the whole project had turned out and seemed to have forgotten she'd ever wanted the spa to be in a separate building overtop the ley lines.

Gwynne turned to Megan as they paused inside one of the treatment rooms and admired the state-of-the-art adjustable massage table. "You're in love with a woman who doesn't believe in energy fields?"

Funny how it turned out that way. Megan warmed at the touch of Kira's hand on the small of her back. "She understands me." Besides, Kira believed her more than she let on.

"What's an energy field?" Kira teased.

"If you keep that up I'm going to teach you how to use dowsing rods," Megan said. She kissed her on the mouth, lingering until she was out of breath, not caring that Gwynne was making gagging noises over the sound of her retreating footsteps.

"Are you still here?" Kira asked Gwynne, drawing back from the kiss.

Gwynne stopped in the doorway. "You both look radiant."

"And when Gwynne uses the word *radiant*," Megan told Kira, "she doesn't mean our cheeks are rosy."

"Goodbye, Gwynne. Thanks for stopping by," Kira said.

Gwynne stayed put. "Seriously, your auras are beautiful—full of light. When you stand near each other they merge into each other and become even brighter."

Gwynne was so sweet. Megan hopped onto the massage table and sat with her legs hanging off the edge and leaned on her hands. "Don't tell me you actually approve?"

"Yup. I can tell you're happy together."

"That easy to tell, huh?" Kira said, not taking her eyes off Megan. She looked like she was about to kiss her again.

Megan put a restraining hand on her chest, keeping it there, dragging her fingertips down Kira's cleavage in a promise that she wouldn't make her wait long to be alone.

"You'll be happy," Gwynne said. "I'm always right about these things."

"One of these days," Megan told Gwynne, "you're not going to be so sure of yourself, my cocky friend." Preferably because of a woman. What would Gwynne's already brilliant aura look like when she, too, found someone to love?

"This is the thanks I get for being supportive?" Gwynne spread her arms and leaned on the doorframe. "I should tell the angels not to bother swarming all around you. Showing that much approval can't be healthy."

There really were a lot of angels hanging around lately. Right now a whole flock was whizzing around them at high speed like kids who had been let out for recess. Gwynne raised her arms and shooed. The angels ignored her.

"Yeah, I tried that," Megan said. "They don't seem to want to leave. I think they might be moving in with us."

"Just don't let them sing you awake in the mornings," Gwynne warned as she made her escape. "They can get really loud." A few of the angels broke off from the group and followed her out.

"Give us some privacy, please, ladies." Kira blindly made shooing motions above her head and the rest of the angels disappeared.

"Are they gone?" Kira tilted her head and traced Megan's lower lip with her fingertips.

"Mm hmm." Megan's heart sped up in anticipation.

"I'm glad everyone approves, but I don't need a group vote." Kira closed the space between them. "As long as you're here, that's all I need."

THE END